THESE FALLEN ANGELS

Wendy Haley

D0041128

DIAMOND BOOKS, NEW YORK

This book is a Diamond original edition,
and has never been previously published.

THESE FALLEN ANGELS

A Diamond Book / published by arrangement with
the author

PRINTING HISTORY
Diamond edition / February 1995

ISBN: 0-7865-0072-7

Diamond Books are published by The Berkley Publishing Group,
200 Madison Avenue, New York, New York 10016.
Diamond and the "D" design are trademarks
belonging to Charter Communications, Inc.

PRINTED IN THE UNITED STATES OF AMERICA

10 9 8 7 6 5 4 3 2 1

SENSUAL. HAUNTING. SEDUCTIVE.

Praise for The Danilov Family Saga
by Wendy Haley . . .

These Fallen Angels

"*These Fallen Angels* is just as hauntingly poignant, chillingly original, and fast-paced as its predecessor. A beautiful love story that stretches the boundary of known reality, this vampire tale is destined to become a cult classic."

—*Affaire de Coeur*

"Lovers of sensitive and sensuous vampire tales, rejoice! *These Fallen Angels* is a chilling masterpiece of love and evil that transcend death. Flawlessly written, this darkly compelling tale will grip you from the outset and hold you transfixed until after the last page." —*The Paperback Trader*

This Dark Paradise

"Aficionados of the sensitive and sensual vampire will love this book. I found it fascinating."

—**LINDA LAEL MILLER,**
New York Times bestselling author
of *Forever and the Night* and
For All Eternity

"A profound vampiric love story . . . highly recommended . . . an emotionally uplifting experience."

—*Affaire de Coeur*

"Stunning . . . a memorable cast of characters . . . one of those rare books that will haunt you long after you finish reading the final chapters . . . a not-to-be-missed masterpiece of both a love and malevolence that transcends death."

—*The Paperback Trader*

Also by Wendy Haley

THIS DARK PARADISE

'Tis all a Chequer-board of Nights and Days
Where Destiny with Men for Pieces plays:
Hither and thither moves, and mates, and slays,
And one by one back in the closet lays.

—The Rubaiyat of Omar Khayyám

1

Summer had come again.

Alex went for a walk along the edge of the marsh, letting the hot, fecund breeze wash over him. Cicadas called madly overhead, and the sweet song of a whippoorwill flowed like honey upon the air.

Peace.

He'd spent almost a thousand years looking for it. And here it was, all around him. He had safety, comfort, the joy of watching the flowering of the next generation of his family. Why, then, did it flow along outside him without touching the hard kernel of discontent deep in his heart?

"Because you're not a peaceful man," he murmured, taking the words Catherine had spoken to him many times. "Never were, never will be."

Blood-Hunger coiled deep in his belly, reminding him that he wasn't a man at all. Sometimes he almost felt like one. But not tonight. Tonight he felt immeasurably old, immeasurably empty; a year ago tonight he'd lost Elizabeth.

He reached up to touch the small crystal pendant that hung over his heart. The gesture had become automatic, the stone the symbol of what he'd lost. If he'd had more time with her . . . If he hadn't left her alone that night . . . The what-if game—if anything showed he still had some humanity left in him, that was surely the proof.

You've never learned to let go. On sudden impulse, he pulled the pendant up and over his head. Perhaps he should lay it to rest, as he had so many of his pasts. Let Wildwood have it; the marsh cared nothing about regret. He drew his arm back, ready to throw, but lowered it again as he sensed Justin coming up behind him. Catharsis should always be private. He slipped the chain back over his head and let the crystal drop back against his chest.

"Alex, you out here?" Justin called.

"Here, by the marsh."

Alex turned to watch Justin approach. No boy now, but a young man, he stood a shade over six feet tall. The mimosa tree cast feathered shadows across his aquiline face, making him seem older. He'd never lost that fey quietness of movement gained that night in Wildwood's embrace; without his revenant senses, Alex wouldn't have heard him coming at all.

He stood beside Alex for a while, silently tossing stones into the quiet water. It wasn't a calm sort of silence; he had an air of tenseness about him that spoke of trouble. Alex, sure that it was the anniversary that was bothering him, let him have the time he needed.

"Alex," he said at last, "I need to get married."

Alex felt his jaw drop. "What?"

"I need to get married."

It took Alex a moment to master his astonishment, a moment longer to digest the implication of that statement. Not "I want to get married," but "I *need* to get married."

"That's an interesting opening to a conversation," he said.

"Kelli's pregnant with my child."

Alex let his breath out in a long sigh. With Sonya off in Switzerland with her Parisian playboy, he was Justin's legal guardian, and this was his problem to deal with. "How do you feel about it?" he asked.

"I want her," Justin said. "And I want my child."

A man's answer, Alex thought. But then, Justin hadn't been a boy since the night Suldris had shattered his family. The memory of it might be gone, but the effect was very real nonetheless.

"You're underage," Alex said.

"In the eyes of the law, yes."

"What about college?"

"Married people go to college. Look, I know we're young and inexperienced. I know I should have been more careful, and I know we've made our lives a lot harder than they would have been. But that's my kid. I want to take care of it, and I want to play a role in raising it. I'm not asking for money or a way out. Just your signature on a piece of paper so I can do what I want to do."

A man's defiance. A man's claim. Pride tightened Alex's throat. Justin had stepped over the threshold. A boy becomes a man when he does, not when he reaches some arbitrary age set by others. And if the truth be told, Alex rather liked the idea of seeing the first of yet another generation of Danilovs come into the world.

"Do you love her?" he asked.

"Yeah."

"Then we'll have to get you married."

Justin let his breath out sharply. "Thanks."

Briefly, Alex put his arm around the young man's shoulders. Man to man, not guardian to ward. "This calls for a celebration. Why don't I take you and Kelli out to dinner?"

"She's home, telling her parents. They're not going to be happy about this."

"Don't they like you?"

Justin's head came up in obvious surprise. "Well, yeah. But any parent is going to be upset at their daughter getting pregnant so young."

"I'm glad you understand that. Go lock up the house. We're going to pay a visit to Mr. and Mrs. Hamlen."

"God. Can't we let them cool down first?"

Alex laughed. "If you *weren't* going to marry her, we'd give them a chance to cool down. Since you're doing the honorable thing, I think we should get right into the thick of it."

"The honorable thing," Justin repeated. "It sounds so old-fashioned."

"Honor never goes out of style," Alex said. "I'm proud of you for choosing it instinctively."

The tension went out of Justin's body. "You're really okay with this, aren't you?"

"Actually, I like babies."

"Most people would have a hard time not giving a lecture about condoms and safe sex."

Alex spread his hands. "I'm not 'most people.' And you're not most teenagers. You seem to have considered all the implications of the situation, and it's yours to deal with."

"Thanks." Justin grinned, bringing youth to his sharp-featured face. "Well, I guess it's time to pay the piper, beard the lion in his den—"

" 'None but the brave deserve the fair.' "

"Not Shakespeare again!"

"Dryden, as I recall."

Justin grimaced. "If you're going to quote poetry all the way there, I'm going alone."

"I'll be merciful. But I maintain that anyone who doesn't like poetry has a barbarian soul."

"Can I drive the Beemer?"

"I rest my case." Alex heaved a sigh. "Yes, you may drive the Beemer."

Hate was a wonderful thing. It filled the prismed emptiness of her dwelling place. She held it close, fanned its heat to white-hot, for it kept her from going mad. Eternity stretched before her, although it seemed as though eternity had already passed. Nothing passed through the walls of her prison. Nothing, that is, except Alex.

She could feel him. Here in the heart of her crystal, her companions were his power, his feelings, and his Blood-Hunger. Oh, yes, she knew Blood-Hunger almost firsthand now, knew the pain caused by his denying it. Knew, too, that he was a fool.

What was death, after all? There were worse things than simply dying. Alex knew. Sometimes living was the worst of all.

"If you could call this living," she said.

The crystal swallowed her words, absorbed them, nullified them. The faceted walls took her voice—or maybe it was only her memory of her voice—and thinned it, turning it bell pure and inhuman.

"I hate you!" she screamed.

Her prison seemed so fragile; spiderweb thin facets of crystal, rainbow-shivered arches, smooth plains of transparent stone that looked like plate glass. But she had no body. If this was her soul, it was pretty damned useless. No fists, no feet, nothing with which to break through. Trapped. Isolated. Nothing to do, nothing to see, nowhere to go. She'd seen hell in the eyes of Suldris's dark god, and had fled here to escape it. And had entered a hell of her own making.

Alex would have appreciated the irony of it all.

"Damn you," she muttered, knowing that, too, would have sparked his amusement. "This is your doing."

That's not fair, a small, reasonable corner of her mind chided. Fair. There was no fairness in this. He may not have put her here, but he kept her here. Damn him for being the only person in the world she couldn't touch! As long as he kept her with him, she couldn't escape. His Blood-Hunger tore at her, echoing his pain, his despair.

Stupid of him to fight it. *She* wouldn't. Blood-Hunger was a powerful urge. Promises of ecstasy more voluptuous than sex, sharper than love or hate or even greed. Pleasure greater than anything she'd ever known. She'd experienced a shadow of it when Alex had made love to her, but only a shadow. The vampire was the one who experienced the reality of it. She wanted it. She wanted it all. Alex's pain came from resisting it.

"Damn you," she said. "If you don't want it, give it to someone who does!"

She'd loved him once. She loved him still. Hated him, too. Him and his damned scruples. Him and his damned *rules*. Love hadn't gotten her what she wanted from him. Maybe hate would.

And what did she want? Immortality. One drop of blood, an endless stretch of tomorrows. Alex had it. He'd lived for a thousand years. Unlimited time, unlimited resources, and all for a few sips of blood.

A few deaths, too, a few souls.

So. It seemed a good enough trade for living forever.

Terror beat dark wings before her eyes as she realized the flip side of that coin: Alex could keep her here forever, merely by continuing to wear the pendant. Immortality of a different sort. Bound. Helpless. Going insane in stages, rattling around the crystal's heart like a worm in a Mexican jumping bean.

"Let me go," she shouted. "Let. Me. Go!"

No one listened. No one cared.

She folded in and over on herself, distancing herself from thought. Blood-Hunger settled over her like a shroud. With a sigh, she folded herself in it, letting it insulate her from her prison.

Even pain was better than nothing.

2

The Hamlen house nestled in the center of a tree-shaded middle-class neighborhood on the north side of Delano. Alex peered up at the two-story frame house. It had been well kept up, the siding freshly cleaned, shrubbery trimmed, flowers nodding in the breeze. A marble birdbath seemed to glow in the moonlight. Suburban America, he thought. Neat. Tidy. And about to be shaken to its foundations.

Justin pulled into the driveway. "There's still time to chicken out."

"Not unless you want to hear more poetry."

"Damn."

Alex smiled. "Some of us doubly so."

The front door opened as they approached, and Kelli rushed out and flung herself into Justin's arms. The top of her head just reached his collarbone. Her short-cut dark hair emphasized her brown eyes and the gentle heart shape of her face. She had moved here from Alabama seven months ago, and had captured Justin's heart her first day here. Small, fragile, with a ready smile and a Georgia accent that flowed like sweet cream, she could turn any young man inside out and upside down.

"Hi," she said, giving Alex a wan smile. "You know?"

"I know." He laid his hand on her shoulder.

"Did you tell them?" Justin asked.

"Yes," she whispered. "They're really upset. Really, *really* upset."

"It's going to be okay," Justin said. "It's all going to be okay." He'd lost all traces of his uncertainty. This was a knight with his lady, protective, reassuring, ready to face any peril.

Ah, to be young! Alex thought as he followed the lovers into the house.

A man and woman sat on the sofa, shoulder to shoulder, as though giving each other strength. Even sitting, the man looked lean and rangy, and was surprisingly young looking despite his receding hairline. The woman had a sharp-featured face that was just softening into plumpness, but Alex didn't miss the stubborn line of her jaw and the ordered intelligence of her eyes. He could tell that she'd already come to terms with her daughter's pregnancy. The man had not.

He jumped to his feet when Justin came into the room. Gently but firmly, he pulled his daughter away from the younger man. "What the hell are you doing here?"

"I want to marry your daughter."

"You're a kid."

Justin squared his shoulders, as though aware for the first time that he was several inches taller than the other man. "I'm a father."

Hamlen's eyebrows went up. "Bold as brass, aren't you?"

"Would you rather I *didn't* want to discuss it with you?"

"I guess not." With an explosive sigh, Hamlen smoothed his palm over his shiny head. "Okay. Talk."

"Thanks." Justin turned to Alex. "Mr. and Mrs. Hamlen, this is my guardian, Alex Danilov."

"I wish I could say it's a pleasure," Hamlen said, reaching to shake hands.

"Perhaps some other time it will be," Alex said.

He looked deeply into the other man's eyes, read honesty there, and a father's outrage. But no hate, no unreasoning anger, nothing to show that he'd sabotage his daughter to satisfy a need to punish Justin. A decent man.

"I've given permission for Justin to marry your daughter," he said. "As a minor, he needs my signature."

Hamlen smoothed his nonexistent hair again. "Look, Mr. Danilov. It's not that we dislike Justin. It's just that they're both so young. We wanted Kelli to go to college—"

"Why can't she?" Alex asked. "Justin is."

"With a baby?"

"A baby is not the end of life, or ambition. She and Justin will just have to work harder, that's all."

Justin stepped forward. "Mr. Hamlen, *how* we do it isn't at issue here. Kelli's eighteen. She doesn't need your permission to get married. But she loves you, and she wants you to accept her decision. So do I."

Justin reached out. Kelli moved into the circle of his arm, an eloquent gesture of loyalty. "We want this baby, and we want to get married."

"Jesus, boy, do you know how hard the world is out there?" Hamlen's voice rose in agitation. "How the hell are you two kids going to take care of yourselves, let alone a baby?"

"We're not completely helpless, Dad," Kelli said.

"You're not even out of high school! You don't have the vaguest idea what being parents means. Why don't you let us contact a good adoption agency—"

"No!" Justin, Alex, and Kelli said together.

The word hung in the air, flat and resolute. While Hamlen was still struggling with surprise Alex turned to the two young people. "Justin, take Kelli for a walk. I want to talk to Mr. and Mrs. Hamlen privately."

"I want—"

"Justin."

Rebellion hardened the young man's jaw. A true Danilov, wanting to fight his own battles, Alex thought. And to take what he believed belonged to him. Alex had to fight to repress a smile; the Danilovs had never been a humble lot.

"Come on, Justin," Kelli said. "Let them talk."

She tugged at his arm, and he followed her with obvious reluctance. Alex waited until they were gone, then turned back to the Hamlens.

"May I sit down?" he asked.

Hamlen nodded, returning to his seat on the sofa as Alex settled into the armchair opposite him. Surveying the two people before him, Alex saw that the man was still struggling to reconcile his picture of his daughter as a child and his daughter as a wife and mother. Mrs. Hamlen, however, had accepted this conversation for what it was: a discussion of practicalities.

"Why do these kids have to do this?" Mr. Hamlen demanded. "I think we've been fair with Kelli, giving her as much freedom as her age warranted—"

"Phil, let Mr. Danilov have his say," Mrs. Hamlen said.

"Say? How about he answers some questions here, like why is he going to let that kid get married when he's not out of high school?" He jabbed his forefinger at Alex. "How's that boy going to support a wife and child? How's he going to pay for college while he's buying diapers and formula?"

Alex leaned his elbows on the arms of the chair and folded his hands across his stomach. "Money isn't a problem."

"Not a problem! Hell, how many marriages break up

over money? Susan and I have had to struggle all our lives—"

"Mr. Hamlen." Alex waited until the other man had taken a couple of deep breaths, then continued. "I wasn't being flippant. You should know that the income from Justin's trust fund amounts to a very respectable living."

"Trust fund?"

"I had planned to turn over the principal to him when he turns twenty-one, but in the light of his new responsibilities, I'll let him have it on his eighteenth birthday."

"Just a minute," Mrs. Hamlen said. "He never said he came from money."

Alex smiled. "Justin doesn't think money has anything to do with who he is. In essence, it doesn't. But *I* wanted you to know that he isn't being frivolous when he tells you he can take care of Kelli and the baby."

"Kelli said his family had a nice house, but I had no idea—"

"Apparently it isn't important to her, either," Alex said.

To their credit, they didn't ask anything more about the money.

"Why were you so upset at the idea of adoption?" she asked.

Alex spread his hands. "Reflex. We Danilovs have been around for a long, long time, and we never turn our backs on one of our own."

Mr. Hamlen turned to look at his wife. She met his gaze levelly for a moment, then nodded. He rose to his feet and held out his hand.

"My name is Phil, and this is Susan. Since we're going to be family, we should be on a first-name basis."

Alex rose and clasped the other man's hand. "Call me Alex."

The storm had blown over.

● ● ●

Justin drove with the reflexes of youth. By the time he pulled onto the bridge leading to the Arbor, Alex had become used to it and had stopped pressing an imaginary brake on his side of the car.

"Kelli wants to have a small wedding at her church," Justin said. "When do you think we should have it?"

"Before the baby is born," Alex replied, leaning back against the headrest and closing his eyes.

"I know this is kinda unconventional—"

"Unconventional!" Alex laughed. "Do you know how many Danilovs have been born on the wrong side of the blanket? And that's not taking into consideration the 'premature' births."

"Look at this, Alex," Justin said softly.

Alex opened his eyes. Mist had risen from the marsh to shroud the bridge, pale, grasping tendrils that coiled like serpents across the roadway. Justin slowed down. The car eased through a river of white, whorls of it spinning in its wake. But fragile as it was, the mist could be torn only briefly; as soon as the vehicle passed, the tendril re-formed, drew together, became a whole once again.

Justin stopped the car, propping his elbow on the back of the seat to look out the rear window. "It's like we never went through it at all."

"Wildwood is reminding us that we're only visitors here," Alex said. "We and our bridges and cars."

Alex rolled his window down. The air-conditioning sucked out, gone as though it had never existed. Marsh air filled the car. Hot, wet, carrying the primordial, fecund smell of mud and vegetation, and the frantic, teeming sounds of summer life.

"It's so big, so old," Justin said. "We don't even register on its scale, do we?"

"Not often," Alex murmured.

A fog tendril quested into the car, leaving a sheen of

moisture on Justin's face. "Sitting here like this, I could almost believe in magic," he said.

"Almost?"

"Maybe a little more than almost."

The young man sat with that hushed, waiting sort of stillness that had become a part of him. It was as though he'd passed into some wilderness inside himself, a place more interesting and compelling than the outside world.

"Sometimes, on nights like this," he said, "I have strange dreams."

Alex turned more fully toward him. "What kind of dreams?"

"Strange. I'm driving, the road is familiar, but I can't place where I am, and I hear this voice . . . calling me. I drive and drive, and then this owl appears in my headlights. Then I'm somewhere else, and I hear that same voice chanting. . . . I can't understand the words. Then everything goes dark and fuzzy."

"Are you afraid in this dream?"

"At the beginning. But then, somehow, I know I'm safe. It just seems . . . I feel that if I can just pin that voice down and understand what it's saying, then I'll remember something real important. I try and try, but the words keep getting away from me."

Dread coiled, cold and hard, in Alex's guts. *Those* memories held Suldris, Barron's death, and inevitably, the truth about Alex Danilov. And those didn't belong in this world. In Justin's world. Someday, perhaps, he should know. But not now. Let him have his marriage and his child. Let him be a simple human being for a while, for once he learned the truth about that night, his life would never again be simple. And how, Alex's cynical revenant mind whispered, do you stop him from remembering?

Distract him. A wife, a child, college. The minutia of

life to keep away the knowledge of death. Humankind uses it all the time.

"Have you ever had dreams like that?" Justin asked.

"No." *Just realities.* "Not like that. But I used to have nightmares when I was young." A thousand years ago, when he was a knight, he'd wake sweating from dreams of swimming in a sea of blood and severed limbs, howling, gut-empty corpses. For a moment that memory washed over him like acid. Then he shrugged it off; it had happened a long time ago, and revenants do not dream.

"How did you get rid of them?" Justin asked.

"I think they kept coming back because I worried about them so much. Finally I fell in love, and then I had plenty of other things to worry about."

"Tell me about it." Justin put the car into gear and eased forward. The mist closed around them, seeming to muffle even the harsh reality of the powerful engine. "I'm scared, Alex. I've hardly started living myself, and now I'm supposed to guide the life of another human being. What if I screw up?"

"Kids are pretty resilient. There's a lot of room for error before they're completely and hopelessly ruined," Alex said, repressing a smile.

"Was that a joke?"

"Not completely."

Justin grinned as he spun the wheel, turning the car into the driveway. But there was an edge to that smile, an awareness of comparisons, of things almost said. Alex knew he was thinking about his own parents—the father who had disappeared, the mother who'd given Justin up to pursue her own life. He'd grown up early because of them, and had learned to tread his own path through their greed, petty selfishness, and hatred of each other.

"If you're looking for my opinion," Alex said. "I think you'll do fine."

"God, I hope so."

The house loomed out of the mist ahead, looking like a graceful ocean liner on a white, moonlit sea. Yellow squares of windows shed beacons of light through the dimness, welcoming Alex as they had for nearly two hundred years. And as always, the sight brought a stirring to his heart. The ghost of lavender scented the air, or perhaps his imagination.

A fey night, as Justin had said. One could almost believe in magic on such a night—fairies dancing half-seen in the fog, a water sprite breasting the quiet water of the marsh, a revenant questing on the night wind with white owl wings.

The front door opened as they drove up, and a woman's silhouette bisected the rectangle of light that spilled out across the porch. Alex tasted anticipation upon the air. He knew this woman, sensed her identity even as Justin drew a sharp breath of surprise.

"Mom." There was joy in Justin's voice, and pain.

He stopped the car and got out. Alex followed him up the steps and across the porch. Sonya stepped forward to meet her son, and her hair caught the moonlight like spun metal.

"Justin, sweetheart!" she cried, throwing her arms around him. He held her tightly, tension squaring his shoulders into awkwardness.

Alex felt the young man's pain acutely. Sonya hadn't been much of a mother, before or after Barron's death. Afterward, when Justin needed her most, she'd left for Europe to search for fulfillment. Judging from the flat disappointment at the back of her eyes, she hadn't found it.

Justin knew. He'd always known. But he held her tightly anyway, loved her despite and because of what she was. Sometimes, Alex thought, we try to hold a thing because we know we'll soon have to let it go.

Sonya stepped back and held her son at arms' length. "My God, I think you've grown a foot since I saw you last."

"It's been seven months, Mom."

"So it has." She smiled tremulously. "Hello, Alex."

"Hello, Sonya. It's good to have you back."

She looked thinner, blonder, and even more beautiful than when she'd left. Chic, with a European flair she hadn't had before. "Where have you two been?" she demanded. "I rushed home from the airport, all excited to see you, only to be left alone for *hours*."

"Isn't Philippe with you?" Justin asked.

"No . . . he isn't." Her smile faltered for an instant. Then she looped her right arm in Justin's, her left in Alex's, and drew them toward the house. "Come on, I'm starving. I asked Eve to fix something, even if it's cold cuts and potato chips."

Suitcases littered the foyer. Many, many suitcases— more baggage than even Sonya would need for just a visit. Alex glanced at Justin, saw that the younger man had the same idea. And didn't like it. Sonya was only going to complicate an already complex situation, on both a practical and an emotional level.

A shame, Alex thought, that the son was more mature than the mother.

"What's going on, Mom?" Justin asked.

"Can't you guess? I'm back for good." She smiled, but her hands were clasped so tightly the tendons stood out like wires. "It didn't work out with Philippe, I'm afraid."

With a sigh, Justin bent and picked up a pair of suitcases. "I'll get these upstairs for you. Are you planning to take yours and . . . your old room?" He flushed, and the almost spoken words "yours and Dad's" hung like fire upon the air.

Sonya didn't seem to notice. "Yes, but you want to hear—"

"Not right now," he said, worlds of weariness in his voice. "It's been a real long night."

He turned away. As he disappeared around the turn of the stairway, Sonya swung back to Alex.

"What's the matter with him?" she demanded.

"It's been a real long night," Alex said. He took her by the arm and led her toward the dining room. "Come on. You can tell me all about Philippe over your sandwiches and potato chips."

And so she did. It was a sordid little tale of blindness on Sonya's part and greedy manipulation on Philippe's part. And then the final, predictable denouement—Sonya finding her lover in bed with another woman.

She cried then, and Alex held her hand while she did. The comfort of a human touch. The thought was revenant cynical, and made him gentler than he wanted to be.

"I'm sorry," he said.

"He . . . he told me he'd never met a woman like me. He'd never felt so strongly about anyone. . . ." She scrubbed the tears from her cheeks with the back of her hand. "Damn. I should have expected it; after all, he *did* leave another woman to come to Switzerland with me."

Alex remained silent, knowing better than to offer a comment on *that*.

"Philippe was the perfect lover," she said. "Attentive, charming, oh so knowledgeable about a woman's wants and needs. And expensive."

Ah. Silence becoming ever more golden as this conversation continued, Alex maintained it.

"Justin told me what you called Philippe. The Parisian Playboy." Grimacing, she pushed her plate away. "It was the classic example of divergent interests, don't you think? I was looking for love, he wanted money. Got it, too; in ten and a half months he went through more than eight hundred thousand dollars of my money. Oh, I knew what he was. But I thought I was different. I thought I could hold him with looks and love." A single tear escaped to trail down her check, and she dashed it away with a sharp, angry gesture. "The woman he left me for was the heiress to one of the world's great fortunes. She was also forty-nine years old, plump and homely. So much for looks and love, huh?"

Alex merely held her hand and let her talk herself out. Poor Sonya, he thought, searching so very hard for love, and missing it because she didn't know what it was. Sad.

She dabbed at her eyes with her napkin. "I think I'd better give up on love for a while."

"No," he said. "Just Parisian playboys."

"How did it happen for you?" she asked. "Did you just look at Elizabeth and *bang!* you were in love?"

"Something like that."

"You still love her, don't you?" Wonderment came into her eyes.

"Yes, I still love her."

"But she left you."

"Yes." Memory shafted through him, a sudden, visceral remembrance of Liz's touch, her scent, the pain of letting her go. Letting her die. And he couldn't even mourn her properly, for the world didn't know she was dead.

"Have you ever heard from her?"

He shook his head. "The police traced her to D.C., then to New York. After that, there was no trace of her."

"She must have tried hard not to be found. Good God, Alex, how can you still love her?" she burst out.

"Because she was perfect for me."

"And Philippe was perfect for me. That doesn't mean they feel the same about us, does it?"

"No."

Sonya sighed. "Do you ever feel like following her?"

"All the time," he said. If he had a soul, he'd give it to be able to follow her. Even to touch her one last time.

Reaching out, Sonya ran her fingertip along the crystal pendant. A heaviness settled in Alex's chest. Grief, perhaps.

"This was Lydia's, wasn't it?" she asked.

"Yes."

"Did you love her, even a little? Be honest."

"No." Regret, yes, for he hadn't wanted the burden of her death. But Lydia had stretched him too thin, wanted too much. She would have cost him his humanity.

"She loved you," Sonya said. "As much as Lydia could love."

Lydia's was a brand of love Alex could do without. He closed his hand around the crystal, feeling its silence. Then, in sudden decision, he pulled it off.

"Here," he said. "Why don't you take this? You were her friend, and she'd probably rather you had it than me."

"As much as two women like us could be friends."

Sonya held out her hand, and he dropped the pendant into her palm. Relief washed through him, startling in its intensity. Was his guilt so easily shed, then? He watched Sonya's face as she slowly closed her fingers around the crystal. Her pupils dilated with what might have been pain.

"Are you all right?" he asked.

"Yes. I . . . was just thinking about Lydia and her crystals." Sonya slipped the chain over her head. The pendant caught the light, a dark glitter between her breasts.

She rose, and he rose with her. Her emotions sharpened. Before his alarm solidified, she wound her arms around his neck and kissed him full on the mouth. Blood-Hunger flared, too long denied. He fought it, fought his response to the warm, demanding lips on his own.

He shook himself free of the Blood-Hunger, reached up to disengage her arms from around his neck. "We've been through this before, Sonya."

She didn't step back. "Philippe didn't look like you. It was the only thing I found unsatisfying about him. Maybe I'll always be attracted to men with tawny gold hair and pale eyes."

"Don't."

"It's never going to happen, is it?"

"I'm as wrong for you as Philippe was," he said. "If for a different reason."

"And you still love Elizabeth."

"I still love Elizabeth."

"Two people don't have to be in love to offer each other a little comfort."

He smiled, but there was an edge to it even he could feel. "If it's comfort we're looking for, how about a glass of good wine and some reminiscences of old times in the study?"

"If you like."

Still, she didn't step back. Alex was the one who moved to create some space between them. His nerves tingled, as though the room were full of static electricity. Or danger.

What an idiotic thought! You've breathed too much marsh air tonight, Alex my lad.

"We've got a lot to talk about tonight," he said. "There's something very important happening in Justin's life that you should know about."

"Justin?" Her lashes veiled her eyes, gold-tipped fans brushing the tops of her cheekbones. "I don't worry about him. He's not the sort of boy to get into *real* trouble."

"In case you didn't notice, he's grown up. He's a man now, Sonya."

"Sure. Why don't we get that wine before we start this discussion? From the look on your face, I'm going to need some fortifying."

Alex bowed, offering his arm. As she tucked her hand into the crook of his arm, he felt a stab of unease. Physical contact did not give him access to her emotions. She was closed off, inaccessible. Maybe it was fatigue, maybe jet lag, or maybe Philippe had hurt her so badly she'd shut everything up inside.

Whichever, he hoped she had enough left to give her son the love he needed.

He glanced at her out of the corner of his eye and found her staring at him. She was smiling, a sly, knowing, female smile that set alarm bells ringing along every nerve in his body.

"Damn," she said. "It's good to be back."

3

Light. Sound. The beating of Sonya's heart, the susurration of blood rushing through her veins. Lydia sighed; it was almost like being alive. Almost.

The moment Alex had given the crystal to Sonya, Lydia had swept out of her prison. She'd settled into Sonya's mind, Sonya's body. The other woman had nothing with which to fight back; a moment's surprise, another moment's struggle, and Lydia took over. She could feel Sonya's psyche hovering just out of the range of consciousness, even her memories stolen.

Tough luck. To the victor goes the spoils.

Lydia saw through Sonya's eyes, heard through Sonya's ears. And the first thing she saw was Alex. Stark, graceful, his dark gold hair bronze in the lamplight, his beautiful pale eyes as transparent as cracked glass. No, not glass. Mirrors. Reflecting the world around them, but showing nothing of what was inside. She felt desire, hers and Sonya's. And hate, which was hotter.

She couldn't have him. No one could. Eternal, he could be borrowed, loved, hated, but never held.

And even knowing that, she kissed him. She could feel the sudden upsurge in his Blood-Hunger when she did. No other man had ever made her feel like this. It wasn't the embrace. A kiss was a kiss was a kiss; different lips, different arms, different taste, but all the same, really. It was the Blood-Hunger that made Alex special. Exquisite pain-pleasure ripped along her nerves, then sank deep, deep, reaching into her core. The tie was still there. Blood-Hunger. His need, too long denied. Hers, unfulfilled.

Blood relatives. Silent laughter skittered through her mind on ticklish mouse feet. She wasn't disappointed when he pulled away. Sonya, after all, wasn't his type. Ah, but this was a new Sonya, and *she* had some surprises in store for him.

She followed him to the study, letting the hijacked body use its own, long-accustomed movements. A fascinating sensation, this slow, languid walk so different from her own.

"Here we are," Alex said, opening the door to the study.

He stepped to one side, gesturing for her to precede him. Always the gentleman, Lydia thought. Urbane, smooth, never letting the Hunger show. Never letting the monster play. Ah, but it was there. She made sure her hip brushed him as she passed, smiling when she saw his eyes turn hot.

The study had become Margaret's again; Barron's things were gone as though they'd never been. She watched Alex. His gaze turned inward, unseeing, he still moved around the room with absolute accuracy.

Men are such fools! Even Suldris. Especially Suldris. He'd made things easy for Alex, even killing Barron for him. All Alex had to do was sit back and collect the goods: Barron's house, Barron's company, Barron's son. Barron's wife, he hadn't wanted. But things change, Lydia thought. Things change.

"What would you like to drink?" he asked, busy at the sideboard.

"Martini," she murmured.

He looked up. "You don't like martinis, Sonya."

Oops. "I do now. They were Philippe's favorite. And you know how we women change to accommodate the men we love."

He met her gaze for a moment, then turned back to the sideboard. She watched his hands move as he mixed her drink. Long-fingered, capable hands. Desire burned along her veins, the memory of what those hands felt like upon her skin. Burning, raising a matching heat deep in her body, a matching need in her soul.

He turned back to her, the overhead light casting knife-edged shadows under his cheekbones. "Here you go," he said, holding out her drink.

"Thanks." Her fingers brushed his as she took the glass from him. The brief contact made her flesh tingle. She took a long swallow from her glass, burying the sensation in alcohol's sting.

"How is it?" he asked.

"Great. Where did you learn to make such good martinis?"

"Here and there."

I bet. Coming to this room had been a mistake. They'd almost made love here. On the floor. She'd come to him, begging for it. Desperately, urgently, because it was as necessary to her as breathing. She almost closed her eyes at the memory of his hands on her, the way his mouth tasted, the way his eyes had burned with the need to consume her. She'd wanted to be consumed. Still did, for that was the way to live forever.

A man to die for. Oh, yes. Cliché that it was, it was true. He held immortality in his hand, a breath, a single heartbeat away. Damn him. He was selfish in his damned morality; even Elizabeth had been denied. Love hadn't been strong enough to pry that gift from him. Lydia almost laughed; maybe hate would work, then.

"Now tell me, what is this momentous thing you simply have to tell me about Justin?" she asked without any real interest, but needing to focus her thoughts on something other than what she wanted from Alex.

"Did he write to you about his girlfriend?"

Lydia pawed through Sonya's memories, came up with what she needed. "Oh, yes. It sounded like a terrible case of puppy love. Ah, he met her, what . . . five months ago?"

"Six. She's pregnant."

Lydia nearly choked on her sip of martini. *"What?"*

"She's pregnant. He wants to marry her."

"Married? Justin?"

Alex nodded.

"He's not even out of high school!" Was that Sonya speaking, or her?

"He's also intelligent, mature, and wants to be a father to his child."

Lydia tapped her chin with her finger as she considered the ramifications of this occurrence. Interesting. *Very* interesting.

"What do you think about it, Alex?" she asked in Sonya's sweetest tones.

"I'm supporting his decision."

"He's too young to be a father."

"Apparently not."

"How do we know the child is even his?"

Alex's eyes turned frost pale. "Because he says it is."

"Don't freeze me out, Alex," she murmured. "It's a natural question to ask under the circumstances, isn't it?"

"Maybe. But I wouldn't ask Justin, if I were you."

"Protective, is he?" She smiled. "How very . . . charming and old-fashioned. You've rubbed off on him."

"Hardly."

"Oh, don't be so modest." She walked around him, knowing he would turn to keep her in sight. Not a man to leave his back unprotected, was Alexi Danilovich. "He admires you more than he ever admired his own father."

"Sonya—"

"Come on, Alex. We both know Barron was a prick. You don't mourn him any more than I do. And neither does Justin."

"Justin loved his father."

"Love and hate are two sides of the same coin," she said. "I should know." Her voice sounded much too bitter. Sonya again? Maybe.

She stopped circling. With the light like this, some of the bottles held a funhouse-distorted reflection of the room. She saw herself in them, but not Alex.

No, not him. No wonder the house was devoid of mirrors. She couldn't stop looking at him. He seemed so nearly human, except for the eyes. Revenant. He seemed unaware of his own power; maybe he'd lived with it for so long he no longer noticed it. But she did. It was like standing on an ocean shore, watching the seemingly placid surface but knowing there was an undertow poised to take the unwary.

Another man might have been uncomfortable with the ever-lengthening silence, but not he. No, he just watched her with those beautiful, inhuman eyes, and waited for her to continue the conversation. He wasn't being rude. No, this was his way of making her spill her guts just to keep the silence at bay.

A thousand years, she thought. How many women had he faced in how many rooms? How many had he loved?

"What did Elizabeth have that Lydia didn't?" she asked.

A subtle tightening of his face betrayed his surprise

at the shift in subject. "Why do you ask?"

"I just wanted to know. Surely you've wondered why you fell in love with one woman and not the other."

"I never wondered."

He gazed at her steadily, a half smile curving his lips, detachment cooling his eyes. She'd been shut out. Again. He'd shut himself in. With Elizabeth, damn him. That precious closed world that had room only for two. Anger sparked to life deep in Lydia's chest. Anger at him, and at herself. For caring. And for being jealous of a dead woman.

Her gaze was caught by the spread of his fingers on the polished wood of the desk. His skin gleamed pale against the burnished old mahogany. If he'd wanted to, he could have crushed the wood, crumbled it like dry bread in his hands. And despite that strength, that wonderful otherworldly power, he couldn't keep Elizabeth. Couldn't save her, because he didn't have the courage to make her revenant.

Lydia saw that his gaze had moved from her to the window behind her. Turning, she stared out at the pale, blind fog. It held nothing for her.

"What are you looking at?" she asked.

His shoulders lifted, fell. "Sometimes, if you look hard enough, you can see faces in the mist."

"Elizabeth's?"

"Among others."

His eyes were stark with loss. Lydia turned to stare out at the mist again, but it remained empty to her. Maybe she needed to carry a thousand years of guilt to see what Alex saw. Guilt. A meaningless word to a being who had outlived history itself. Stupid of him to let it chain him.

Elizabeth Garry didn't matter. The one woman who could hold him, truly hold him, was the one who could live forever.

And that's going to be me.

He wouldn't give immortality to her, any more than he'd given it to Elizabeth. She'd have to take it from him.

But how? If Suldris hadn't been able to make him break his vow, how could she? On impulse, she stepped forward, reaching out to smooth his hair back from his forehead. He caught her wrist, denying her the intimacy. He couldn't deny her the sudden flare of Blood-Hunger in his eyes, however.

Triumph slewed along her nerves, raising the tiny hairs on the back of her neck. This was hers, this link to his Blood-Hunger. Suldris couldn't touch him this way, or Elizabeth.

She disengaged her wrist from his grasp, watching the sudden, swift need drain from his eyes. *Get ready, Alex. The ride has only just begun!*

"I suppose I'd better get to bed," she said. "Jet lag."

"I was hoping we could talk about Justin—"

"Let's wait until tomorrow, hmm? I'm too tired to make sense right now. And I doubt the baby's going to go away overnight." She smiled at him, anticipating. "Good night, Alex. Sweet dreams."

Alex woke to silence. He would have welcomed a ghost to help him out of Oblivion. Catherine's portrait looked down at him, benign and empty. For a moment he wondered if the scent of lavender followed her through the Abyss.

He closed his eyes, imagining that empty blackness. How long had the past year felt to Catherine as she floated in nothingness?

"I'm still trying, love," he murmured. "I'll find a way to get you out. I'll save—" He broke off, both appalled and amused by his own hubris. Savior of her soul, indeed.

And Elizabeth. There were times when he could almost hear her calling him, times when he had to resist the urge to turn to see if she stood behind him.

First love, second love, both gone. He smiled, not in humor but in self-deprecation. Sometimes he thought he ought to flap in the wind like a piece of old Swiss cheese, more holes than substance.

He swung his feet over the side of the bed and got up. The contents of his lair had changed. He'd added a large oak table, which filled some of the room's space but took little away from its austerity. The table had become his office, his laboratory, and his hope. Neat stacks of books competed for space with ancient, moldering papers. The scent of mildew tainted the air.

Unhampered by the darkness, he crossed the room and picked up the book he'd had to abandon when Oblivion claimed him. An ancient book, this Grimoire, obtained at great cost and trouble. He'd had hope for it. But it was as full of inaccuracies as the rest, scribblings of pseudo-sorcerers who only hoped to be more. Nothing that could open a path to the Abyss.

"Halloween tricks," he muttered, "when I need the stars, the moon, and perhaps an earthquake or two."

With a hiss of frustration, he tossed the book aside and headed upstairs. Life was the issue of this day.

He found Sonya, Justin, and Kelli in the family room. The two young people sat on the floor, the girl secure in the circle of Justin's arm. His fingers spread out over her hip, tender and yet openly possessive. Although the television provided the only light in the room, he knew Justin's gesture would have been no different in daylight or before God Himself. How very Danilov.

Sonya sat on the sofa, her bare feet propped on the coffee table. Her strapless sundress pooled around her calves, the soft gold of the fabric making her skin look even paler than it was. She watched her son, not the television. A tall glass sat in a pool of condensation beside her right foot. The harsh light from the television bleached her eyes and cast odd, flickering shadows across her face.

"Hello, everyone," Alex said, stepping into the room.

Sonya turned to look at him. "Hello, Alex. Come to howl at the moon?"

"That's for werewolves," he said.

"Werewolves?" She smiled. "Someone else would have said *wolves*."

"Would they?"

Justin rolled to his feet and switched on the overhead light. "Anyone for going into town and catching a movie?"

"Sure," Kelli said.

"No," Sonya countered. "We need to talk."

Her eyes held no emotion, no sign of what was going on inside her. Their very blankness made foreboding bloom in Alex's stomach.

"You see, Alex," she said, "I've grown up in the past few months. I'm tired of letting men run my life. It's time for me to take responsibility for me and mine."

"And . . . ?" Challenging.

She met his gaze levelly. Challenge accepted. "For his own protection, I'm moving to regain custody of my son."

"What?" Justin shouted, jumping to his feet.

"And," she continued, her gaze never straying from Alex, "to protect his interests, I'm also suing for control of Danilov Industries, this house, and all properties that were conveyed to you under Margaret's will."

"No!" Justin cried. "Alex, do you see what she's doing?"

"Yes, I see."

"I don't," Kelli said.

Justin swung around to face her. "She's not going to let us get married."

"She's . . ." The girl's face turned pale. "Wh-why not?"

"Because Justin is simply too young to be tied down, Kelli," Sonya said. "You're a nice young woman, I'm sure, but I'm afraid I can't allow him to ruin his life."

"Can she do that?" Kelli asked, turning to Alex.

"No," he said.

"Yes, I can. I'm his mother."

"You gave him up," Kelli cried.

"So what? I want him back."

Sonya reached for her glass and took a drink. Against his will, Alex's gaze fastened on the smooth length of her throat. Beautiful. Something had warmed her languid passion; he could almost see the heat beneath the pale skin.

"I won't let you do this," he said.

"Alex, darling. I don't think you've got a snowball's chance in hell of stopping me."

Justin stepped forward, fists clenched. "You're not going to get away with this. We'll fight you—"

"You, young man, are a minor. And Alex is not your father. Do you think a court is going to choose him over your own mother?"

"You just want the money," Justin said.

His voice seemed calm, almost resigned, but anger rolled from him in almost palpable waves. With a stab of surprise, Alex realized that Justin had expected this from the moment he'd seen Sonya's suitcases in the foyer. The surprise came, not from the young man's perception, but from the fact that he'd been less foolishly idealistic than his thousand-year-old guardian.

Alex knew Justin; a long time ago he'd been very much like him—strong, stubborn, and smart. Good qualities, yet edged with a young man's needs, a young man's recklessness. And recklessness carried a price. Alex had paid it many times over and had found it too high.

He put his hand on Justin's shoulder. "Take it easy."

"Take it easy! I've got a baby due in February. Would you take it easy if you were me?"

Alex leaned close. "Trust me," he murmured.

Feeling the younger man's body tense, he tightened his grasp. It must have hurt. Justin didn't seem to notice. For a moment he looked very like his father.

Then the tension went out of him. Acquiescence, if not acceptance. Alex released him.

Justin turned on his heel, disgust evident in the taut line of his jaw. Kelli reached out to him. Her face was still pale, her eyes shadowed with fear. Alex sighed. Her world, steady and content a few moments ago, had become an insecure place run on the whims of others. Her world, and her child's.

She's too sweet, too vulnerable for this game. And Justin can't protect her.

Alex took her chin and tipped her face up. Tears shone in her eyes. "Try not to worry," he said.

Justin slipped his arm around her and drew her in. Without a word, he led her from the room. Slowly Alex pivoted to look at Sonya. She returned his gaze coolly, strands of her moonlight-pale hair lifting in the faint draft from the air conditioner.

"This is poorly done," he said.

Her eyes were clear and guileless. "I'm just protecting my son's future."

"Are you?"

She crossed her legs, a languid movement that exposed her thighs almost to her hips. Pale. Perfect. He imagined touching her, running his hands along her skin. It stirred him even as it repelled him. Her skin, like her heart, would be cool and smooth, untouchable even if possessed. No wonder Philippe had strayed.

Smiling, she met his gaze, her fingertip stroking the length of the crystal pendant. "I want nothing but the best for my son. Come on, Alex. Justin's handsome, he's rich—or he will be someday—and his family's the closest thing to royalty around here. Do you think that little girl is the best he can do?"

A surge went through Alex, but he couldn't tell if it was anger or Blood-Hunger. This was not the Sonya he knew. Even at her most brittle, she'd been more destructive to herself than to others. "Is this all you learned from Philippe?" he asked.

"What do you mean?"

"You dared something new with him—being in love. Did you learn only the lessons about taking, and not the ones about giving?"

She rose to her feet and came toward him. The overhead light cast platinum sparks in the smooth fall of her hair and deepened the blue of her eyes. "What do you give, when you love?"

"Everything."

"I see." She stopped in front of him, so close that the crystal cast miniature rainbows on the front of his shirt. "And what do you take?"

It was a trap. He knew it and, despite the knowing, was unable to keep from stepping into it.

"Everything," he said.

The words seemed to hang in the air between them. Stark truth. Too stark. Too true.

Ah, Elizabeth!

His gaze refocused on the woman before him. Triumph gilded her eyes, turned the corners of her mouth up in a supercilious curve.

"This playing with other people's lives," he said, "can be dangerous."

"The risk is less for the player than for the pawns. Barron taught me that."

Alex considered appealing to her love for her son, but there was an edge to her, a hardness as smooth and polished as the crystal she wore, that told him it would be useless. He had to try, however. For Justin and Kelli, for the unborn child who had become a pawn in an adult's game.

"Justin was very hurt when you left for Europe," he said. "He might have forgiven you. But you ignored him. One letter and three phone calls in nine months' time—" Her eyes didn't soften, and he broke off in frustration. "Look. Your relationship with Justin is a fragile thing right now. What you're doing is likely to strain it beyond repair."

"But he has you, after all," she said.

"He'd rather have you, if you'd give him half a chance."

"Or else." She smiled. "I know him. He'll just walk away emotionally. Write me off as a lost cause and go on with his life. Mother, father, lover—it doesn't matter who, just whether they're doing what Justin wants them to do. Very Danilov, don't you think?"

There was enough truth to her statement, however twisted, to hurt.

"Don't you care?" Alex asked.

"Why should I let him blackmail me? Gee, Mom, if you don't do what I want, think what I want, I'm not going to love you anymore."

"He'll always love you, Sonya. But as you say, he's capable of going on without you. Do you want to risk that?"

"I don't seem to have a choice."

"He's your son," Alex said.

Her smile was brittle, humorless. "He might as well be *your* son, Alex; he's more like you than he ever was like either of his natural parents."

"I'll take that as a compliment."

"If you like."

Anger sparked a coal deep in his chest, fanned it into heat. His hands itched with the desire to shake her into understanding. Into *feeling* something for her son.

"What is it you want, really?" he asked. "Another million?"

"Are you offering one?"

"Would it work?"

She tilted her head to one side. "This time money can't buy me what I want."

"I'm going to fight you," he said.

"Be my guest. You've got unlimited money. I have unlimited time and the fact that I'm Justin's mother. Even if you win this in court, you won't do it before that baby's born."

Too true, damn her. "Why are you doing this?"

This time she smiled at him with what looked like genuine amusement. "Let's call it spite. Or maybe perversity."

"Or greed," he said softly.

She raised one pale, bare shoulder, let it drop. "Whichever. As the saying goes, let the games begin." Rising on her tiptoes, she kissed him on the mouth.

Then she walked away. Alex was left with the flesh memory of her lips on his, and a burn deep inside that surely must be anger.

4

The afternoon sun lay hot on Lydia's shoulders as she walked. She smiled. Sonya *never* went out without a hat and sunscreen; she'd have a stroke if she knew how her body was being used. Then again, maybe she did know. How entertaining.

"I'll see if I can find something else you've never tried," Lydia murmured.

A lock of hair blew across her face, surprising her with its paleness. She and Sonya were a poor fit. For all this body's cool, blond beauty, it didn't feel right. Lydia wanted her own body back. Living in someone else's took a great deal of strength, and she wouldn't be able to keep it up more than a day or two at most. Then it would be back into the crystal, without the resources to break out again.

Imprisoned forever. No, no, no.

Anyone else would have enjoyed the bright golden day, the sun sparkling on the roofs, flowers nodding their heads lazily on the hot, humid breeze, a pair of butterflies whirling in a mad mating dance. But Lydia didn't see the beauty. Her sight, smell, hearing were tuned only to the taint that hung in the air like a wound. All that was left of Suldris—a shadow, a faint almost scent of corruption. Touching it brought a shudder to her soul. Still, she followed it.

It took her down a street, an alley, then another street, always moving closer to the waterfront. Her feet began to hurt. It was a shame she couldn't remember more about what happened a year ago—like where she'd hidden her body. But that night had been a whirlwind of power, of loss and death and pain. And all flavored with Alex.

Suldris was dead. But his evil remained, her only guide. As much as she abhorred its touch, she followed it. As the saying went, the end justified the means.

"Hello, gorgeous."

Startled, she looked up to see a man standing in front of her, almost, but not quite blocking her path. He towered over her, muscles bulging, mouth turned up in a leer. His face hadn't seen a razor in days, and he reeked of beer and sweat. A real charmer.

Beneath the sour man-smell lurked the essence of Suldris's power. Beckoning her.

Her nostrils flared. "Excuse me?"

"I said, hello, gorgeous. Lonely?"

"You've got to be kidding."

"Aw, come on. I been on a ship for nearly five months, and you're goddamned beautiful. How about it? I'll show you a real fun night on the town."

Lydia stepped to one side, then shifted to the other when he blocked her path. He blocked that, too. She glanced up and down the street. Empty, as were the warehouse windows overhead. No help there.

He's an animal. Show fear, and you've had it.

"I don't have time for this," she snapped. "Let me by!"

"Later," he said, taking hold of her arm in a grip that numbed it to the elbow. "First I want to get to know you better. Maybe then you won't *want* to leave, huh?"

Her shoes rasped on the pavement as he pulled her toward him. She twisted, hurting her arm even more. "Let me go!" she panted.

The scent of corruption grew thicker, darker. It drew around her, enclosing her, seeping into her pores, her flesh, sinking deep into her soul. Evil. Terrifying. And also compelling, in its own way as intimate and seductive as Alex's Blood-Hunger.

Something fluttered in her mind. Not a voice, not even a thought. But she got the message with utter clarity. *Use me, and I will set you free.*

Yes, she thought, tasting power. *Free.*

The blackness rushed through her veins like a sweet, dark liqueur, smooth even though it burned all along its path. The crystal caught its echo, matching it, amplifying it. She gritted her teeth as she struggled to bring stone and power into harmony. And won.

It had taken only an eye blink in time; the man's smile was only now fading, his arm tightening in preparation to pulling her closer.

"Take your hands off me," she said.

Surprise bloomed on his face. "Your eyes. They've . . . what the hell?"

She lashed out at him with everything inside her. All the hate, frustration, and anger came out in one enraged outpouring. For a moment the world turned black. She heard a choked cry, thought it was hers. It wasn't until the darkness eased that she saw the man slumped down against the curb.

Silent. His back heaved with his labored breathing, and blood ran from his ears, mouth, and the corners of his eyes. Even as she watched, his breathing stopped.

"Jesus," she whispered. "Jesus."

Jesus had nothing to do with this. Shaking, she drew the back of her hand over her mouth. Then she turned and ran. She ran until her breath gave out, until her pulse roared in her ears. Finally she stopped, propping her back against a building's brick wall while she tried to recover.

She'd killed a man.

No, Suldris's power had killed him. But she'd used it. She hadn't meant to kill.

Didn't you? Didn't you really?

"Yes," she said aloud.

Liar.

Liar. She hadn't cared what happened to him; she'd only wanted to get away. Any way she could, whether she killed or not. Just the way she'd have immortality. Any way she could, whether she killed or not.

The darkness moved within her, questing. She straightened. Her body was somewhere close; she could feel it, a nagging ache like a sensitive tooth. Even in her wild flight, Suldris's power had drawn her in the right direction.

She followed eagerly as the taint drew her down the street to a warehouse. Ivy bearded the building's brick walls, and weather-grayed plywood shrouded its windows. A rusted padlock secured the front door. This was the place; she could sense her body inside. Impatience shafted through her. She had to get *in*!

"Come on," she muttered, rattling the door.

The lock held. She went around to the back, only to find the back door secured as well.

She scanned the building, smiling when she noticed a gap between the plywood and the frame of one of the first-floor windows.

"So that's how you got in!" She wedged the heel of one of Sonya's fine Italian pumps beneath the plywood, then levered it away from the window.

Getting in was easy, a matter of sliding the unlocked window upward and climbing in. Daylight filtered through a filthy skylight two stories over her head.

Judging by its size, this room must have been a warehouse. Corpses of packing boxes littered the floor, silent confirmation of her guess.

She moved forward, toward the double doors at the far end of the big room. Dust sifted up from beneath her feet to hang suspended in the sunbeams. Tiny tracks crossed and recrossed the floor, left by the small creatures that dwelled here. Lydia left her own footprints, a giant moving through a Lilliputian world.

She passed through the double doors into a hallway. Doorways pierced the walls at regular intervals, some closed, some open. She peered into each one, waiting for the grinding ache to sharpen. All were empty, ordinary. Finally she came to a doorway where the mouse and insect trails did not enter. Neither did the light. Darkness filled the room, shadows so thick they looked as though they'd been painted.

The smell of power was strong.

She stepped over the threshold, walking into a world where the creatures of this one dared not enter. But not without fear. This was Suldris's power, and he had killed her.

The room seemed to resist the sound of her footsteps, as though it had somehow forgotten human things. Even her breathing sounded strangely hushed.

Something gleamed in the darkness, catching light that wasn't really there. Lydia moved toward it. Terror and anticipation rocketed through her body, mingled with the dread of what she might find. And what she might not.

She stumbled over something. Bending, she retrieved the offending object. A shoe, one of the pair she'd worn that night. The night she died. The leather was as supple as it had been a year ago, unmarked by mildew or rot. She dropped it back to the floor, noticing that the room swallowed the sound.

As she moved forward she found herself gripping the

crystal in one hand. To keep herself in, she wondered, or maybe to keep something else out.

Not some vague something—Suldris. Her master, mentor, murderer. The essence of his power was all around her. In her. He'd be pleased, she thought. Even in death he possessed her.

"No, you bastard," she whispered. "You're dead. It's my turn to use *you*." Gripping the crystal in one hand, she moved toward that faint glimmer.

A sudden surge of heat stung her palm, and she let the crystal drop. She drew her breath in with a hiss. Light had sprung to life within the depths of the stone, a spark that kept the surrounding shadows from quite touching her.

Let there be light. Triumph flooded through her. *I could get used to this*.

And then, at the very edge of the illumination, she saw . . . herself. Lydia.

Her body sat on the floor, back propped against the wall, legs extended. The left one was broken, bone sticking out of the shredded flesh of the thigh. That was shocking enough. But it was the utter bloodlessness of her skin that made her stomach lurch. White. Pallid. Corpse skin, stark and dead against the fiery-red hair.

"God!" she muttered, whirling away from the sight.

She took a couple of deep breaths, then forced herself to turn around again. Forced herself to look.

I've got to inhabit that? She swallowed against an upwelling of vomit.

Tell yourself it isn't so bad.

"It's not so bad," she said, disbelieving.

Then she thought about the network of tracks that crisscrossed the floors outside. What if *they*'d gotten in here? Her mind conjured up the vision of tiny mouths chewing, chewing. Liking the soft parts best.

A shudder rippled up her spine.

She forced herself to touch that still, white face. The skin felt cool despite the stifling heat of the room, and the flesh strangely hard, as though muscle and fat had congealed into a solid mass.

"Okay," she said. "Let's get to work."

Reaching into her pocket, she pulled out the crystals she'd prepared the night before. Their vibrations set up an answering hum in the back of her mind. The hovering shadows seemed to press closer, as though attracted to the crystals.

In a hurry now, Lydia stretched her body on the floor. But she took a moment to straighten the broken leg that hung pitifully to one side.

"I will be whole," she said.

The crystals sang.

She arranged them upon the body; garnet at the base of the spine, agate just over the pelvic area, yellow citrine upon the navel, malachite on the center of the chest, blue topaz on the throat, and finally, a brilliant sapphire at the center of the forehead.

Lydia abandoned the usual procedures; they were as obsolete here as the dodo. She'd learned a better way. The danger no longer mattered. Safety was for those who had something to lose.

Closing her eyes, she opened herself to the darkness. Or Darkness, as Suldris would have said.

Resonance ran through her, the stones, and back again. She drew in a sharp breath as the crystal over her heart began to pulse with the cadence of her—Sonya's—heart. Sparks bloomed in her mind, red, orange, yellow, green, blue. They, too, began to pulse with the rhythm of her borrowed body.

"Move," she muttered.

Move, move, move! In time with her beating heart.

No, Sonya's heart. No. Two hearts. One echoing the other. Sonya's, Lydia's, Lydia's, Sonya's.

"I will be whole," she whispered. "I will not be that poor, broken thing on the floor. I will not be mutilated . . . I will not be *ugly*!"

The power contracted around her. For a moment she thought she heard laughter. But it was only the crystals, humming together in eerie cadence. Something wrenched the world from beneath her, whirling her adrift in a sea of multicolored light. Pain. Awareness, helplessness. Like being born again, or maybe like dying.

Two voices merged into the scream, then more. She realized that the crystals had joined her agony, amplified it. Impaled on pain, she howled their collective protest. It went on until she was sure she'd die, then went on even longer.

Darkness washed over her, extinguishing the voices and the light. She spiraled down into the velvety blackness. Like a leaf in autumn, circling gently down to its final resting place . . .

The darkness changed, softened. With a shock, she realized that she was looking at the insides of her own eyelids. She opened them. The ceiling hung above her, tendrils of shadow encroaching into the light reflected there.

"What . . . ?"

I'm me! This is my body!

She turned her head to see Sonya kneeling beside her, head down, her face hidden by her hair. A faint pulse of light lingered in the crystal pendant she wore. Gingerly, then with mounting confidence, Lydia moved her arms and legs, fingers and toes. Everything worked. The broken leg was whole again, not even a scar to show where the terrible wound had been.

"I did it," Lydia whispered. "Oh, God, I did it."

God isn't the one you should be calling on. The thought was an odd one, but no odder than the next: God wasn't the only one who could perform miracles.

She got to her feet, pushing the tumbled mass of her hair back with her hands. What wouldn't she give for a trip to the salon for a wash, a cut, and a set of Solar Nails!

Sonya still hadn't moved. Lydia smiled. This, too, was going according to plan. The other woman would be in control of her own body, but her actions would be ordered by Lydia. And she had a lot of things to ask of Sonya.

Lydia touched her lightly on the shoulder. "Wake up."

Sonya raised her head. Her eyes remained unfocused, her jaw slack. Gently, Lydia lifted the pendant from around the other woman's neck and slipped it on. Then she took another, similar crystal necklace out of her pocket and handed it to Sonya.

"Put it on," she said.

Sonya obeyed. Lydia touched her own stone and saw an answering glow deep in the other crystal. Good. It was working perfectly.

"Thank you for bringing me back," she said. "Now it's time to go home. Run along, Sonya. When you reach the main street outside, you'll wake up. Can't have you walking around like a . . . zombie."

Lydia laughed, but it wasn't really funny.

She led Sonya to the back. "Let's give that door a try, shall we?" she asked, knowing she'd get no answer. "I'll be damned if I'm going to be climbing in and out of that window all the time."

She grasped the handle and gave the door a hard shove. With a scream of snapping metal, the lock broke. She snatched her hand back, staring at her own fingers in astonishment.

Absently she said, "Go home, Sonya."

The other woman walked out. Lydia closed the door behind her and returned to the room that had housed her body. She picked up a piece of wood, a brace for a packing case. And broke it easily between her hands.

"Wow," she said, stacking the wood double and breaking that as well. Was this the result of using Suldris's power? Or did it have something to do with using the crystals the way she had?

Then she shrugged. It didn't matter. What did matter was the fact that this fight was getting more and more even as time went on.

"You're not going to brush me away this time, Alex," she muttered.

She opened a window and tore off a section of plywood, letting the ruddy afternoon sun stream into the room. A sudden glitter of reflected light caught her gaze. She turned, abruptly realizing it came from the crystals that had tumbled, unnoticed, from her body when she'd gotten up.

The glitter was not red or orange, yellow or green or blue. Every stone had turned black.

"Why is she doing this?" Justin raged. "Did she come back here just to ruin my life?"

"She can't stop you forever," Alex said.

"Right. But my kid will be born before that happens."

Alex nodded. "It will still be a Danilov."

Justin spun, putting his back to Alex, and raked his hand through his hair. "Can't we pay her off? You can take it out of my trust fund."

"She says she's not interested in money."

"Then it's just for spite, or what?"

Alex spread his hands. "I don't know. She's . . . changed. I wouldn't have expected this of her, Philippe or no Philippe."

"Hell, maybe we should bribe *him*. I bet she'd go running back to Europe fast enough if he asked her to."

From the mouths of babes. "I'll look into it," Alex said, amused despite the situation. "You know, maybe you *should* take some business courses. I think you've got a real flair for cutthroat dealings."

"This isn't business," Justin snarled. "This is my life."

Alex stared at the young man's back. The shoulders were a bit bony, without the heavy musculature that would come when he matured. But they were square and wide, stubborn like their owner. What would Catherine have said to him if she were here? She'd raised a brood of these headstrong Danilovs and had somehow managed to guide them without either giving in or breaking their spirits. It was only now that Alex realized how little he'd contributed in the day-to-day raising of his children. With Margaret he'd held favorite-uncle status; he could tease her, spoil her, give in to her, and leave the discipline to her father.

And now, in Justin's crisis, he could do nothing. He could think of no words of reassurance, no comfort.

"Justin," he said, "I'm trying. I've got Charles McGinnis working on this."

"Yeah, yeah. But all that takes time, and I don't have it. How do you think Kelli's going to feel walking down the aisle with her belly out to here—"

"Proud," Alex said. "Just as we will be, no matter where her belly is."

Justin turned around. His eyes had turned black with rage, but it was a cold and determined kind of anger. The kind that took action.

"Let me work on this," Alex said, wanting to defuse the anger—and the action. "As the proverb says, there are many ways to skin a cat."

"Yeah. Too bad I'm the one getting skinned."

Justin stalked out, slamming the door behind him. A moment later Alex heard the front door slam, too.

"Ah, Sonya," he murmured. "Whatever you're looking for, is it worth losing your son's love?"

With a sigh, he sat down to contemplate the chess-board. He'd talked the young man into a game of chess, hoping to channel some of his restlessness. Of course it hadn't worked. Human beings weren't ordered like games, nor was life. Chess was much easier; move this over here, that over there, and voilà, you win.

Sonya had a lot to learn.

He got up and went to the sideboard to pour himself a glass of wine from the bottle that had been chilling since dusk. Something new, white and Californian. Cautiously he took a sip. It was quite good. But on nights like tonight, he missed the old things—candlelight sparkling amid the chandelier's prisms, the smooth lilt of a waltz, the windows open to let in the summer breeze.

"Well, why not?" he asked himself.

He set his glass aside and opened the window. The hot, humid air slid into the room like a questing serpent, bringing the scent of roses and beading the wineglass with moisture.

The marsh echoed with life tonight—frogs croaking, insects humming, whining, droning, and below that, supporting it all like a refrain, the cicada's shrill summer call. This alone did not change; uncounted generations of insects had lived and died since the first time he'd listened to it, but the song was still the same.

A shame the lavender was no longer in bloom.

Alex retrieved his glass and raised it in a toast. "To you, Catherine."

But it was Elizabeth he wanted. Elizabeth for whom he ached in the dimness between Oblivion and wakeful-ness, Elizabeth for whom he listened in dark hallways and the hushed stillness of almost dawn.

His Blood-Hunger stirred, wakened perhaps by his need. Claws stroked along his spine, taunting but not quite digging in; a reminder of what he was. He pushed it aside. Revenant he might be, but it didn't control him. But he knew this respite was only temporary; soon the Blood-Hunger would stab deep. And only blood could blunt its edge and make the agony bearable.

A knock at the door brought his head up. "Who is it?"

"Mr. Danilov? Detective Rhudwyn to see you."

The bulldog is here. Not an unwelcome presence, as Alex had discovered months ago. "Please show him in, Eve."

The detective came in a moment later, walking into the room like a man who was comfortable with his surroundings. As indeed he was. He'd become a regular visitor here, dropping in every few weeks to play chess and engage in conversation that was outwardly innocuous, actually sharp and deadly—a rapier sheathed in velvet. Alex liked him, cautiously. And welcomed him, for his chess game was as cunning as his mind.

"Hello, Martin," he said, coming forward to shake hands. "Would you care for a drink?"

"Not tonight, thanks. Eve is bringing me coffee; I'm on midnight shift." Rhudwyn indicated the open window. "Is something wrong with your air-conditioning?"

"No," Alex said. "Sometimes I just like to feel the outside world."

"Most people would go for a walk."

"Most would." Alex smiled. "But I'm lazy tonight. I want to feel the world from my easy chair. Would you care for a game?"

Rhudwyn returned the smile. "Don't I always?"

Neither supplied the word *chess*. They knew which games they'd be playing. Alex closed the window, shutting out the frantic summer song of the marsh. The sudden cessation of sound was startling.

"Loud out there, isn't it?" Rhudwyn asked.

"The beat of their lives is fast and furious. One brief

summer. If they don't mate, breed, and raise their young in that time, then their living was futile. Nature is very hard on futility. White?"

"Thanks."

They settled into their respective places at the chess table, Rhudwyn taking white, Alex black.

The detective looked over the board. "Three moves, and black would have won this game."

"My opponent had his mind on other things," Alex said.

Rhudwyn began putting the pieces back into their starting positions, his fingers quick and sure on the board. He then moved a pawn, initiating the play. "I heard that Sonya Danilov filed to regain custody of her son."

"News travels fast."

"Bad news always does."

Alex knew the mention of the custody suit hadn't been a request for information. Just a reminder that anything Danilov happened to be of interest. Leaning back in his chair, Alex regarded his opponent over the small forest of white and black spindles. Frustration hovered at the back of the man's eyes, belying the relaxation of his hands and body.

An interesting man. Secretive, perhaps more so than the people he hunted. Welsh blood ran strong in him, an intuition almost strong enough to be psychic. It had made him a very good detective. In another age, he might have been a knight—or perhaps a priest. Certainly he had a streak of inflexibility a mile wide, the complete surety that there was a clean division between black and white, right and wrong. That surety had been outraged by the deaths of the Garrys. Those deaths could not be put aside until the murderer was found and the scales of justice set right.

"Something's bothering you, isn't it?" Alex asked.

If he hadn't asked the question, Martin would have wondered why not. A challenging man, as well as interesting.

"Bothering me?" Rhudwyn echoed, touching his knight, then abandoning it in favor of a bishop. "You could say that. My boss reduced the Garry case to pending status last week. Seems we've got fresher murders. But I've been working it on my own time."

"Of course," Alex said. "It doesn't sit well to let something like this go."

"And don't start that nonsense about me being Welsh. Anyone would be bothered by this case. In the space of a single night, two people are burned to a crisp in their beds and three people disappear off the face of the earth. Two are prominent area citizens, one the daughter of the two murdered people. Kinda strange, wouldn't you say?"

"Very," Alex said. "As I told you before."

"I'm going to solve this case."

Alex smiled. "If anyone can, you can."

"Don't you wonder what happened to your fiancée?"

"I think about her every day."

"Do you think she's dead?"

Alex met the other man's gaze squarely. "Yes. So do you."

Elusive as always, the detective sidestepped. "We found out about the money Barron embezzled from the company."

Feint and thrust, Alex thought. Answer a question with a question, attack in order to defend. He wasn't surprised at what the police had discovered; he and Charles had worked hard to make that information available without letting the police know they *wanted* it found. Alex and his opponent continued to move chess pieces around the board, echo of the larger game they played.

Rhudwyn was the first to break the silence. "I can't

believe your people didn't find the missing funds."

Alex inclined his head, accepting the charge. "This is hard enough for Justin without having him find out his father was a thief."

"Telling the police isn't the same as telling the boy."

"No? I recall certain details regarding Barron and Lydia's disappearance that cropped up in the newspapers. There's a leak in your department, Martin. Until you find it and plug it, I'm afraid I can't be free with Danilov business."

Alex had deliberately drawn a distinction between Rhudwyn and the possible leak, and the lack of tension in the man's shoulders showed that he understood that distinction.

"As it is," Alex continued, "this custody business will be in the paper within a day or two."

"I'll plug the leak. Check."

Startled, Alex surveyed the board. His king was indeed in check. He moved it.

Rhudwyn smiled. "Does it bother you to know that Barron—and probably Lydia with him—is probably living it up in the sun in Rio on Danilov Industries money?"

"Is he?"

"Isn't he?"

"Does every embezzler run off to Rio?"

"A man with several million in embezzled funds is unlikely to hole up in, say, Kalamazoo. Check. Mate in two."

Alex glanced down at the board, then spread his hands. "Looks like you've beaten me."

"Maybe someday." Rhudwyn glanced at his watch, then pushed his chair away from the table. "Got to run. I've inherited a strange one—a sailor who died when every blood vessel in his body ruptured simultaneously."

Alex raised his brows, astonished. "You're kidding."

"I wish I were. Pleasant dreams, Mr. Danilov."

"I never have dreams, Martin. Pleasant or otherwise."

"Maybe that's why you keep losing at chess. Dreams are good for the soul." He walked to the door, then paused with his hand on the knob and turned back to Alex. "You do believe in the soul, don't you?"

"More than most."

Surprise sparked in Rhudwyn's eyes. And interest. "Good night. I'll see you . . . next time."

"That sounds like a threat," Alex said, smiling.

Rhudwyn turned away. Alex felt the man's presence long after he was gone.

5

Alex flew over the marsh, his owl wings almost touching the water on every downstroke. It was eerily quiet in this hour before the dawn, the only sounds the gentle splashings of feeding fish and the occasional hoot of an owl. He never answered those calls. A man in the shape of an owl, a revenant in the shape of a man—in both his worlds, an intruder.

A predator. Perhaps not the monster he'd once thought, but always the hunter.

Only Wildwood accepted him. But the marsh accepted everything, predators and prey, amphibian and bird and mammal, mouse and alligator. And why? Because they were too small and too short-lived to affect it. Even he. His thousand years meant nothing here. Nor did his Blood-Hunger; all who lived here fed on one another, and all eventually fed the marsh's eternal fecundity.

As he neared Wildwood's edge the house became visible between the trees. The starlight lay gently upon its white walls, making it seem almost as ethereal as the mist surrounding it. A lit window marked the second floor. Lydia's room.

Alex flew into the dark recesses of the big mimosa,

then shifted into man-form before entering the house. He could sense only Sonya's presence in the house, and that quite a distance from Lydia's room.

He drifted silently upstairs. The darkness of the hallway leading to Lydia's room was broken only by the bar of light that came from beneath the door. Ominous, somehow, like a snake coiled to strike.

Alex pushed the door open and went in. Crystal song greeted him, the voices of the stones that had once served Lydia. The pain of the great quartz crystal shivered along his nerves like an accusation.

"I'm sorry," he said, reaching up to touch the pendant that was no longer there. "I haven't the power to heal you."

He walked toward the bookcase where the injured crystal lay. He'd removed the mirrors from the closet doors and the one over the bureau, and even the small, handheld one that had lain beside the brush on the dresser. Not because they could give him away, but because they'd seemed to reflect his guilt back at him, if not his face. So he'd removed them. The guilt, however, remained.

"And why not?" he asked the crystals. "Lydia died because of me."

So had Elizabeth. He took the injured stone down from its shelf and held it in his hands, letting its pain flow over him. A penance, perhaps. His mouth curved in a smile he didn't feel inside.

Still punishing yourself, I see, whispered his cynical revenant self.

"Of course," he said aloud. "No one else can."

The crystal's voice went up a notch, making his skin prickle in response. He closed his eyes. If he lived another thousand years, he would never forget that note. Part pain, part plea, as pure and plaintive as a Gypsy's violin. It drew him into himself, drowning him in his past, his present, and the long, undefinable future.

"Alex?"

Justin's voice brought Alex swinging around with a jerk. The young man stood just inside the doorway, Kelli behind him. Shock momentarily robbed Alex of his voice—and wits. *He hadn't sensed either of them!* It had been nearly a thousand years since someone had sneaked up on him.

"Sorry if I startled you," Justin said. "I saw the light, and figured I'd better check it out."

Alex set the crystal back on its shelf and tried to ignore its song. "I was just . . . deep in thought." He glanced at his watch. "Is there a reason why the two of you are up at this hour?"

"We spent the night talking about what to do," Justin said.

"Do Kelli's parents know where she is?"

Guilt spread across both their faces.

"Well . . ." Justin began.

"I climbed out the window," Kelli said.

Alex almost smiled. "I think you'd better call them."

"I'll do it," Justin said. "This is my fault."

He disappeared from the doorway. Alex expected Kelli to follow him, but instead she came into the room.

"What is this place?" she asked.

"This was Justin's aunt Lydia's room," Alex said. "As you can see, she was into crystals."

"She disappeared, right?"

"Right."

The girl made a circuit of the room, touching first one stone, then another. "They're beautiful."

Alex watched her, saw fascination bloom on her pretty, open face. Justin had been in this room a hundred times, and had even handled the stones, but had never responded to them at all.

She stopped in front of the bookcase and reached

up to stroke her fingertips over the big quartz crystal. Before she quite touched it, however, she pulled her hand away.

"Oh, God," she muttered.

"Is something the matter?" he asked.

"I'm feeling . . . kind of nauseated," she said, blushing.

Alex slipped his arm around her shoulders. She's so young, he thought. Such naïveté—to blush at the mention of nausea. "That has a habit of happening to pregnant women," he said. "I understand that it's worse on an empty stomach. Have you had anything to eat since supper?"

She shook her head.

"Let's get you some crackers and maybe a little hot tea. That always helped my"—he paused, erasing the almost said word *wife*—"sister during her pregnancies."

"I didn't know you had a sister." Justin's voice came from the doorway.

Alex turned, mentally cursing himself for allowing the crystal's pain to make him careless. "I did, a long time ago. She died."

"What was her name?" Justin asked.

Alex pulled for a name, any name. She'd have to be French. "Céline."

Memory washed over him; not the fiction named Céline, but the sister whom he'd left behind nearly a millennium ago. Varina. Sweet Varina with her golden hair and gray eyes. She married a soldier at fourteen and died in childbirth a month after her fifteenth birthday. Yes, a long time ago. A chill slid up along his backbone, flesh memory of the glacial Ukraine winter. He could almost hear the tinkle of icicles being tossed by the wind. Or perhaps it was the sound of crystal lattices crumbling.

Apprehension shot through him. *If I were psychic, I'd call it fear.*

"Are you okay?" Justin asked.

He looked up, startled again that he hadn't sensed the boy's return. "I'm fine," he lied. "Just reminiscing. How did things go with Kelli's parents?"

"Well, they weren't as upset as they're gonna be when they find out we're not going to be able to get married right away."

Alex rolled his eyes. "That leaves it somewhere between being upset and going into a homicidal rage, doesn't it?"

"Good description," Justin said. "Let's just say that if I don't have Kelli home in an hour, we'll pass into the homicide phase even without bad news. By the way . . . Isn't that my woman you've got your arm around?"

"Why, yes," Alex murmured. "She wants to go downstairs and have some crackers and tea before—"

"Before I throw up all over your nice house," Kelli finished for him. "And as far as Mom and Dad's homicidal tendencies go, well, I'll talk them around in an hour or two."

"I don't want you getting upset," Justin protested.

"I'm not going to get upset. Trust me on this one, Justin. I know how to deal with my parents. Bottom line is that they love me, and want to see me happy." Turning, she winked at Alex with open mischief. "Right, Mr. Danilov?"

That wink made Alex instantly revise his opinion of her. Sweet-natured she might be, but perhaps there was enough fire in her to handle a Danilov. Good. "Call me Alex," he said.

She smiled. Alex returned it.

Ohhhh, Johnny! Better get your seat belt on. This one reminds me an awful lot of Catherine.

"Take her downstairs, Justin," he said, shooing them out the door. "And mind the time."

He waited until they'd disappeared around the corner,

then left the room. He'd delayed almost too long; he could feel the nearness of dawn like the promise of flame on his skin. Time to go downstairs.

Echoes of crystal song followed him down the hall. *Help me, help me.* The sound of pain, the cry of broken rainbows, and the echoing emptiness of a shattered stone heart. He would have helped if he could.

As it was, all he could do was try to drown the voice, to erase it and his guilt from his memory. In this he wasn't different from men. Men, however, had liquor and drugs, religion and self-delusion to help them in their drowning.

He had only Oblivion, and that only until darkness came again.

Lydia stopped at the entrance of Colonial Cemetery. The mist lay heavily on the ground, coiling up among the dripping, moss-hung branches of the trees. This was the end of yet another trail of Suldris's power.

Why this destination? she wondered. What could be here that sent this strong trace wafting on the hot summer air? Whatever it was, she had to have it.

Had to.

She'd tried to ignore the strange numbness in her body. It was almost unnoticeable at first, just the faintest dulling of the edge of feeling, like a tooth throwing off the effects of Novocain. But as time went on she became more aware of it.

And the numbness was getting worse. Little by little she seemed to be losing the integration with her body. She reached out, running her hand over the trunk of a nearby tree. The roughness of the bark felt blunted, as though the ridges of the bark weren't quite so high as they seemed, the crevices not so deep.

But she sensed the trail of Suldris's power with utter

clarity. That, and her hate. "What have you hidden here?" she muttered.

The cemetery remained silent, as it had for hundreds of years. She moved along the quiet lanes between the graves, her feet leaving dark tracks in the wet grass.

The ghostly shadow of a crypt materialized out of the mist ahead. A stone angel guarded the entrance, its wings fading off into the swirling fog. Lydia moved closer, saw the name Danilov carved on the lintel. So, this was the old family crypt! Nobody had been buried here since around the turn of the century, when the family started to use the more modern Georgian Cemetery in Delano.

She ran her fingertips along the warm slickness of the metal door. The sensation of power was stronger here, more centered. A shudder ran through her. Something lurked in the room beyond the door, something that exuded power and danger in equal parts.

"What are you?" she whispered, drawn to both.

She stepped back from the door. The brass lock was new and bright, apparently having been replaced within the last several months. It felt strangely cold in her palm, especially after the warmth of the door. Something put there to keep intruders away? Or maybe just to discourage the curious.

With a wrench, she broke the lock. The door moved at her touch, but grudgingly, its hinges squealing protest. She stepped inside. The fog accompanied her, white, ghostly tendrils swirling across the stone floor like questing fingers.

"Hello?" she whispered.

Deep shadows shrouded the far end of the room. Shrouded . . . it. The aura of power and danger coiled in that darkness. Waiting. To greet or destroy, Lydia had no way of knowing. Whichever, she had to wake it.

She waited for her eyes to adjust. Finally she began to see something in the far end of the crypt, an amorphous dark shape that nonetheless had more substance than the shadows around it. She moved closer. From here, it looked almost like a woman.

Lydia's breath went out in a gasp as she finally realized what it was. Elizabeth Garry! Alex's fiancée, laid out on the floor with her hands folded over her chest like a sleeping child. She was dead, of course.

"So this is what happened to you," Lydia said.

A year dead. And yet she remained perfectly preserved. No sign of rot, no degeneration even in the hot, humid staleness of the crypt. Hesitantly Lydia bent and touched the woman's hand. It was cold, but no colder than her own. Then she felt . . . She snatched her hand back. Power ran just beneath Elizabeth's skin, unawakened yet, but definitely there. It tasted of Suldris. Tasted of him, smelled and felt like him. And why not? It was part of him, just as she was. As Elizabeth was.

> *Deep in the cavern of the infant's breast,*
> *The father's nature lurks, and lives anew.*

Where had that thought come from? she wondered. Alex, maybe; he was always quoting ridiculous poetry. But no, Suldris had made this shadow of Lydia Danilov. If anyone's poetry showed up in her brain unbidden, it had to be his. A moan bubbled up in her throat, and she pressed the back of her hand over her mouth to keep the sound in.

Her crystal beat like a heart upon her chest. It knew. Her gaze riveted to Elizabeth's pale, still face, she sank to her knees. For all the stifling heat of the chamber, cold radiated from the floor, numbing the flesh of her knees even more.

"Why did he love you and not me?" It was the faintest of whispers, a mere breath of sound.

Lest we wake the dead.

Black wings of terror flapped along the avenues of her mind. She wanted to run and run, and never come back. She almost did. Then she realized that she'd been clenching her fists so tightly that her jagged nails had sunk into the flesh.

She stared down at the dark half-moons in her palms. No blood welled in those cuts, and no pain. Suldris had taken that from her. Only Suldris could give it back.

Yes, Alex had destroyed the man. But the power could not be destroyed. It had merely found another host. For a year it had lain here, sleeping like the woman who now possessed it.

To wake the power, she had to wake Elizabeth. A gamble—life or death, knowing what she'd want, what she'd need. But then this isn't exactly life, she reminded herself. The numbness would continue to worsen until she had no sensation at all. She'd have to look herself over a hundred times a day to make sure she was all there. A mind suspended, denied touching the world around it. She didn't have the strength to take over Sonya's mind again. Control it, yes; replace the resident personality, no.

Trapped again.

"It's the devil or the deep blue sea, Liz. I guess I've got to pick the devil; drowning has never appealed to me. Hey, what's that?" she said, noticing a glint of gold between Elizabeth's clasped hands.

Lydia pried the corpse's fingers loose, shuddering at the cold-wax feel of the flesh. Curiosity replaced her revulsion as she held the gold necklace up by its chain. It revolved slowly, catching hints of starlight on its carved surface. A cabochon ruby winkled at her from its place between a griffin's claws. The stone exuded a feeling of great age, of awareness of vast power stored and spent. But not all. She tried to tap into that wraith of power within the ruby, but was rejected. Gently but firmly, the way Alex had refused to make love to her after he'd met Elizabeth.

"This is yours, Alex, isn't it?" Lydia murmured, stroking the medallion with her fingertips. "It feels like you."

She dropped the necklace into her left hand and squeezed. The medallion resisted the pressure more than any normal gold should, but she did manage to crush the chain into a shapeless mass. Then she tossed it over her shoulder, dismissing it.

"Elizabeth," she called.

No response.

"Elizabeth." Fear in her voice, fear running with cold little mouse feet down her spine. Sensation, however given, was better than none at all. She squared her shoulders. "Elizabeth. Wake up."

Still no response.

"I don't want to touch you," Lydia said, trying to control the involuntary chattering of her teeth.

Her own crystal throbbed frantically upon her chest, demanding that she do it. She took a deep breath and squared her shoulders.

I will live forever. I will live *forever. I'll kill for it. I'll die for it—again—if I have to.*

Laying her right hand on that cold, pale forehead, Lydia clasped the ghost crystal in her left. It almost seemed to move in her palm—hungrily, as though sensing the power.

"Wake up, Elizabeth," she called, willing it.

Echoes of Suldris howled in the hills and valleys of her mind, ran like hot wine through veins that had forgotten the sensation of life. A surge of power shot through her arm, coiled deep in her body, then spread outward to her skin. *Now* she remembered what she'd been missing, what she'd never have again if she didn't succeed. The feel of the warm air moving across her skin, the hardness of the floor under her, the faint tickle of her hair as it slid across her cheek—all hers, for one glorious moment.

"Oh, God!" she sobbed.

Suddenly the warm rush of power was sucked away from her, and sensation with it. Lydia cried out, bound once again in her deadening flesh.

Then she looked down. And down, down, down into twin amber pools in which galaxies of gold stars spun.

Elizabeth had awakened.

6

Lydia stared down into the other woman's eyes, seeking awareness, seeking recognition. But there was only hunger. No. Blood-Hunger. This wasn't Alex's brand of Blood-Hunger with the damped-down ferocity and heightened sensuality, but a raw, primitive tidal wash of need that made Lydia shake with terror.

Helplessly she was drawn into the depths of those eyes. She leaned closer, and closer still, until she could feel the cool touch of Elizabeth's breath on her throat. The need enveloped her. Became hers. It spiraled in her belly, coiled upward into her throat like a lifetime's thirst. Elizabeth's. Hers.

She closed her eyes in anticipation. A moment more, and she'd step through the doorway. She might not *be* alive, but she'd feel like it. And that was enough.

The touch and the desire drained away. Abruptly. Completely. She cried out with the sudden swift loss, scrabbled frantically to regain it.

"No," she gasped. "Oh, no!"

Elizabeth lay still, apparently unaware of what she'd done. Sobbing, Lydia flung herself forward, pressing her throat against those cool, unresponsive lips. She shouted, cried, beat her fists on the other woman's shoulders.

Finally, exhausted, she pushed herself back to a sitting position. Elizabeth's dark amber eyes remained blank. No constellations of gold whirled in their depths now. But Lydia could feel oceans of Blood-Hunger beneath that indifferent surface. The beast had not been tamed. There just wasn't anything here to interest it.

If I were alive, she'd see me.

Spurned.

Left out.

Found wanting.

Lydia's eyes ached from tears she was no longer capable of producing. "Elizabeth," she whispered.

Not a flicker. Not even a sign that anyone had spoken.

She doesn't remember anything.

Yes. And so . . .

She doesn't remember Alex.

The thought rang through Lydia's brain, carrying reverberations of possibilities. With no memory of her life, Elizabeth was a clean slate. To be written on as Lydia chose.

She touched Elizabeth's hand. When there was no response, she dared clasp those cold fingers in her own. "I'm Lydia. I want to help you."

The crystal began to pulse again. With her free hand, Lydia grasped it. She cried out as she plunged into a sea of dark sensation. Pain. Need. A desire so profound it made the body cringe, submerged the mind.

Instinct screamed at her to push it away. But she forced herself to hold on to the crystal despite the agony. *This* was her lever. Gripping the stone until it cut into her palm, she poured a message into it. Her vision dimmed. A storm raged in the crystal's depths, a dark and screaming torrent of wind that swept her up and spun her like a dry leaf.

She convulsed as white-hot lancets of lightning stabbed into her, through her, pinning her in the arms of the storm wind. Shrieking, she clutched the crystal, knowing that to let go would be the end of her.

Then she felt the echo of Suldris's touch in the shadowed places of her mind. It was elusive, a mere breath of presence. But it gave her what she needed. Just as she'd learned to tap into Alex's Blood-Hunger, she set about tapping Elizabeth's. Suldris had taught her well. She wasn't about to waste this legacy he'd left for her.

Not for you. For him. A year ago he'd created this being, poised her at eternity's threshold with a single drop of his blood. And waited for Alex to take her over.

The irony of it made Lydia smile in her light-shot nest. A single drop of blood. It gave him power over his creation. And Lydia, his creature, carried echoes of him in her mind.

I'll use you, as you used me. It's little enough payment for what you took.

Reaching out with her free hand, she gathered the shards of lightning.

Claimed them. Tamed them. Taught them to obey.

I can help you, she shouted into the whirlwind.

Something touched her then. A cool touch, but possessing the potential of great power. The soul of that-which-has-no-soul, the heart of that-which-is-no-longer-alive.

Vampire.

Ah, if only Alex knew.

Deep in that secretive heart of his, he mourned his dead lover. Oh, yes. Dreamer that he was, he comforted himself with the thought that he had saved her from . . . a fate worse than death. Amusement ran in hot little torrents through Lydia's mind. Alex. After a thousand years he still hadn't learned not to trust.

Lydia called to the vampire along the waves of the wind. *I'm your sister. We were . . . born of the same father. I know what you need. Trust me, and I will give it to you.*

Elizabeth's eyes remained blank, but Lydia could feel acquiescence in the crystal. The Blood-Hunger knew. It wanted to be fed, and recognized that Lydia was the only one who could help it.

Sisters. Born of blood, Liz. Born of the voice you feel inside you. The Dark Revenant.

Lydia rose to her feet. Elizabeth followed her lead, moving with a fluid, graceful power the woman envied. Like Alex. It was a deadly sort of grace, but seductive.

"Do you know what you are, Elizabeth?" Lydia asked.

Those dark amber eyes remained blank. She looked much more beautiful now than she had in life, but her beauty had an inhuman quality to it that both attracted and repelled.

Monster. Driven by Blood-Hunger, unchecked by the conscience that kept Alex from realizing his true potential.

"Feel what's inside you," Lydia murmured, grasping the crystal again. The stone pulsed with dark desire against her skin. She took that desire, amplified it, sent it back to the beautiful, deadly creature before her. "Feel its power, Liz. *This* is what you are."

Need etched shadows on Liz's face, made her lips part and swell as though a man had kissed her. Lydia shifted restlessly. Wishing the sensation were hers, wanting to taste, to feel, to be alive again. Her own brand of Hunger—different, but no less powerful, than the vampire's.

"Come," she said, holding out her hand. "Let me help you find yourself. Your true self, Elizabeth."

Alex went downstairs at dusk, picking up the newspaper that had been set on the foyer table for him. The scent of animosity hung strongly in the house. Tucking the paper under his arm, he followed the trail of anger into the living room.

He found Justin and Sonya locked in a silent battle of wills, the boy determined to ignore his mother, she apparently determined to make that as difficult as possible.

"Are we having fun?" Alex asked.

"Indeed we are," Sonya said.

The lamplight lay golden upon her skin and warmed the paleness of her hair. Blood-Hunger stirred in his belly, plucked fretfully at the fringes of his mind. "Is this anything we can discuss?"

"Ask Justin," she said. "He's the one being silent and sullen."

Justin switched the television on, swiveling his chair to shut out the rest of the room. Alex met Sonya's gaze, saw amusement there. An odd reaction from a mother who'd just been rejected.

Interesting. Alex sat down on the sofa, a figurative midpoint between the two opposing camps.

"Why don't you call into the kitchen for a sandwich?" Sonya asked. "I think there's some roast beef left over from dinner."

"I'm not hungry, thanks."

His cynical revenant self tittered at him. Sonya smiled, almost as though she'd heard it.

"Why don't we ever see you during the day, Alex?" she asked.

He studied her from beneath lowered lids. "Because I conduct business elsewhere."

"Where?"

"At my place of business."

"And where is that?"

"I have offices in the Drayton-Thomas Building in

downtown Savannah." It was the truth, although he seldom actually went there. But the small subterfuge gave him an excuse for his days.

"So," she said. "You've given up on your genealogical research for the crass pursuits of business?"

"Not at all."

She crossed her legs. The crystal shifted, and the lamplight struck a ruddy spark in its depths. "I'd like to see what you've found so far. The Danilovs seem to have been a very interesting family."

"They have. And continue to be."

"Alex, look at this," Justin called.

Alex's gaze shifted to the television screen. The news had just come on, the anchorman's smooth voice flowing into the room.

"The bodies of two Causasian males were found in Forsyth Park this evening," he said. "The men haven't been identified as of yet, but sources say they appeared to be vagrants. The police aren't officially calling this a murder, but homicide detective Martin Rhudwin has been assigned to the case. We interviewed him a few moments ago."

A square bloomed in the corner of the screen, showing Rhudwyn standing against a backdrop of hoary live oaks. He looked grim and tired.

"Detective Rhudwyn, can you tell us how these men died?" the reporter asked.

"Not until the coroner takes a look at them."

"The man who found them said they looked terrified."

Rhudwyn's eyebrows went up. "Really?"

"He also said that although they had wounds in their necks, there wasn't any blood. Do you agree?"

"I can't agree or disagree until I get the coroner's report," the detective said. His voice remained bland, but Alex saw anger in his eyes. "Now, if you'll excuse me, I've got a lot of work to do."

The square disappeared. The anchorman stared into the camera, his forehead creased with concern. "That's all we have right now on the double murder in Forsyth Park. On other fronts, a body of a woman was found floating in the Savannah River. Police spokeswoman Norma Harrison says there was no sign of violence. . . ."

Alex tuned out, and the man's voice became a background drone. The killings in Forsyth Park bothered him. They also bothered Justin, and had evidently triggered some of the almost-memories that had haunted him since he'd been touched by the Dark Revenant. His dark eyes had a fey look to them, a knowing beyond what could be seen and heard.

"Justin—" Alex began.

"Yes, Justin," Sonya interjected. "There's something I've been wanting to say to him all night. Are you ready to listen, young man?"

Justin's gaze shifted to his mother. "What is it?"

"I had a chat with Dr. Janeway this afternoon. He said he'd be glad to do a nice, safe abortion for us. With privacy guaranteed."

Justin stared at her openmouthed for a moment, then stood up. "I need to get some fresh air."

He slammed the door behind him when he left. Alex got up to switch off the television, then leaned against it and crossed his arms over his chest.

"I think you've got your answer," he said. "And even if Justin and Kelli were willing, I wouldn't be."

"Old-fashioned?"

"If that's what you want to call it." He closed his eyes, thinking of the tiny life now blooming in Kelli's body. A fetus, as they called them nowadays. Cells. Everything in him rejected that label. It was a child, a human soul. A *Danilov* child. A Danilov soul.

With a grimace, he pushed away from the television.

"Wait," Sonya said. "Don't go all cold and judgmental, Alex. I'm only thinking about Justin's welfare."

"Not in this you're not."

The light lay like a caress on her pale skin. "Of course I am. He's so young. He's got worlds of things to do, he'll probably fall in and out of love a hundred times if he's allowed to. He'll grow away from her in a few years."

"That's the future," Alex said. "Neither you nor I can predict what Justin will be or what he'll want."

"This girl and this child will hold him down."

He raised his brows. "Do you really think anyone or anything can hold Justin down?"

"Yes. And I don't intend to let it happen. My son is all I have, and I'm not about to let that little girl ruin him. Think about it, Alex. If he has to wait to marry, chances are he'll have gone on to something or someone else. He'll have gotten out of the situation with a minimum of inconvenience."

Alex leaned back and studied her. Something lurked beneath that cool, perfect beauty of hers, something he'd never seen before. It tasted of ruthlessness. In a way, that had been the one thing she'd been lacking before. Yes. Always before, she'd been the martyr, hurting herself to punish others. Somewhere along the way she'd learned to change that.

He liked her less for it. And wanted her more.

A regrettable vice, this fascination with selfish women. They abounded in every generation. All lovely, all compelling, all dangerous to the unwary. Dangerous, too, to the wary. He'd wiled away many empty centuries with them: Russian countesses, Parisian courtesans, noblewomen of Renaissance Italy, and once, an English queen. And last, but certainly not least, Lydia Danilov. He'd known better than to love any of them, but each had extracted a high price.

Sonya smiled, as though she'd read his mind. She got to her feet with a languid seductiveness that both amused and aroused him.

"Let the boy get married, Sonya," he said. "You'll only lose him by doing this."

"I'll have to take that chance."

"Why?"

"Because she's not good enough for him."

"Who is?"

She smiled again. "No one."

"Shall I buy Philippe back for you?" he asked.

"That was a low shot, Alex darling."

"But worth a try. What do you say?"

"No, thanks," she said. "I realize now that Philippe was only a substitute for what I really wanted."

She moved to stand in front of him. Reaching out, she put her hands on his shoulder. Her fingers spread out over the muscle, the long, gold-painted nails digging gently into the fabric of his shirt. Her perfume enveloped him, but it was a pale thing compared with the sensuality she exuded.

Blood-Hunger flared. Raw. Powerful. It sank sharp claws into his being, raked furrows of need through his brain.

"What is it you really wanted?" he asked.

"Don't you know?"

"No."

"It's always been you, Alex."

He reached up and grasped her wrist. Her pulse beat steady and slow, odd counterpoint to the sensuality.

"I don't think so," he said.

"Of course you do. I *had* to leave; how could I stay here with you, knowing that you didn't want me?"

"You seemed eager enough to go at the time."

"I was fooling myself," she said. "Philippe was as dark as you are fair. Black hair, black eyes, Latin temper and passion, the works. But it was all surface. Inside, he was as smooth and bland as pudding. Now you"—she slid her free hand along his shoulder and down his arm—"have the darkness inside. It's big and powerful and dangerous; a woman could get swallowed up in it and never come out again."

Her perception startled him. "Don't you think you're being just a little melodramatic?"

"No."

She leaned down and kissed him. For a moment it seemed as though he'd fallen into a volcano. She tasted like desire, like honey and spice and a woman's need. Blood-Hunger roared through him. He tightened his grip on her wrist, intending to pull her against him.

Sudden realization spurred through him: her pulse still beat slow and steady against his palm.

He straightened. Gently he turned her face into the light with his free hand. "You're lovely," he said. "But too cold for me."

"I'm not cold," she whispered, leaning toward him.

He smiled. "Why did you come back?"

"This is my home, after all."

"Ah. Then why did you leave it in the first place?"

"I told you before. You—"

"Didn't want you," he finished for her. "Yes, you told me before."

She slid her hand down the front of his body. "I'm glad you changed your mind."

"What makes you think I did?"

"This."

"That," he said, "is mere reflex."

"Liar."

Alex looked down at her hand, then up into her face. A man would have seen the beauty, the lowered eyelids, the smile, and called her passionate. But he was not a man.

"Is this what you want in return for letting Justin go?" he asked.

"It's a start."

Only just. He watched the pulse beat in her throat. Blood-Hunger dug razor claws of need into his brain, urging him to take her. *She won't remember; it can't cost you anything.*

Ah, he thought, it always costs. Always.

He clasped her throat gently, feeling her life surge against his palm. She closed her eyes.

"You know," he said, "I liked you better last year when you were screwing for revenge instead of gain."

Her eyes opened. "What . . . ?"

"I'd much rather pay a prostitute to satisfy my . . . appetite. At least then I'd get value for my coin. And no strings attached afterward."

She flushed scarlet, the first genuine sign of warmth he'd seen, and snatched her hand away from the front of his body.

"Thank you," he said. "If you have a business proposition to make—"

"We're talking about my son here," she snapped.

"Precisely. If you've got some sort of bargain in mind, make it. If not, leave me alone and let the courts decide it."

The flush drained from her face, leaving it even paler than usual. "If that's the way you want it."

"That's the way I want it. Now, if you'll excuse me, I've got things to do." He turned on his heel and headed for the door.

"Alex," she called.

He stopped, turned to look at her.

"You'll never win in court," she said.

"Perhaps not. I can only try."

"I'm his mother. I'm just trying to do what's best for him."

"Sonya, you may win this battle. But you'll lose your son for it."

"That's your opinion."

Alex sighed, truly feeling his years. "I hope it's worth it. Whatever it is you're after."

"Where are you going?"

"Out."

She smiled. "To find yourself a prostitute?"

He matched her smile. "It would be safer, wouldn't it?"

"Maybe."

Blood-Hunger rolled through him in a dark tide. He wanted her. It had nothing to do with like or dislike. Just appetite. A powerful draw, both unsettling and familiar. In all his long life, only one woman had ever roused his need this way.

And she wasn't Sonya.

7

Death lay rank in Forsyth Park. Violent death, filled with terror and disbelief and, finally, despair. Alex felt his nostrils flare as the scent hit him.

A crowd had gathered to watch the detectives and lab technicians work. Avidity filled the onlookers' faces. Murder always held fascination for humans . . . as long as it wasn't their own.

Alex turned back to the men working the crime scene. Martin Rhudwyn walked among them, taking notes, occasionally pointing to something. A thorough man, Martin. The bodies had been taken away. To the morgue, no doubt, to have their tissues and fluids analyzed.

Alex already knew what would be found. And what would not.

Technology couldn't solve this double murder; it belonged to another realm, one beyond the reach of scalpels and laboratories. He sniffed the air, drawing in the taint that lay below the scent of dying.

Revenant.

It had hunted here, and it had killed. It had left an aura of rawness behind, something unbridled and savage. Blood had run onto the ground. There had been no finesse to the taking of these lives; the men had died swiftly, brutally. He could almost hear the echoes of their souls being torn away and consumed.

"Not in *my* city," he murmured.

Suddenly Rhudwyn looked straight at him. Alex saw his own outrage reflected in the detective's eyes and felt a powerful kinship for this man. In another age, they might have been friends.

Rhudwyn joined him. "Come to join the party?" he asked, thrusting his thumb at the clot of onlookers.

Alex shook his head. "I've never liked ghouls."

"Happens every time. I wouldn't be surprised if somebody scooped up the dirt and tried to sell it for souvenirs. Why *are* you here?"

"I just happened to be passing by on my way through town," Alex said. "You look lousy, detective. Can I buy you a cup of coffee?"

Some of the grimness left Rhudwyn's face. "Give me a minute to finish up here, and then you're on."

While Alex waited he opened himself to the eddies and currents of emotions around him. Morbid curiosity charged the air, distasteful but not unexpected. He ignored it, focusing instead on the fading traces of murder that still clung to the area. The breeze shifted the tree branches overhead. A whisper of sound, as though even the wind was afraid to speak of what had happened here.

His Blood-Hunger stirred, almost as though someone had tugged at it. He tilted his head back, questing the hot night air. He'd come to Savannah to trace something that tasted of Lydia, and found something else entirely. Another revenant. And a hungry one. His own Blood-Hunger resonated with that need.

Two lives had not been enough. Not nearly enough.

"I'm ready," Rhudwyn said.

Alex blinked, focusing on the man's face with an effort. "I . . . Sorry. I was woolgathering."

"Murder tends to do that to people."

"Not to you."

Rhudwyn smiled. "I'm a homicide detective."

"There's a nice little coffee shop a couple of blocks away. Why don't we walk?"

"Sounds good to me."

Rhudwyn paused at the fountain. He cupped his hands and splashed water into his face, then smoothed his hair back. His widow's peak seemed deeper now, the narrow bones of his face more prominent.

"Bad one?" Alex asked, knowing the answer.

The detective nodded, dipping his hands once more into the water. "I don't know why I'm doing this; it's not like I can wash it away."

"No," Alex agreed. "You can never wash it away. Would you like to talk about it?"

"What's to talk about?"

Rhudwyn shoved away from the fountain and headed toward Gaston Street. Alex fell into step beside him. The streets were quiet in the moonlight, the air heavy with the scent of flowers. If he'd been human, he might have been able to ignore the feeling of foreboding that seemed to shadow the city's beauty.

The detective walked silently for a couple of minutes, then said, "I've got a pair of corpses, identity unknown, cause of death unknown, suspects unknown."

"It's already been on the news."

"Yeah. The bodies were found by some guy out walking his dog. He phoned us, then the media."

"Politician?"

Rhudwyn grinned. "Ad executive."

"Ah," Alex said. "Somebody owes him a big favor."

He watched the pattern of tree shadows move across his companion's face. The moonlight etched creases in

Rhudwyn's face and made his eyes look more yellow than brown. Call it a policeman's hunch or a Welshman's intuition, Rhudwyn was bothered by the killings.

"The newspeople said there wasn't any blood in the bodies," Alex said.

"I haven't gotten the coroner's report yet."

"But?"

"But there wasn't a trace of lividity."

Alex nodded. "Time element?"

"Rigor had begun to pass off. If I had to make a ballpark guess, I'd say they were killed sometime between midnight and dawn last night. Here's the coffee shop."

Alex glanced up at the sign overhead. TEAGUE'S COFFEE AND CROISSANTS, it said in tasteful script. Years ago it had been called simply the Coffee Shop. He and Margaret used to come here late at night sometimes, to chat and sip coffee while the city went to sleep around them.

The interior had changed, too. The heavy English tearoom decor had been replaced with modern Art Deco, a great deal of etched glass and plants. Alex liked it.

"Table or booth?" Rhudwyn asked.

"Booth, if we're going to be talking murder."

"Are we?"

"How can we not?"

"Do you ever have a normal conversation?" the detective asked, leading the way toward the back of the shop.

"Not with you," Alex said. "And what's a normal conversation, anyway?"

"Beats me."

Rhudwyn ordered eggs, hash browns, Danish, and sausage, then raised his brows when Alex ordered only coffee. "Aren't you hungry?" he asked.

"Murder puts me off my feed. Apparently it doesn't affect *your* appetite."

"I'm a homicide detective."

The waitress left, rather too fast.

"Martin, have there been any other . . . odd deaths?"

Rhudwyn leaned forward, propping his elbows on the table. "What makes you ask that?"

"The tension in your eyes."

"Damn. I should have stuck to chess with you." With a sigh, he raked his hand through his hair. "We found another body three days ago. Same characteristics. It was fresh when we found it, say, an hour or so after death. Male, Caucasian, no ID. Probably a vagrant."

"No others?" Alex asked.

"Three isn't enough?"

No. Not for the Hunger I sensed. "It was an innocent question, Martin."

"By innocent, do you mean the definition of 'artless' or the more usual 'sinless'?"

Alex smiled. "Which would you choose?"

"What brought you into town tonight, Mr. Danilov?"

"Boredom."

"And what brought you to Forsyth Park?"

Again Alex smiled. "The smell of something wrong. I've a finely tuned nose for trouble."

The waitress returned, a tray balanced on her table. Rhudwyn leaned back to let the waitress put a plate in front of him. Alex drew in the fragrance of the food, trying to remember what it had been like to be a man. To eat, to be replete. To be, if only for a short time, free of hunger. But a thousand years had dimmed those memories, leaving him merely revenant.

"So," the detective said when the waitress had moved away again, "what does your nose for trouble tell you about the killings?"

"That there will be more of them."

Rhudwyn's eyes shuttered. "Why do you say that?"

"You think so, too," Alex said.

After a moment the detective inclined his head. "Unfortunately."

"If there's anything I can do to help—"

"We'll handle it."

Rhudwyn's face closed. Alex probed the mind behind the mask, but found it, as always, to be shielded. Poor Martin, always holding close against the intuition that was his heritage and his nature.

With a sigh, Alex leaned back against the cushioned booth. Outside, the breeze kicked up, making the branches of a climbing wisteria scrape gently across the glass. Rhudwyn ate with swift efficiency; obviously a man accustomed to having his meals interrupted.

"I saw your cousin in town this afternoon," Rhudwyn said between bites.

"Sonya?"

"She was just coming out of Fleetwood Tera's office. Is he her lawyer?"

Alex nodded. Suddenly his attention shifted outside. A cloud scudded across the moon, making the shadows shift. It almost seemed as though the world had taken a subtle half turn.

"Tera's a wild man," Rhudwyn said. "You've got a hell of a fight on your hands."

Alex blinked. The world settled back into its normal pattern, and he could almost convince himself nothing had happened. Almost.

"Do you know the man?" he asked.

"I know *of* him." The detective shrugged. "He's good, and he's effective. Doesn't mind stepping on a few toes to win a case, from what I've heard."

"Are you warning me?"

"Ah, Charles McGinnis is a gentleman. That's somewhat of a handicap when his opponent isn't."

"A gentleman isn't quite an anachronism, Martin. At least not yet. Perhaps I should just call Mr. Tera out.

Pistols at twenty paces and voilà. End of problem."

"You'd have to shoot half the lawyers in the state. Besides, I'd have to arrest you. Dueling was outlawed in 1828."

"Eighteen twenty-six," Alex said.

"You've looked it up."

I lived it. "I wanted to find out if it was actually illegal or merely passé. Some social customs should be revived, don't you think?"

Rhudwyn snorted. "They'd use Uzis now."

"A pity. There should be more finesse to killing."

"Finesse!"

"Do I shock you?" Alex asked. "Think about the rules of dueling, my friend. You faced your opponent at a predetermined time and place. There were rules. You each had one chance—an equal chance. If your aim was better, you walked away vindicated. If you missed . . ." He shrugged. "You were buried a gentleman."

A shrill electronic tone sounded. Rhudwyn grimaced, pushing his plate away. "There goes my beeper. I've got to find a phone . . . there it is," he said, getting up.

Alex rose, too. By the time he'd paid the bill, Rhudwyn came back. His face had settled back into grimness.

"Another one?" Alex asked.

"How much do I owe you for the meal?"

"Nothing. It was my treat."

"No, thanks."

"I'm a rich man, Martin."

"Then let me pay for your coffee. Maybe it'll relieve your boredom." Rhudwyn took a ten-dollar bill out of his pocket and thrust it into Alex's hand.

"If I were going to bribe you," Alex said, "I'd try something better than eggs and sausage."

The detective stood looking into Alex's eyes for a moment. Then he turned and walked out. The line of his shoulders didn't invite company, so Alex waited a minute or so before following him.

Shadows hung hot and heavy beneath the trees. Alex walked into one of those thick patches of darkness, flew out the other side. Cupping the breeze with white owl wings, he caught up with Rhudwyn.

The detective got into his car and headed toward the waterfront. Alex followed, hovering high overhead to get a view of the city. Catching sight of flashing lights near Ellis Square, he glided down ahead of Rhudwyn's car.

Death had claimed the quiet little square. Live oaks stood sentinel over the scene, Spanish moss dripping like tears from their twisted branches. Echoes of Blood-Hunger were strong here. So was terror, the last emotion of a man whose fate came upon him unexpectedly. It had been a swift death, but not a merciful one.

Alex focused his revenant senses on the psychic spoor left by the other revenant. Again he felt the harshness of it, the raw, uncontrolled Hunger. This revenant knew little of caution and nothing of restraint. He'd come across revenants of this sort many times in his long, long life; he'd never left one behind to continue its depredations.

The trail of Blood-Hunger led him toward the waterfront. He flew over Factors Row, taking a steep glide down the lee side of the buildings that clung to Yamacraw Bluff. A moment later he entered Emmett Park. Trees lines both sides of the walkway, their branches twining into an archway overhead. At another time it might seem a charming bower; now, however, it looked like a dark tunnel into hell.

He found the victims near the fountain. Three of them, their remains tossed into the bushes like discarded rag dolls. Alex flew down to the ground, resumed human form. Kneeling, he touched each man's face. He didn't feel flesh or skin or bones; he felt the jagged edges of their dying, the howl of their souls as they were torn from their moorings and consumed. Bile rose in his throat, and rage in his heart.

Not in my city!

Gently he closed the wide-open eyes of the corpses. Then he rose. The scent of the revenant was still fresh. His own Blood-Hunger responded, a reminder that he was not so different from the being that had feasted here. A philosophical difference rather than a spiritual one, he supposed. Both monsters. Both driven by things no man could conceive, let alone understand.

And then, almost in midstep, the trail vanished. It shouldn't have happened. Not to Alex Danilov.

"Hubris again, Alexi," he murmured.

He closed his eyes, testing the spot where the trail ended. A subtle closing, that. Too subtle for a revenant whose Blood-Hunger tasted of such raw mindlessness.

The police weren't going to solve these murders; policemen dealt in facts and clues and laboratory results. Cold, hard reality. And so this was, but a different sort of reality. The police weren't equipped to deal with it . . . or even to recognize its existence.

An odd thought flitted through Alex's mind: If Martin Rhudwyn *had* become a mystic or a priest, he might have had a chance of solving these murders.

The breeze stirred his hair playfully, then went tittering off among the trees. So, he thought, it's a challenge.

"You knew I'd be coming," he said aloud. "Very well. A contest it is."

Lydia shivered as the backwash of the vampire's Blood-Hunger surged through her. Elizabeth moved with deadly grace through the quiet late-night streets. The moonlight made her pale skin gleam and struck golden sparks in her hair. Beautiful, eternal, infinitely deadly. Only the form was human; inside, where it counted, she was all predator.

"Look at them, Elizabeth," she said, indicating the houses around them. "They live out their boring little lives, not knowing or caring that there's more to the world than what's on the television screen."

There was no response, but then, she didn't expect one. "Are you thinking anything at all, Elizabeth?" she asked. "Do you sense them? I bet you'd like to take every one of them. Maybe you should. They're expendable, after all; an hour after they're gone, the world will have forgotten them."

Lydia couldn't seem to stop talking, although she knew why she felt compelled to fill the vampire's silence. It had been a reckless night; one victim after another going to feed that inhuman appetite. Appetite. It was this that Alex controlled so savagely, and at such cost. Blood-Hunger. But she realized now that it was far more than just the blood. Vampires craved the death itself, the taste of the human spirit as it left its mortal home. How long had it been since Alex had experienced that exquisite pleasure? Five hundred years, eight hundred, a thousand? Self-inflicted torture. And for what? Guilt? Morality?

She saw Elizabeth's head go up, saw her nostrils flare. The hunt had begun again. Suddenly the vampire broke into a run. Lydia followed, drawn along with the torrent of Blood-Hunger. So powerful, so compelling . . . Morality couldn't have stopped her from following that pull, nor could fear.

She caught sight of the quarry just ahead, a middle-aged man just emerging from his car. Elizabeth swept him up. Blood spattered down on the asphalt beneath his feet. His dying echoed through Lydia's brain, and even the reflection of it was glorious. She shivered. Wanting more.

Elizabeth looked up at her. Those dark amber eyes seemed almost to glow with a light of their own. Pleasure filled them, born of dark need. Blood-Hunger. Even after four lives tonight, it still craved more.

Lydia grasped the crystal that hung against her chest. "It's getting near dawn, Elizabeth," she said. "Time to go home."

She could feel Elizabeth's reluctance. The stone throbbed with the vampire's hunger and the lives that had already gone to feed it. Lydia tightened her grip, using the crystal to channel that mindless need into a preservation of self.

The sun will kill you. Let me help you. Let me show you how to live in the world of men.

The vampire let her victim fall. Reading acquiescence in that gesture, Lydia smiled.

"Now, first things first," she said. "You can't leave bodies lying around everywhere. Not only is it gauche, but it's bad for business."

Elizabeth didn't even blink. With a sigh, Lydia bent and picked up the body. "Let's go," she said. "We'll drop this off somewhere on the way home."

She glanced back to make sure the vampire was following her. Elizabeth, the Blood-Hunger quiescent now, looked as blank and beautiful as marble. Power beat like a heart beneath that cool exterior, however, power that would grow with every life she consumed.

Lydia smiled. "And what will you do when you find her, Alex?" she murmured. "Will you kill her, or will you let her kill you?"

8

"Alex, are you paying any attention at all?" Charles McGinnis asked.

"I'm sorry, Charles," Alex said without turning away from the window. Savannah lay spread out before him like a star-dusted cloak, beautiful against the velvet darkness. But a taint lay beneath that beauty. Blood-Hunger. He could feel it along the nerve paths in his body, feel it creeping through the caverns of his mind.

Charles sighed. "Alex, listen to me. With Barron, ah, disappearing under such strange circumstances, his contesting of Margaret's will unresolved . . . Well, there's a chance Sonya might be able to get a piece of Danilov Industries."

"So?"

"Make her an offer."

"I did. I even offered to buy Philippe back for her." Charles snorted. "And?"

"She turned me down. So far she hasn't said what she wants, other than to make life difficult for everyone."

"How's Justin taking it?"

"Like a Danilov."

Alex spread his hand out over the glass. feeling the

pulse of the other revenant's Blood-Hunger, and his own. The beating of Charles's heart, the scent of blood and flesh and quick human life surrounded him.

"Alex."

Charles's tone was sharp, imperative, and brought him swinging around. The lawyer sat in the same battered chair in which he always sat, his dead wife's portrait hanging above him like a benediction. The room hadn't changed in the past year, except for a few additions to the clutter of a lifetime. A pleasant room, marred only by the loneliness of the man who occupied it.

"You don't seem very concerned about any of this," Charles said. "Damn it, Alex, we're talking about the Danilov fortune here!"

Alex shrugged. "I've won and lost more fortunes than any living man can imagine."

"And the house?"

"It's only a house. It's the people who matter." Alex glanced up at Meg McGinnis's portrait. "As you know."

The lawyer didn't turn; Alex knew he'd looked at that portrait so many times it had become ingrained in his mind.

"You should let the grief go, Charles," he said.

"That's an odd statement, coming from you."

"I let mine go."

Charles smiled crookedly. "You let the *women* go. Not the grief. You, of all people, should understand mine."

Of all people. But he was revenant.

"Now," Charles said. "Why don't you tell me what's really bothering you?"

"It's been three weeks," he said.

The lawyer blinked. "I don't . . . Oh. The other . . ."

"Revenant. It tears at me. Every waking moment I can feel its need, its bestiality. Until I stop it, it will kill and kill and kill."

Charles sighed. "Have you seen today's paper?"

"No."

The lawyer retrieved the newspaper from the chair beside him and held it out. The headline screamed VAMPIRE KILLER STALKS CITY! POLICE HELPLESS AS NINTH VICTIM FOUND!

"Not nine victims," Alex said. "Seventeen."

"Seventeen!"

"The revenant started hiding bodies after the first few days. Most were homeless men, the sort no one looks for, no one reports missing."

"You found them?"

"Yes."

"You aren't going to tell the police?"

"This isn't their province. I'm the only one who can deal with this creature." *If I can find it.*

Charles brushed a lock of sandy hair back from his forehead, then propped his elbows on the chair arms and steepled his fingers beneath his chin. "What if you can't?"

"Deal with it?"

The man nodded.

"I have to. Seventeen lives, Charles. And it won't stop. It can't stop."

"You did."

With a sigh, Alex leaned his head back against the window behind him. "Not all revenants return with their faculties intact. Some are as mindless as they are soulless, mere slaves to the Blood-Hunger."

"And this is one of those?"

Alex, remembering how the revenant had slipped away from him, shook his head. "This is something I've never come across before. Its Blood-Hunger is raw and brutal, about as subtle as an ax."

"But you haven't been able to track it down."

He nodded.

"And you feel it's your fault."

"I should have been able to find this revenant, Charles."

The lawyer pushed up from his chair. "Come with me. I've got something to show you."

Alex followed him up the stairs and into one of the bedrooms. Charles strode across the room and opened the curtains with a flourish. Plywood, painted the same soft green as the walls, covered the room's one window.

"I caulked all around it," Charles said, rapping the plywood with his knuckles. "No light's getting in here. And the drapes are lined with the same fabric they use in darkrooms. Turn and look at the door."

Alex swung around. A curtain rod had been hung above the door to hold another set of heavy draperies.

"The hallway's pretty dark, even in daylight," Martin continued. "Shut the door, bolt it, pull those curtains across, and you'll be perfectly safe."

Astonishment rolled through Alex. "You're inviting me into your home?"

"We can't have you running out of night while you're chasing after that revenant. Seriously, though, feel free to use this room whenever you need it. I expect you won't have any trouble getting in if I'm asleep."

Alex looked into the man's eyes, read compassion and understanding in those cool blue depths. He didn't need Charles's room; burrowing into the earth was as good an escape from the sun as any. But friendship had been offered here, trust given. It had to be accepted, and returned. Alex inclined his head. "Thank you."

"Good. Now let's go try some of that wine I found—"

Alex reeled as Blood-Hunger shot through him, need so powerful that it felt like a white-hot stake spearing through his brain. The world blurred. He gripped the top of a nearby table, hanging on to it as his one anchor in the stormwind of dark desire.

Out there in the city, a man was dying.

"Alex." Charles's voice lashed at him, sharp and imperative. "Alex!"

He held on to the humanity of that voice. Slowly, like a man swimming through gelatin, he climbed out of the pit of revenant need. Charles's face came back into focus, his expression one of concern and just a little fear.

With a start, Alex realized that the table had come apart in his hands. Gently he laid it aside. "I'm sorry, Charles."

"What happened? You looked—"

"Like a man who'd seen hell?"

Charles nodded.

"I did," Alex said. "And I've got to go."

He walked away from the lawyer's protest, down the stairs and out into the night. Between one stride and the next, he shifted into owl form.

The taste of the other revenant was strong. Tantalizing. It called to him, to that black, howling place deep inside. The creature he hunted was part of him. Like him. In a way, more like him than all the human beings sleeping so close and unaware.

Suddenly, so suddenly that he almost lost his hold on the owl form, the trail ended. He winged into the shadows beneath the feathery branches of a great mimosa tree and resumed his human form. Power tainted the air. It seemed to leech the night of modern things, as though the city had passed through a portal into another world entirely. The noise of man's inventions faded, leaving the night to nature's sounds: the shrill whine of mosquitoes hunting on the night air, the leaves overhead whispering fey tree secrets to one another, the soft *drip-drip* of water from a nearby rainspout.

This shouldn't be happening; the revenant feels new and raw, all Hunger and no restraint.

He closed his eyes, searching for the anomaly. Searching for death. Flesh and blood all around him, beating warm, beating fast. Blood-Hunger raked along his spine, sent daggers of pain shooting through his brain.

"Hello, honey."

A woman's voice. Alex turned, unsurprised that she'd been able to approach him; with his senses overwhelmed by the clamor of life force all around, he might have missed a dozen women. As he got a better look at her, his interest sharpened.

Her profession was obvious; short, tight skirt, see-through blouse over a bra that revealed more than it covered, too much makeup covering a too-young face and too-old eyes.

"A little out of your neighborhood, aren't you?" he asked.

She smiled. "Some. I had a special . . . delivery to make."

Her life surged high. He tasted joy in her, youth undimmed as yet by her profession. It called to him. Need long-denied clamored in his mind, and it was all his. He accepted it; being his, it could be controlled. Used. Strength for the fight that was soon to come.

"How old are you?" he asked.

"Ages," she said aloud.

Perfect. "Me, too," he replied.

She thrust one hip forward. Her skirt rode up an inch or so, revealing her lack of clothing beneath. "What's your name?"

"Alex."

"Alex. Mmmm, that's a nice name. I'm Tammi." Her perfume mingled with the scent of the bougainvillea behind her. "Are you lonely tonight, Alex?"

"Yes," he said. "I am."

Lydia slowly loosened her grasp on the crystal. Alex had nearly found them that time. He'd become attuned to Elizabeth's Blood-Hunger, and the danger increased with every kill.

"How about taking a night off?" she asked, turning to her companion.

Elizabeth's gaze lifted to the twin Gothic spires of the Cathedral of St. John the Baptist. Interior lights made the stained-glass windows gleam like old blood.

"Come on," Lydia said. "Let's go home. You're wearing me out."

She put her hand on the vampire's arm. Elizabeth's gaze locked with hers, and she found herself awash in those tawny depths, sucked down into a need as deep and dark as hell itself. Pure appetite.

"Elizabeth." Lydia tried to pull the vampire away, but she'd have had more luck pulling the cathedral itself down. "Elizabeth. Listen to me—"

She staggered as Elizabeth pulled free. The vampire, her gaze once again fixed on the spires towering overhead, stalked toward the cathedral's massive front entrance.

Lydia started after her, then realized in horror that her legs weren't working properly. No, not legs; just clubs of bone and muscle without grace or feeling. She gripped the crystal, trying to regain lost sensation. But the stone, drained by the effort of keeping Alex at bay, felt as sluggish as her body.

She lurched up the stairs, sobbing in frustration as she saw Elizabeth moving so effortlessly ahead of her. She seemed almost to drift on the night wind. Graceful, purposeful.

"Wait," Lydia called as Elizabeth disappeared into the church. "Wait!"

The vampire had no trouble in the dimness of the interior. Lydia followed her, trying vainly to bring her legs under better control. Lurch. Scrape. Lurch again. A whimper rose in her throat.

I'm ugly. Ugly!

Not her. Not Lydia Danilov. She'd always been beautiful. She'd always hated ugliness, despised it in others. It was going to get worse. A real catch-22: refrain from using the crystal, and Alex would track them down; use the stone's power, and fall apart piece by piece.

There had to be a way out.

Ahead, Elizabeth had stopped in front of the altar. Head thrown back, gold-shot hair rippling down her back, she stared at the crucifix above her. Something stirred in the vampire's still, beautiful face, something that might have been the beginning of memory. Panic fluttered like a trapped bird in Lydia's chest.

Don't remember!

She gripped the crystal with both hands, every ounce of her will going into the command.

Don't remember!

The spark faded. Elizabeth's eyes resumed their blank revenant stare, and the urgings of Blood-Hunger rankled the air.

"Okay," Lydia whispered. "Okay. Come on, Liz. Come with me."

She reached out, beckoning. Gaping cuts marked her palms where the crystal had cut into the flesh, and the skin of her hands and forearms had shriveled and darkened.

"No," she moaned.

A door opened at the rear of the sanctuary, spilling a rectangle of bright yellow light into the church. A man stood silhouetted in the doorway. The priest, Lydia thought. She caught a glimpse of wispy gray hair and a startled face before Elizabeth reached him.

His feet dangled helplessly as the vampire lifted him into the air. She bent toward him, her eyes seeming almost to glow with Blood-Hunger. Sweat broke out on his forehead as he strained to break free.

"Help me," he gasped, looking straight at Lydia. "Help me!"

His terror hit her like a palpable force. And with it, revelation.

"Elizabeth," she said, gripping the crystal. "Stop."

For a moment she thought the vampire would ignore her. The priest hung in her grasp, his legs flailing in a solitary dance of fear. His desire to live burned like a beacon.

"Liz," Lydia called again, sharply.

Elizabeth half turned. The priest's crucifix caught the light, cast it back in a whorl of bronze. Slowly the vampire let him drop to the floor. She stood for a moment looking into his eyes, then turned and glided out of the church.

Lydia watched the priest slump to the floor, his back heaving, his face flooded with the relief of a man who'd stared death in the eyes and walked away.

She bought herself movement by draining a dangerous amount of the crystal's power. A necessary risk. Her legs moved almost normally as she went to stand over the priest.

"Thank you," he said.

"You're welcome."

"What—" He broke off with a gasp as she bent and lifted him into her arms.

"You see, Father, I couldn't let her have you when I needed you so badly myself."

His astonishment turned to realization, then horror. She drank in his rocketing emotions, feeling them rush through her veins like sweet, hot wine. Life. She'd almost forgotten what it felt like.

She laid him on the altar, immobilized him with the stone's power. "Don't try to scream, Father," she said. "I've enclosed us in our own private little universe here. There's no help for you and no way out."

His gaze left her, focusing instead on the crucifix hanging overhead. Something strong and serene came into his face. "Our Father, Who art in heaven—"

"That's not going to do any good," she said.

"Hallowed be Thy name—"

"He's not going to help you. He didn't help *me*." The memory of her death whorled through her mind, black and terrifying. The pain. Pain and darkness, the draining of her soul. "I called out for Him, too. He didn't bother. We're details, Father. Minor characters in the play."

He shook his head.

"Believe what you want," she said. "It won't change what's happening."

His gaze returned to the crucifix. His terror had gone; he'd placed himself in the hands of his God. For whatever good it might do him.

Denied his fear, Lydia settled for pain. He screamed once, near the end.

So did she.

The woman stirred as Alex left the bed. She looked very young now with the tawdry clothes and most of the makeup gone. A small, red bruise marked the skin between her breasts. His mark.

Bending, he kissed the spot. He felt renewed. Stronger, faster, more enduring. And for a time the Blood Hunger would be his companion instead of his scourge. The woman called Tammi would never know what she'd done for him.

"Thank you," he murmured.

He took five hundred-dollar bills out of his wallet, folded them, and pressed them into her sleep-lax hand. She'd find them in the morning, earnings from a night she wouldn't remember. Then he dressed and walked back out into the night.

The weather had changed in the time he'd spent with

her; the breeze had strengthened, sending pockets of clouds scudding across the moon's face. Gray specters of Spanish moss stirred beneath the twisted branches of live oaks, and the cicadas chirped madly. A fey night. Alex lifted his head, his nostrils flaring. He could almost smell Wildwood on the air.

Suddenly the rustling of the leaves turned crystalline around him, and he tasted something different on the breeze. A subtle thing, and one not flavored of the night. Something new. His awareness focused, sharpened.

He followed that touch through the quiet streets. It grew stronger and more compelling, until he finally pinpointed its source: the Cathedral of St. John the Baptist. Police cars surrounded the church, their flashing lights strobing Christmas-bright colors on its stucco walls.

Cloaked in revenant power, Alex walked through the encircling cars and up the stairs. Once inside, he tasted murder on the air.

Menace filled the great, arched space of the sanctuary. Alex moved forward, silent and unseen, past the clots of men and equipment that filled the aisle. A contained, powerful pocket of evil surrounded the altar, and entering it was like being taken into the devil's hand.

Blood stained the altar, had even dripped down its sides to pool on the floor below. There was no body, only a scattering of sodden ash. Sacrilege. Sacrifice. Alex gazed up at the crucifix overhead; if his own eyes hadn't been blurred with tears, he might have thought the figure of Christ was crying.

A sense of distress penetrated his outrage. Turning, he saw Martin Rhudwyn striding down the aisle. A woman walked a few paces behind him, and it was from her that the feeling of distress came. She appeared to be in her early fifties, with a plump, broad-shouldered body and hair that was more silver than brown. Her face was the sort that would have been placid at another time.

Alex probed the mind behind the face, then recoiled with shock. *She'd sensed his touch.* Even now, her gaze darted around the sanctuary, seeking the source of contact.

A psychic. One with the true gift; even now, she'd focused on the spot where he stood, her brow furrowing as she tried to see beyond his illusion. Her mind felt like sunlight on a summer meadow. Complex, yet simple, deep, yet possessing the clarity of pure spring water.

So precious, Alex thought. Each generation spawned one or two such talents; few managed to grow into any realization of their potential. This woman shone like the sun, her mind strong and compassionate, her spirit serene. A good woman. In her own way, she was far more dangerous to him than Suldris had ever been. Alex retreated from her, shielding his mind as he'd shielded his body from view.

"Francine, are you ready?" Rhudwyn asked.

She looked away, and Alex breathed a sigh of relief.

"Yes, Lieutenant," she said. Her voice, like her mind, was years younger than her body.

"It's not pretty," he warned.

"I've been to a lot of crime scenes in my time," she said. "I don't expect pretty."

The detective took her hand and tucked it into the crook of his arm as he led her toward the altar. Alex watched her face as she reached the containment that surrounded the dais. The evil seemed to coalesce around her, as though attracted by her brightness.

"Dear God in heaven!" she cried. Then she crumpled, so suddenly that her hand tore from Rhudwyn's grasp.

Even as Alex sprang forward he knew he'd made a mistake. But the instinct to preserve her overrode for a moment the need to preserve himself, and he managed to catch her before she hit the ground. As the evil pressed close, reaching for her, he lashed at it with his own revenant power. Insulating her.

The woman's eyelids fluttered. A moment later he found himself staring down into irises the color of new leaves. He had no defense against her; it was all he could do to keep her safe. She touched his mind in one sweep of glory and danger, and he felt the hair rise up on the back of his neck.

She knew.

9

Rhudwyn's hand fell heavily on Alex's shoulder. "Alex! What the hell are you doing here?"

Alex, still gazing into the psychic's eyes, smiled at the irony of the situation. After a thousand years destiny had caught up with him; he might be able to erase this memory from Martin's mind, but not the woman's.

"I want an answer," Rhudwyn said, his voice grim.

The psychic's gaze shifted to him. "I asked him to meet me here, Martin."

Astonishment flooded through Alex, then relief. He didn't know why she'd acted to protect him; he'd expected fear, horror, betrayal. But this wasn't the time for explanations. So he merely nodded, accepting the gift.

"You know him?" Rhudwyn asked, his voice echoing Alex's surprise.

"I do get around," she said. "We met in—"

"Paris, three, no four years ago," Alex said. "It was raining."

"You've a better memory than I." She pushed herself to a sitting position. "Help me up, Alex. I seem to be having a bit of trouble."

He lifted her to her feet, keeping his hand on her arm to steady her.

"No. Away from this," she whispered. "I can't bear it."

She wouldn't, he thought. It tore at him, and he'd had many years to become used to the taste of evil. He bowed, offering his arm in a courtier's gesture. She leaned on him more than he expected as they moved away, and probably more than she would have liked. He sat her in the front pew. The polished wood enclosed her in a buttery glow that complemented the warmth of her mind.

Rhudwyn followed, his face set in that bulldog stubbornness Alex had come to know so well. "What the hell's going on here?" he demanded. "Where did you come from? One minute this sanctuary was empty, the next—"

"I was only standing in the shadows," Alex said. "Did you think I stepped out of thin air?"

"None of my men saw you come in. If they had, do you think they'd let you walk right up to the crime scene?"

"I didn't try to hide. Maybe this abomination held too much of their attention."

"They're professionals. It would take a lot more than this to shake them."

Alex sighed. "Martin, this is an extraordinary thing. You can't change that by calling it something else."

"Bull."

"Then why did you bring"—Alex paused, casting back to the beginnings of this meeting—"Francine into this case?"

"My captain ordered it."

"Always the skeptic, eh?"

For a moment anger turned the detective's eyes more yellow than brown. Then he relaxed. "Always digging, aren't you?"

"I just want you to realize your full potential, Martin."

"Are you two always like this?" Francine asked.

"Always," Alex said, without looking away from Rhudwyn.

The detective raked his hand through his hair. "Frank!" he called to one of the men behind him. "Get over here, will you? We need samples of that blood. And the ash."

"It's only blood and ash," Alex said. "It won't tell you what happened here."

Swiftly Rhudwyn turned back to face him. "We can tell a lot of things from blood. And the ash . . . We can tell whether it had been bone or wood, fabric or paper, and we can tell what burned it and when."

"And the why?"

"There are plenty of nuts running around out there. We'll run a computer check on known cults or known Satan worshipers who might be responsible for something like this."

"Very thorough," Alex said. His voice sounded drier than he'd intended. "But since Francine is here, why don't you listen to what she has to say?"

Rhudwyn turned to the psychic, reluctance plain in every line of his face. "Do you feel up to it?"

"Yes. I'm up to it."

She closed her eyes. Alex could feel her revulsion as she reached out with her mind to touch the aura of evil surrounding the altar.

"I feel pain," she said. "Terrible pain. And fear."

"Did someone die here?" Rhudwyn asked.

Alex let his breath out sharply. "Can you doubt it?"

"I," Rhudwyn said, "can doubt anything. Go on, Francine. Is there anything else?"

"Yes. I feel the image of a . . . a cross—"

"Big surprise," the detective muttered, glancing up at the large crucifix.

Francine opened her eyes. "Not that one. A smaller one. Worn around a man's neck—"

"The priest," Alex said. Outrage flooded through him.

"Father Genovese," Rhudwyn said. "His housekeeper said he went out for a walk and didn't come back. But why a priest?"

"For the sacrilege," Alex said.

The detective glanced at him, then away. "Did the killer take the body with him?"

Francine shook her head. "I don't think so. This has a . . . a sense of closure about it. Finality. A job done. The person who committed this murder got what he or she wanted, then walked out."

"So where's the body?"

She pointed to the altar.

"No go," Rhudwyn said. "It takes a lot of heat to burn a human body to ash. There's no sign of a combustible here."

"None you're familiar with," Alex said.

"Don't give me that crap, Alex. Facts are facts."

"True. But to understand this crime, you're going to have to take some things on faith."

"Faith!"

Alex smiled. " 'Faith is to believe what you do not yet see; the reward for this faith is to see what you believe.' "

"St. Augustine." Rhudwin smiled sardonically. " 'Faith,' " he retorted. " 'Belief without evidence in what is told by one who speaks without knowledge, of things without parallel.' "

"Ah, *The Devil's Dictionary,*" Alex said. "What an interesting source. You're an unbeliever, then?"

"I'm a Methodist."

"Stop it, both of you!" Francine snapped.

Rhudwyn swung around to face her. "Why did you ask Alex to meet you here?"

"I—"

"I'm an historian," Alex interposed smoothly. "But one of my hobbies happens to be the paranormal. Francine and I happen to have some . . . parallel skills. She thought we might complement each other in this."

"I see."

"No," Alex said, "you don't."

He met the detective's challenging stare levelly. Resentment rolled beneath those yellow-brown eyes and, with it, a touch of fear. Rhudwyn didn't like the taste of the evil here, and liked even less the fact that he could feel it.

"Hey, Lieutenant!" the technician called from the dais. "Take a look at this."

Rhudwyn strode to the altar. Alex followed, uninvited, and was in time to see the technician lift something out of the ash with the tip of a pen. Light caught on the tips of a cross, gleamed golden among the links of a chain.

"How interesting," Alex said. "The priest's crucifix."

"Looks like it," Rhudwyn snapped.

Alex cocked his head to one side. "I wonder what sort of combustible burns a human body without melting the crucifix he was wearing."

Silently Rhudwyn pulled a plastic Ziploc bag out of his pocket and held it open. The technician dropped the crucifix inside. Ash gritted beneath Rhudwyn's shoes as he turned to face Alex.

"Until I get the lab results, I'm not going to admit there *was* a body here," he said.

"You should listen to your instincts more, Martin."

"You mean the ones that say you were involved in last year's disappearances and the Garry murders, and now you've managed to become involved in another set of weird happenings? If you're talking about those, my Welsh instincts are working overtime."

Alex shrugged. "Think what you want, as long as you're not foolish enough to disregard Francine's talents."

"Quite a coincidence that you happen to know each other."

"Yes, it is."

"And how convenient that you happen to have complementary talents."

"Isn't it?"

"Do you have any other skills I don't know about?"

Alex spread his hands. "Probably."

"I don't know why I keep talking to you."

"You just like beating me at chess."

Rhudwyn closed the plastic bag with an audible snap. "Somehow I come away from every win feeling as though I've lost something more important than a game of chess. Why is that?"

"I wouldn't know."

Alex jerked in surprise as the surrounding aura started to shiver. It broke up around him, fragments whirling toward the ceiling as though sucked by a great psychic vacuum cleaner. And then they were gone. He tried to trace the source, but it came and went so swiftly that he lost it. Glancing over his shoulder at Francine, he saw her shake her head.

"What the hell was that?" Rhudwyn demanded.

"Look at the technician," Alex said.

The man still poked amid the mess on the altar, seemingly unaware of what had happened. He *was* unaware, for the simple reason that he didn't have the ability to sense it. Alex saw the realization flash in Rhudwyn's eyes.

"Something to think about, hmm?" Alex said. Without waiting for a reply, he turned and strode back to Francine.

"You've annoyed him again," she murmured.

"I always do."

"Maybe you shouldn't try so hard to wake him up. He'll be very dangerous to you then."

"As you are."

"Me?" Faux innocence.

He smiled. "Where are you staying?"

"A little bed-and-breakfast just off Orleans Square. Charming."

"Ah. The Whyte-Bragton House."

"You know it?"

Indeed, he did. The house had been built by his friend Edward Whyte in 1838. Memories flooded in, unbidden: Edward proudly showing off his new dwelling, his wife walking arm in arm with Catherine; Alex's daughter Cybelle flirting with the oldest Whyte son; a fire roaring in the parlor fireplace, adding piquancy to the Christmas smells of roast goose and pine garlands. And Catherine's perfume. Lavender and musk . . .

Abruptly realizing that Francine was staring at him, Alex wiped the memories from his mind. This woman was too dangerous to allow her into his past. "So," he said, "shall I take you back to your charming bed-and-breakfast?"

"Thank you, but I'll wait for Detective Rhudwyn."

Ah, she doesn't trust the vampire. It might be for the best. Of all the dangers he'd faced through the centuries, this plump, sweet-faced woman was perhaps the greatest. She'd stripped away his facades, broken through the layers of carefully applied humanity to find the truth. To a revenant, truth meant exposure. And exposure, destruction.

Another of his kind would have killed her. Alex lifted her hand to his mouth, then turned and strode out of the church.

The crystal pulsed between Lydia's breasts. The priest had fought hard. In the end, however, he'd given her what she wanted. He'd begged for his life, offering his soul in exchange for a few more heartbeats, a few more breaths of air. It had been like drinking champagne.

She held out her hands. Turned them over, over again. The skin had become smooth again. She rose up on her tiptoes, turned like a model on a runway. Graceful again. Beautiful again, plumped by the life she'd taken.

"Now I understand," she said to Elizabeth. "Really understand."

The vampire looked at her, unresponsive. She lay on the floor of this windowless room in the old warehouse. An inelegant setting for such a creature, but safe from the coming dawn.

"I'm almost like you," Lydia said.

She clasped the crystal, feeling Blood-Hunger rolling like a great dark sea beneath Elizabeth's flesh. An undercurrent washed through that, a tide that tasted of Alex. His Blood-Hunger, tied to Elizabeth's, augmenting and augmented by it.

"You must have been feeling mighty randy last night, Alex darling," she murmured. "I hope you're enjoying it."

Lydia took that Blood-Hunger, fed it, teased it, stroked it like a lover. She smiled as she saw Elizabeth's hips lift in unconscious response. Oh, yes. This was going to do very well.

Elizabeth's eyes closed. Lydia's hold on the Blood-Hunger loosened, fell away. Dawn had come. Awareness—what little there was—fled from Elizabeth's face, leaving it as pale and blank as a wax doll. She'd never seemed less human, even when draining the life from one of her victims. Lydia tried to imagine Alex lying like this, pale and still and cold, and failed.

"Do you dream?" she asked softly. "Probably not. You don't know how lucky you are."

Lydia dreamed. Oh, yes, she dreamed. Sleep wasn't even necessary; whenever she relaxed her guard, dreams came into her mind. Sharp, Technicolor dreams that hurt as much as reality: the feel of the cold altar beneath her, the pain of Suldris's entry into her body, the violation, the fear. A black wind howling as the knife poised above her, the glitter of the blade as it plunged downward. Her soul shrieking as it was torn away. Her mind fleeing, darting into the ghost crystal, running, hiding, going so deep she couldn't find her way out again.

Trapped. Wandering through a rainbow-shot world that tasted of Alex Danilov. Pain resonated through the crystal, a cry that was taken up in every arch, every diamond-sharp angle. A primal wail of loss. Hers. His.

With a gasp, she clawed her way free. She found herself crouched on the floor, her cheek pressed to the cool concrete. It took several minutes for her to regain her composure. Finally she sat up and brushed the bright, tumbled hair back from her face.

Elizabeth lay before her, beautiful and unaware. Her chest didn't rise and fall with breath, and there was no sign of a pulse in her throat. But behind that pale skin beat immortality. Lydia wanted it. Craved it.

Not now. She needed the day. The sunlight gave her freedom from Alex, freedom she had to have to take him down.

Echoes of Blood-Hunger coursed through her. It pooled in her belly, desire as quick and hot as life.

She abandoned the cool darkness of the warehouse for the hot, humid streets of the city. The sun seemed to feed the heat within her. She felt molten, heavy, rich with life. A man passed, made eye contact, then turned around to follow her.

"Hi," he said.

Just a man. Compared with Alex, found wanting. But he was tall and well built, and in the sun just now, his hair was almost the same color as Alex's. Good enough.

Lydia smiled. "Hello."

"I was on my way to work," he said. "Then I saw you."

"And?"

"And now I don't want to go to work anymore."

The crystal pulsed, and it felt like a dark song in her veins. He took her to brunch. She pushed food around her plate while desire grew and warmed beneath the light conversation. His eyes echoed what she felt. His gaze dropped to her chest; she glanced down, saw that her erect nipples were plainly visible beneath her blouse. He pushed his plate away.

"My place is only a couple of blocks away," he said, his voice heavy with arousal.

She smiled. "That far?"

His apartment showed money and taste, a decorator's touch in the color scheme and accessories. While he went into the kitchen to fix her a drink, Lydia moved around the living room, picking up a carved jade box here, a picture frame there. As she held a vase up to the light to admire it, she saw a striation of fine lines on her wrist and forearm.

She didn't have much time. Logic told her to husband what power she had; maintaining this artificial life was draining the crystal. But just this once, she needed to be a woman. She needed to be desired. To be loved.

The lines deepened, and she could feel, actually feel, the skin of her face loosening. Aging. *Is that all the time I get?* Apparently so; only a vampire seemed to get the youth *and* the time. Quickly she drew the curtains closed, plunging the room into an intimate half dark.

The man returned, carrying a pair of tall glasses. She couldn't remember his name.

"You're beautiful," he said.

She unbuttoned her blouse, enjoying the flare of desire in his eyes. It called to her. For a moment she almost felt like Lydia Danilov again—beautiful, sensual, the woman who had nearly brought a thousand-year-old vampire to heel. No one, not even Elizabeth, had touched Alex like she had.

And as for this man, well, he belonged to her. His name didn't matter, or his past. He was here.

"I want you," she said, spreading her hand across the front of her skirt.

He set the glasses aside and strode to her. Stripping the blouse off her shoulders and down her arms, he tossed it away. Her breasts swung free. He dropped to his knees, suckling first one, then the other. Her flesh responded, her nipples hardening, her belly tightening in response to the pull. But something wasn't there; her skin had begun to lose sensation again. Still, desire burned in her, desire that couldn't quite be touched, at least by human hands.

She became more aggressive, searching for a way to breach that invisible barrier. "Stand up," she said.

He obeyed, his face tight with arousal. It tightened even more when she undressed him, and more yet when she pushed him to his knees again. She offered her breasts. He suckled her again, harder this time, almost hard enough. Almost. Damn it, almost. She sank her hands into his hair.

With a moan, he reached up under her skirt and jerked her panties down. She kicked them away. Here, too, her body responded, swelling beneath his caresses, wetness welcoming him as he thrust two fingers inside her. It was . . . almost right. Almost there. But again something lay between her and true sensation.

Alex. You could touch me, you could make me feel again.

She let the man pull her down to the rug. He knelt between her wide-spread legs and pushed her skirt up over her hips. "God, you're beautiful," he muttered. "So wet."

He started at her breasts and worked his way down. Lydia rocketed between arousal and frustration as she watched his head move between her legs.

The crystal throbbed in time with her body. Without thinking, she closed her hand over it. Waves of heat went through her. Desire. Hers. His. Alex's.

"Now," she said.

He raised his head. Crystal fire sparked in his eyes, bright reflections of power. Lydia trapped those sparks, held them, pulled them—and him—in. He moaned.

She rolled him over, straddling him. Possessed him, body and mind. Her vision blurred, became his. Interesting, this moment of maleness; desire centered in the scrotum, intense and focused, the sensation of being buried deep in another person's body, enclosed, surrounded. Exquisite. She closed his eyes, quickening the pace of his body and hers.

Lydia could feel him fighting this ostracism of self. Swirled in almost too intense passion and even sharper fear, he pressed close, struggling for reentry. She wasn't going to be able to hold him long. Maybe long enough. Somehow she summoned the strength to push him away; denied her own release, she'd take his.

Close, so close. Friction pulling the sensation to a single spot at the front of his body, the overwhelming feel of slick flesh surrounding him, pressure building, swelling, bringing her closer to the brink . . .

Every nerve screaming, she opened her/his eyes. And saw herself. What was left of her. Her face had withered, the gray-green eyes sunk in a nest of wrinkles. Awful. Ugly. Old. Patches of discoloration beneath the skin. Her breasts had deflated, turning into mere flaps of dried skin that slapped against her ribs as she moved.

Horror shrieked through her mind. Hers and his, merging into a silent howl. She was thrust out, back into a body she didn't want. His penis shriveled within her. He bucked, trying to dislodge her.

Sobbing, she pressed clawed hands on his chest to hold him down. He opened his mouth to scream. She bent down, caught his exhalation in her mouth. It gave her strength. Staring into his eyes, she invoked the power of the stone. He stopped struggling. His penis lengthened and swelled, belying the horror in his mind.

Lydia straightened. "Good," she said. "That's my boy."

She started to move again. His terror poured through the crystal and was amplified by it. Fear—black and howling, deep and wild as a thunderstorm. It tasted like life, like power. Lydia drank deep. Bracing her hands on his chest, she drove herself harder, drove him. He gasped, arching beneath her.

"Yes," she said.

He shook his head, denying it. Lydia smiled. Looking down, she saw her hands begin to fill out, twisted claws becoming fingers again, the skin smoothing. Her breasts swelled, became full and rich and aching with arousal.

"I'm beautiful again," she said. "Feel me."

His hands came up, trembling as he fought not to obey. He cupped her breasts, slid down her belly and beneath her hips. She hung poised on the razor edge of feeling, impaled on a desire she didn't have the ability to fulfill.

Ah, but he did. He cried out as a climax ripped through him, cried out again as she stole it from him. Raw sensation poured into her: pleasure, terror, pain, the gut-clenching feeling of something being given, something more torn away. She shuddered, closing her eyes against the sheer sensuality of it.

"Alex," she gasped.

The world slowly fell back into place around her, and she opened her eyes, made her skin smooth and elastic. Between her thighs, the man lay still.

His skin started to crease. Decades passed through his face, melting the flesh, layering wrinkles atop wrinkles. His hair whitened and fell out. He drew one breath, let it out with a wheeze, drew another. Then his chest stopped moving. The crystal throbbed against Lydia's chest, glowing with a dark light of its own.

"Oh, I *see*," she said.

She slipped off his lax penis and stood up. He'd become an old man, now the corpse of an old man. How quickly life can be lived, she thought. Spreading her arms, she twirled around the room. Young again. Powerful again. She might not be immortal, but this was the next best thing. Until.

"Thanks for the life," she said, glancing down at the body. "I appreciate it."

10

Wildwood had awakened.

Alex stood at the edge of the sea of grass, watching the raindrops fall softly on the surface of the dark water. Blood-Hunger beat in him, in its own way as vast and eternal as the marsh. It could be contained but not denied, managed but not controlled. He'd never felt less human.

"Do you feel it?" he asked. "Old powers are at work, my friend."

Wind stirred the grass, nodded the branches of the trees. An insect skated madly across the surface of the water, only to disappear down the quick-snapping mouth of a fish. Concentric rings spread out over the water to be obliterated by the rain.

The predator and the prey. Always the way of nature, always the way of man. And revenant.

The claws of his Blood-Hunger were sharp tonight, honed by the taste of the other revenant's need. Brother/sister/cousin/kindred . . . It called to him more than any he'd ever encountered. He could feel it rushing through his veins, seeping through the fabric of his being, touching those things he'd rather deny.

Wildwood responded to the beat of his need. The cicadas' song deepened, grew faster and more imperative. Mist, strangely independent of the breeze, drifted amid the spiky grass. Alex raised his head, savoring the fecund swamp smell. There were times when he wished he could lose himself in the quiet fastness of the marsh, to walk in and never come out again. Perhaps the dawn would be gentle here.

"You look like you're about to dive in," Justin said from behind him.

Surprise spun Alex around in a fighting crouch, brought his hands darting forward to grasp the boy's forearms. He almost broke bones before he managed to stop the motion he'd begun.

"Sorry," he said, making sure Justin had his balance before letting him go.

"Jeez, Alex. Kinda jumpy, aren't you?"

"You took me by surprise. Not many people take me by surprise."

"I wonder why."

"Do I detect sarcasm?"

"My arms are numb to the elbows."

"It could have been your neck. Next time make some noise."

Justin shrugged, moving up beside him. "Did you talk to Charles McGinnis?"

"Yes. He's doing his best on this."

"But . . ."

"But Sonya *is* your mother."

"Don't remind me."

"Relax, Justin. We have time yet."

"Not much."

"No," Alex agreed. "But maybe enough."

The young man swung one fist into the palm of his other hand. The marsh absorbed the sound, the rain playing a soft counterpoint patter. "I can't believe she's getting away with this."

"In the law's eyes, you're still a child."

"The law's wrong."

"Yes," Alex said, "it is. Look, I know it's hard to be patient, but waiting Sonya out is our best bet. She'll find something to do—"

"And then she'll dump me again."

"I wouldn't put it quite that way."

"Why not? It's the truth. Another Philippe, and she'll be gone so fast you won't even see her dust."

So cynical, Alex thought. "Strange as it seems, she does love you."

"Spare me."

"You're a fortunate person in that you have focus," Alex said. "Sonya has no structure on which to hang her life, so she drifts. Reacting to life instead of controlling her own destiny."

"Why do you sound so bitter?"

"Do I?" Alex asked in surprise.

"Yeah."

Alex wasn't sure he liked being read so easily. A lie rose in his throat, but died beneath Justin's level gaze. "I . . . empathize with your mother. I've done my share of drifting, and more than my share of not taking charge of my destiny."

Justin turned to stare out over the marsh. In the rain-shrouded darkness, his profile had the predatory sharpness of a young hawk. "Something's bothering you," he said. "And it isn't the legal stuff."

"Why do you say that?"

With a suddenness that caught Alex by surprise, he swung back around. His eyes seemed as dark and fathomless as the marsh itself. For a moment Alex saw something strange spark in those black depths, an awareness of things older than House Danilov, older than time itself. Mist coiled along the ground to wreathe his ankles. Wildwood claiming its own.

"Something strange is going on," Justin said. "It's like the seconds before a storm hits, when you can almost feel the lightning running along your nerves."

A brushfire of alarm rushed through Alex, carrying the fear that Justin's memory of that night a year ago might return. "Maybe it's the moon," he said, striving for lightness. "They say people feel weird things with the waxing and waning of it."

"The moon's got nothing to do with it. You feel it as much as I do. It's in your eyes."

"Those are my sins," he said. "Not anticipation."

"Bullshit." Mist seemed to coil in the depths of the young man's eyes. "You're not what you pretend to be."

"I've already confessed to being a dilettante—"

"Stop treating me like a kid," Justin snapped. "And a stupid one, at that."

"I'm sorry."

Justin took a deep breath, then nodded. He turned to look out over the marsh. "I can feel it, the marsh. It's huge and old and . . . powerful. It fills my dreams."

"Which dreams?" Alex asked, wanting not to.

"The dark ones. Ones where something awful grabs me and drags me into blackness. I fight, I scream, but my arms don't work and my voice is caught somewhere inside. Then I hear a voice. Calling me. Taking me back. It's a familiar voice. I try and try to place it, but somehow it wiggles away before I can quite . . . pin it down."

He's almost remembering. "That's not a good dream," he said aloud.

"No." The young man stretched his arm out, pointing into the shrouded darkness of Wildwood. "It knows. Whatever it is I'm trying to find, it knows."

"Some people might call that the working of an over-active imagination," Alex said.

"Do you?"

Lie. It's time. And it's for the best. But the lie wouldn't come. "I wish I knew. It would be easier to be so sure."

A scream shivered on the air. A woman's voice, shrill with fright.

"Kelli!" Justin whirled and pelted toward the house.

Alex caught up with him at the edge of the garden, caught up and passed him. As he neared the house he heard the wail of crystal song. *Danger,* it cried. *Danger, dangerdangerdanger . . .*

Glass shattered as he flung the back door open. He raced up the stairs and down the hall to Lydia's old room, only vaguely registering the sound of Justin behind him. Ahead, the crystal cried.

Alex caught the doorjamb to swing himself into the room. He found Kelli standing beside the bed, the large crystal cradled in her hands. Terror pooled in her brown eyes. Gently Alex took the crystal from her. Broken shards of song vibrated through his palms.

Justin hurtled through the doorway. He skidded to a halt, his gaze encompassing the room. Then he walked to enclose Kelli in his arms.

"So much pain," she said, visibly shaking. "Like a well. You go down and down and never stop, and everything's black and howling and—"

"Stop it." Justin swung to look at Alex, savagery in his eyes. "What is it? What happened to her?"

"Kelli seems to have some sensitivity to Lydia's crystals," Alex said.

"*What?* But that's a bunch of crap! My father—" Justin broke off, his lips thinning to a line.

Alex set the crystal gently back on its shelf. His flesh seemed to retain the memory of its pain. "Yes. Your father said the same thing. He had no use for anything mystical, anything that couldn't be bought or sold or owned. To your aunt, however, the power of the crystals was very real."

"Yes, it's real," Kelli said. "I felt it."

"Have you ever experienced anything like this before?" Alex asked.

She shook her head. "Never. Some of my girlfriends were into New Age stuff, and I handled their crystals and everything. But tonight was different. I was in"—she paused to blush—"in Justin's room. I felt something . . . calling me. I came in here, and it was like . . . like fog closing in on me. The next thing I knew, I was holding that stone in my hands. It's in pain, you know. Like having your heart torn out and still living. And hiding beneath it was something even bigger and stronger, with teeth and claws that sink into your brain and pull and tear until you do what it wants."

Blood-Hunger, Alex thought in shock. *She sensed the Blood-Hunger!* Dangers within dangers. He wished he knew whether she was at risk, or he.

"I suggest," he said, "that you not touch that particular stone again."

She shuddered. "I didn't mean to touch it this time."

"We'll lock the room from now on," Justin said.

Alex nodded. He could sense the life growing inside Kelli, small, vulnerable, infinitely precious. A Danilov life. He didn't want it sullied by the crystal's pain. Or by his own Blood-Hunger.

"Why don't you take her home, Justin?" he said.

"This *is* her home."

Alex let his breath out with a hiss. Margaret had had this quality of surprise, of depths below depths and quicksilver changes that not even a millennium-old revenant could pin down.

"Do your parents know?" he asked the girl.

She nodded. Echoes of strife darkened her eyes; evidently the Hamlens' acquiescence hadn't been easily won. If at all. Alex sighed, noting that *his* approval hadn't been asked for, either. Then amusement bubbled through him. This was Justin's counter to his mother's game. A risky move, perhaps, but one calculated to tilt the playing field.

"Do you mind me being here?" Kelli asked.

He looked past her eyes into the shadowed places beyond. He found traces of crystal song and the memory of things dark and fearful. Those, he expected. But he also discovered strength in her, a solid buttress against the ugliness she'd touched.

Alex inclined his head, accepting the power of her spirit. No wonder Justin had chosen her; no wonder he fought so hard to keep her now.

"We'll have to see about finding larger accommodations," Alex said. "May I suggest the suite at the far end of the west wing? With a few minor alterations, you'll have plenty of room for a nursery."

"How close is it to Sonya?" Kelli asked.

Alex smiled. "At the opposite end of the house."

"Then we'll be glad to have it."

"Shall we draw lots to see who tells Sonya?" Alex asked.

"Oh, let me," Kelli said. "I've been looking forward to it."

Taking her hand, Alex raised it to his lips. A rare find, he thought, enjoying the prospect of watching her mature. "Be my guest," he said. Blood-Hunger raised its ugly head, focusing on a presence downstairs. "I believe I just heard her come in."

"Let's go," she said, tugging on Justin's arm.

Justin glanced over his shoulder, his dark eyes urgent.

Alex nodded. He waited until the young couple turned the corner, then locked the door to Lydia's room.

"Well, *that* went well," Justin said.

"With Kelli upstairs crying and Sonya in the study drinking herself into a stupor?"

Justin spread his hands. "Kelli's more mad than upset, and as for Mother . . . This isn't anything new. The most important thing is that Kelli's in."

"It might not work."

"What?" Justin asked.

"Don't play innocent with me," Alex retorted. "Of all the people in the world, *I* should know how your mind works."

Justin's brows went up. "What makes you the expert?"

"I'm a Danilov."

"So was my father, and he never understood anything."

"True." Alex slipped his raincoat on and patted his pockets for his keys.

"You're going out?"

"Yes."

"It's pretty foggy for driving, isn't it?"

"I always manage to find my way."

Justin shrugged. "I'll walk you out to the garage. I've got to get Kelli's suitcase anyway."

Going outside was like stepping out into another world. The scent of Wildwood hung heavily on the air, a fecund, primeval smell that eclipsed the lighter smells of magnolia and jessamine. Fog spread clammy arms over the garden, twining like a lover around the trees and turning the garage into a ghostly outline. An alligator's bellow echoed in the distance.

Wildwood cast the fog around them like a net, seeming to suck them farther and farther from the comforting glow of the house's lights. Alex walked carefully; the boundaries between marsh and dry land had blurred, as had the strict line time had drawn between the present and the long ago, when Wildwood had reigned supreme.

It won't work, my old friend. The sun will rise in the morning and burn away this fog. Like me, you'll have to retreat. Our powers are for the darkness.

"Alex," Justin said, breaking into his thoughts. "What did Kelli touch in the crystal that scared her so much?"

"If you asked that question of twenty people, you would get twenty different answers, depending upon their belief."

"I asked *you*."

"So you did." Alex sighed. "And I don't know what to tell you. There are people in this world who can sense things the rest of us can't. Lydia definitely had a special touch with crystals, and there are those who swear they can contact the dead or read facts from a crime scene or predict the future."

"I thought they were fakes."

"Some are."

"Do you believe this stuff?"

"Sometimes."

The young man's gaze lost the edge of focus, and for a moment Alex saw reflections of fog in his eyes. "What about tonight?"

"Just now," Alex said, "I could believe almost anything."

"What did Kelli touch? She kept talking about pain."

"That particular stone is . . . flawed."

"Why did Lydia have it, then? She was always talking about 'perfect' crystals."

Alex thrust his hands into his pockets. "I don't think Lydia was capable of sensing another's pain."

"You said 'was.' "

"Did I?"

"Yeah. Did you love her?"

With a sigh, Alex shook his head. "It wasn't love. For either of us."

"Elizabeth?"

"She shone like the sun."

Justin nodded. *He understands,* Alex thought. *It's like that for him and Kelli.*

The garage loomed out of the fog, an island of reality in a Wildwood sea. Alex opened the door and switched on the overhead light. The fog swirled in behind him, reaching up to bead water on the cars' metal skins.

Justin retrieved a bulging suitcase from the trunk of his car. "Well," he said, swinging around to Alex, "I guess I'd better go in. Kelli's probably wondering where I am."

"I envy you," Alex said.

The young man studied him, compassion deepening his eyes. Then he turned and walked away. The fog closed around him welcomingly, and Alex realized that Justin was more at home with Wildwood than he himself would ever be. A rectangle of golden light bloomed in the dimness, then died again as the door closed.

These Danilovs. Always a surprise.

The door opened again. A figure stepped into the opening, platinum hair backlit to gold. Sonya. Alex sighed; just now he would rather have dealt with a dozen revenants.

"Alex?" she called, moving out into the garden. "I know you're out here. Come on, we need to talk."

His Blood-Hunger focused, sharpened. He could smell her perfume on the heavy air, smell the headier scent of the woman herself. Life beat hard in her tonight; she moved through the darkness like a pale flame. Revenant need raked talons through the fabric of his mind, promising exquisite pleasure, even more exquisite torment. He took a step toward her without realizing he'd done it.

No! He clenched his fists, striving for a control that seemed as ephemeral as the mist.

"Alex, I want to talk to you," she called. "Alex!"

He slapped the button that opened the big doors, then slid behind the wheel of the Lincoln. Catherine would have said he was running away, and she would have been right. But she would also have understood that there were times when running was the only option.

Sonya appeared in the doorway behind him. Her dress swirled around her as she walked, and her white-blond hair seemed part of the shrouding mist. Her pale skin seemed almost to glow with a light of its own. Moon goddess, Alex thought. Born of the night.

Only there was no moon.

His Blood-Hunger roared. He wanted her, needed her with an intensity that made his hands tremble. Desire— a revenant's and a man's—that could only be slaked by having her.

He slammed the car into gear. The Lincoln shot forward, away from her, and it was like climbing out of a well. He made the turn onto the causeway much too fast, preferring to risk a crash into the marsh than to face the woman behind him.

"I don't have time for this," he said aloud, wrenching the car back into the lane. "I've got a revenant to kill."

A cynical voice chimed at the back of his mind. *Yes, Alexi. Save the city, save the world. You're damned if you do, damned if you don't. You're just . . . damned.*

"I knew that," he said.

11

Savannah lay peacefully beneath the dripping sky, lights burnishing its rain-wet streets as Alex drove through the city. He could feel the other's Blood-Hunger lurking just beneath the threshold of his perception. Tantalizingly near, but elusive.

"Why can't I find you?" he muttered.

Thousands of hearts beat around him, humanity unaware of what walked in their midst. He felt alien tonight, barred from being one of them, unable to be what his nature dictated.

Impulse took him to the Whyte-Bragton house. His watch read midnight as he parked at the curb and got out, tilting his head to gaze up at the brownstone facade. The windows were dark, the occupants sleeping. He located Francine on the third floor. Even asleep, her mind couldn't quite be contained; he felt it surging, warm and vital, fathomless as a sunlit sea.

Compelling. Dangerous. If he had any sense, he'd stay away from her. Stooping, he picked up a handful of pebbles and tossed them, one by one, against her window. He sensed her awakening. Sensed, too, the recognition in her mind as it touched his.

He went in, slowed only briefly by the locked front door. A single lamp lit the foyer. The house had changed greatly in the past hundred years, although some attempt seemed to have been made to return it to its former condition. The banister felt the same beneath his hand, however, as he went up the curving staircase. He and Catherine had climbed these stairs many times; for a moment he could almost hear her slippers upon the wood.

Too many memories. And too much guilt; Catherine may have accepted her imprisonment in the Abyss, but he had not.

He'd descended into grimness by the time he reached the third floor. The psychic's door lay ajar, spilling a sliver of light across the polished oak floor. He pushed it open and slipped inside.

Francine stood in the center of the room, her hands clasped in front of her. Her mind was tied as tightly as the sash of her velour robe. Even so, he felt the shadows of her fear.

"You don't have to be afraid," he said, closing the door behind him. "I've only come to talk."

She studied him for a moment, then gestured to the pair of wing chairs in front of the fireplace. "Have a seat." Her fear shaded to caution as she settled into the chair across from him.

"Why didn't you say anything about me to Martin Rhudwyn?" he asked.

"How do you know I didn't?"

He smiled. "I know."

"This isn't comfortable for me," she said, clasping her hands over her knees. "Usually *I'm* the one who knows things."

"You still are."

"Not really. You're not nearly as easy to read as you think you are."

"Oh?"

"Oh. You've got a stubborn mind."

"And what did you see?"

The light picked out the silver strands in her hair and cast curved shadows along her cheeks and throat. "I've met people you could call 'old souls.' But you're . . . truly old. I sensed centuries in your mind, ages of experience. Ages of nights. Always darkness, never the sun."

"Is that all?" he asked, knowing it wasn't.

"Such power." She closed her eyes. "And such pain. You control it well."

"I have to."

"You call yourself a monster."

He grimaced; she saw too much, understood too much. "At times," he said. "At times. Tell me why you protected me."

"Because you opposed the horror that had taken over the sanctuary . . . And because you were the only one strong enough to do so."

"The answer of a pragmatic woman. So this is to be a truce, then, not a permanent peace?"

Her eyes opened. "You are what you are."

"A monster?"

"I can't tell that yet," she said. "It depends on how you live your life."

"I don't live at all."

He saw her recoil, mentally and physically. His words had driven a wedge between them, and he welcomed it. It took her a moment—a blink of time—to compose herself.

"You bother Detective Rhudwyn," she said.

He spread his hands. "Everything bothers Martin. He allows himself to see and feel only a fraction of what's going on around him, and it clamors to be set free."

"It's every man's God-given right to be blind," she said.

"I . . ." Jagged shards of Blood-Hunger pierced him. He fought it, only vaguely registering the groan of the chair arms beneath his hands. His gaze focused on Francine's bright green eyes and the flame of her spirit behind them.

He saw her shoulders tense as the power of the Blood-Hunger hit her. Emotions flitted across her face: astonishment, disbelief, and finally, horror.

"There's another one," she gasped.

Surprise rent the shield over her mind. It was the merest instant of exposure, but enough for Alex to realize that she'd suspected him of the murders.

"You wound me," he said.

She didn't pretend not to understand. "Well, who else?"

"Even the priest?"

"No, not him. That had a completely different feel to it. A . . . deliberate sort of evil. The other killings were . . . ah"—she waved her hands, obviously frustrated by her inability to explain the unexplainable—"just sort of *there*."

"Appetite," Alex said.

"But not yours."

He shook his head.

"This other . . ."

"Revenant," he supplied. "Vampire is a harsh word, one full of ugly connotations."

She nodded. "You're hunting it."

"I'm the only one who can find it."

"The police—"

"Are prey, like anyone else." Alex said it as brutally as possible so she'd understand. "This is my domain. For obvious reasons, I'm uniquely suited to deal with this problem."

"I want to know," she said. "I want to understand."

He looked into her eyes, read truth there. "Why?"

"Because no one else can." She reached out both hands, inviting his touch.

"That's not quite true," he said. "The other—"

"Is nothing like you. You're alone, Alex. Just like me."

Her words touched something in him. Recklessly he grasped her hands and took her with him into the morass of Blood-Hunger. He let her share it as no human being had before, let her feel the red-hot drill of pain in her brain, the torn-entrail rake of the revenant's thirst.

With a cry, she broke contact. "Dear God in heaven," she gasped. "Is that what you are?"

"No," he said, gentle now. "It's what I *could* be."

She covered her face with her hands as though to isolate herself from what she'd seen. "I don't . . . I can't. . . ."

"You wanted to understand," he said.

"So I did." Taking a deep, shuddering breath, she dragged her hands down her face. "You certainly didn't sugarcoat it."

His senses had been brought to a fever pitch by the brief but powerful contact. He could hear the beating of her heart, the suspiration of air moving in and out of her lungs, smell the scent of flesh and blood and quick, pulsing life. And her horror; that hung in the air between them, thick and rank as spoiled meat.

"I'd better go," he said, rising to his feet.

The phone rang, and she leaned over to pick the receiver up. "Hello? Ah, Detective Rhudwyn. No, I wasn't asleep."

Alex turned to go. Frowning, she lifted her hand in an imperative gesture to stay.

"What?" she said. "Another one? What's . . . All right, I'll come. Alex is with me; may I bring him? Thanks. You'll pick us up in fifteen minutes? We'll be ready."

She tossed the receiver back into its cradle, then jumped up from the chair and started going through the clothes in the armoire.

"I can't go with you," Alex said.

"You have to. I think this latest murder is going to fall into what you call 'your domain.' "

"I don't need to see—"

"This one died during the day."

His attention focused, sharpened. "What?"

"Ah, I see I piqued your interest." Clothing in hand, she retreated into the bathroom.

Alex sank back into the chair. A revenant that could bear the daylight? It was impossible, of course. *Or I'd do it myself.*

"You're not protesting," she called through the door.

"Aloud, anyway."

"But you're still here."

"How could I leave?" Long ago he'd learned the necessity of knowing the enemy: strengths, weaknesses, habits, vices. Just now, this situation was unique, and uniquely dangerous.

Francine emerged wearing pants and a cotton sweater that brought out the green in her eyes. She looked pink and placid and harmless. If it hadn't been for the tremendous talent lying beneath that soft-seeming exterior, she might have been someone's grandmother. Her confidence seemed to have returned, although her mind was now closely shuttered to him.

"I've got some bourbon in my suitcase," she said, taking him by surprise.

"So there *is* justice in the world."

"There are also two glasses over there on the bureau. Will you be mother and pour while I do something with my face?"

"Try to stop me."

"Make mine a double. Neat." She returned to the bathroom, this time leaving the door open.

Alex found the bottle and held it up so that the light played golden in the amber liquid. Half-empty. He shook his head; maybe this was the only way she had of dulling the cacophony of minds around her. Or maybe loneliness drove her to it. Talents of her caliber were as rare as hen's teeth. Or revenants. He raised the bottle in a silent toast, then poured two generous portions.

"Thanks," she said, taking the one he offered her. "By the way, what are you going to do if and when you catch up to this other, ah, revenant?"

"It has to be destroyed, of course."

"Some people would say the same about you."

"Some would." He took a sip of his own drink. The bourbon burned his throat on the way down, and he took another. "There are times when I'd agree with them."

A car horn sounded outside, imperative and impatient. Alex finished his drink and set the glass aside.

"There's our ride," he called. "Ready, Francine?"

She came out of the bathroom, lipstick in one hand, drink in the other. With a practiced motion, she knocked the liquor back, then applied the lipstick in two sweeping, surprisingly accurate arcs. "There," she said, tossing the glass to him. "Let's go."

"Take a good look," Rhudwyn said, pulling the sheet away from the still form on the gurney.

The corpse was that of an old man: wrinkled, slack-jawed, a few wisps of hair straggling from his scalp. He'd been autopsied, then neatly sewn up again with black thread. Alex saw no wounds upon the body, no sign of violent death.

He glanced at Francine, who shook her head. "What's going on, Martin?" he asked.

Rhudwyn picked up a clipboard from a nearby table. "The deceased has been identified as Roger Walton Essler, 681 Charlton Street. He died at approximately eight o'clock this morning of apparent heart failure.

Traces of semen and vaginal fluid indicate he had intercourse shortly before he died."

"Why did you need us?" Francine asked.

"It seems cut-and-dried, doesn't it?" Rhudwyn asked. "An old man, maybe having sex with a prostitute, getting too excited and giving himself a heart attack. Kaput. So simple, happens all the time." He tossed the clipboard back onto the table. "Except that Roger Essler was twenty-seven years old."

Alex stared at him in astonishment. "Surely there's some mistake."

"Dental records check out. Fingerprints check out. His mother ID'd the small birthmark there on his forearm. Before fainting, that is."

"People don't age fifty years from having sex, Martin," Alex said.

"This one did."

Alex shook his head, trying to assimilate the possibilities. A revenant took its victim's blood, and with it his life, his soul. But youth? This was something very different.

"Roger, here, was a methodical fellow," Rhudwyn said. "He paid his bills on time, went to work on time, had his car serviced every six months whether it needed it or not. He even paid his taxes on time. His landlady saw him leave for work at seven-thirty on the dot, like always. But for some reason, he met a woman, turned around, and brought her to his home. Had sex with her and died of old age."

"How would *you* explain it?" Alex asked.

"I can't." Frustration roughened the detective's voice. "A corpse drained of blood I can understand; there are a multitude of ways that can happen. But this"—he thrust his thumb at what was left of Roger Essler—"shouldn't have been possible. And then we get into motive. We've seen it all—cultists, devil worshipers, nuts who think they're vampires."

Alex didn't blink; he, too, had encountered human beings who wanted to be revenant so badly they lived the illusion.

"Taking someone's blood is one thing," Rhudwyn continued. "But this . . . Hell, I don't even know what it is."

Gently Alex pulled the sheet up and over Roger Essler's face. "Don't you?"

"No."

"This is the unexplainable," Alex said, giving in to the need to goad Rhudwyn out of his only-what-I-can-see-and-hear complacency. "This is the case that computers and laboratories and hard physical evidence cannot solve. One of those 'faith' things."

Rhudwyn scowled. "Faith in what?"

"The impossible."

"Damn it, Alex—"

"I want to see the place where he died," Francine said, overriding the detective's retort.

Alex met Rhudwyn's hot yellow-brown gaze levelly and smiled. He knew the danger to himself mounted with each step Rhudwyn took toward believing the unbelievable. Ah, but the challenge of it!

The detective's gaze was the first to falter. He turned away, retrieving his keys from the table. "Let's go."

The drive was a silent one. Alex watched his companions out of the corner of his eye, noting Francine's nervousness and Rhudwyn's almost surly introspection. It had been a difficult couple of nights for them both.

"Here we are," Rhudwyn said, pulling up in front of Roger Essler's home.

Alex helped Francine out of the car, then turned to look at the building. It had once been a single-family home, but had been broken up into apartments many years ago.

Fortunately the exterior had been left almost intact.

"Nice place," he said, cupping his hand beneath an iron dolphin-headed downspout to catch the trickle of water.

Rhudwyn nodded. "Essler was a stockbroker. Did very well for himself."

"Let's get this over with," Francine said.

Alex turned to look at her, alerted by the harsh tone of her voice. Her lipstick stood out sharply against the paleness of her face, and dread had turned her eyes to jade. He touched her shoulder lightly.

Rhudwyn led the way inside. Two doors opened off the small entryway, two more on the landing upstairs. A police seal marked the door to the right. Rhudwyn broke the seal, then pushed the door open and stepped aside.

"After you," he said.

Alex admired the courage it took for Francine to go first. He followed her, his nostrils flaring at the scent of death and black malice. Whoever had stolen Roger Essler's life had enjoyed doing it.

Sex hung in the air, a heavy, rolling sensuality that ran like brandy through his veins. Hot. Powerful. Sickly-sweet, a honey-rich well to trap a man's soul. Roger Essler had leapt into that well, unknowing, and had never come out.

Succubus.

The name sprang to his mind, unbidden and unwelcome. In a thousand years of existence he'd never encountered anything to make him think the succubi other than legend. And to come across this at the time he was hunting a revenant . . .

"This feels like the priest," Francine said, her eyes stark with emotion.

Rhudwyn, who'd gone to look out the window, turned abruptly to look at her. "The circumstances were completely different. The sex—"

"The method was different," she said. "But the killer is the same."

"How so?"

"There's a kind of . . . glee about both killings. A sense of triumph, something important gained."

Alex found himself nodding agreement.

"What was gained?" Rhudwyn asked.

She shook her head. "You'll have to ask the killer."

"I'd like to, damn it." With an explosive sigh, the detective ran his hand through his hair. "Okay. Is this the same person who's been doing the so-called vampire slayings?"

"No." Alex and Francine spoke together.

Rhudwyn turned back to the window. Bracing his hands on the sill, he leaned forward to rest his forehead against the glass. "How exactly do you go about stealing someone's youth?"

"I haven't worked that part out yet," Alex said. Echoes of sensuality flowed through him, almost memories of a pleasure hot enough to drain a man's youth.

Rhudwyn's shoulders hunched. "You're telling me I have two nutball killers running around my city. I've got eleven corpses, no fingerprints, no witnesses, and very little physical evidence."

"That appears to be so," Alex agreed.

"How the hell am I going to solve these cases?"

Alex smiled, felt it twist. "Maybe it's time to start believing in miracles."

12

Lydia strolled down Oglethorpe Avenue, shoulder to shoulder with the tourists who'd come to gawk at Savannah's summer beauty.

She smiled at a man, received a polite nod in return. Something sharp dug beneath her ribs. Lydia Danilov did not get polite nods. *Not anymore*. She'd begun to lose the youth she'd gained yesterday. One life, one day of beauty. There simply wasn't enough power in a human being to sustain her for long.

Alex had the power. Enough to make her young again, enough to keep her young forever.

A woman bumped into her, hard enough to send them both staggering "Oh, my fault! Sorry!" the woman gasped, dropping a shower of envelopes onto the sidewalk.

Lydia started to walk away. Then she noticed the keys dangling from the woman's hand and turned back. "That's okay," she said, crouching to help pick up the scattered mail. "I wasn't watching where I was going, either."

With so many people around, her options were limited; of all the things she didn't want, attracting attention headed the list. No, this had to be done subtly.

"Thanks," the woman said, reaching for the letters as she rose to her feet.

Lydia rose with her, the crystal pulsing between her breasts. Their gazes met, held. The woman's eyes lost their focus.

"You've got a ton of stuff to carry," Lydia said. "Why don't you let me walk you to your car?"

Her hand dropped to her side. "Y-yes, sure. Right over here."

She led the way around the corner and a few yards down the next street, where a new red Nissan sparkled in the sunlight.

"Forget you ever saw me," Lydia said, plucking the keys from her hand. "And take the bus home. You lent the car to a friend for a few days."

She sent the command spiraling through the crystal, felt it sink deep into the woman's mind, an ice-pick desecration of reality. True memory faded, replaced by the false.

Lydia peeled rubber as she left. Behind her, she could see the woman standing in the shade of a huge old maple tree. Leaves cast dappled shadows over her face.

"Thanks a lot," Lydia said. "I appreciate it."

The greenery seemed more lush the closer she got to the Isle of Palms. Not overgrown; that might catch the attention of the road crews. But more primitive, somehow, more vibrant, more full of life. Alex's doing, no doubt. If it hadn't been for the concrete ribbon of the road in front of her, she might have thought she'd flipped back a century or two.

She pulled off the road a short distance from the house. The sun hung just above the horizon, a great red ball that bloodied the clouds and sent a riot of color sweeping the western sky. Home. The house rode on a sea of afternoon light.

"Welcome back, Lydia darling," she murmured. "If nobody else can say it, I can."

She could feel Alex's power. Quiescent now, as he was, but there. It permeated every brick, every piece of wood, and set the Arbor apart from the rest of the world. The vampire's domain. His shelter from humanity, his link to his own past.

The rim of the sun touched the western horizon. Time was running out; if she was still here on the property when Alex awakened, he'd sense her for sure.

She walked around to the back of the house, to the spot where garden gave way to marsh. Stepping into the shelter of the trees, she grasped the crystal and summoned Sonya. A few minutes later she heard a door open and close, then the rustle of leaves as Sonya made her way through the brush.

A shaft of hot envy shot through Lydia as she came face-to-face with the other woman's beauty. If she'd had the power, she would have ripped Sonya's mind out of that body and taken it for herself. But she couldn't; even now, Sonya struggled against her control.

Lydia grasped her own crystal, bore down hard. "Lift your hand," she said.

Sonya's hand shook as she fought the command. But it came up. Lydia bared her teeth in something that didn't feel at all like a smile.

"Go on, touch your face," Lydia said.

Twitching, the hand lifted more, until the fingertips rested on Sonya's cheek.

"Now scratch yourself." Lydia's grip on the stone tightened. "Draw blood."

Sonya's hand tensed. The fingers curved, and the long coral nails indented the skin of her cheek. Then it stopped. Black disappointment weighted Lydia's belly. She raised her own hand, saw the cross-hatching of lines upon the skin, the wattle of loose flesh on her forearm. Even that small expenditure of power had cost her. She'd been trapped in a body that seemed to crumble faster after every rejuvenation, and there seemed to be no way out.

Only Alex could help her. But that damned stiff-necked morality of his . . . If he knew she existed, he'd move heaven and earth to destroy her.

"Damn you," she said, releasing her hold on the crystal.

Sonya's hand fell to her side. With a sigh, Lydia leaned back against the trunk of a tree. Frustration dug deep. She could control another person—up to a point—but she couldn't do what she really needed: take another body.

How long did zombies live? Did they go on and on until the last limb fell off, or even until the last shred of flesh rotted off the bone? Maybe longer . . .

No! Alex has the power you want. He won't give it, but you can take it.

"Yes," she said.

She had to try. The possible gain was worth any risk, any cost. And caution belonged to another lifetime. She reached out to touch the twin ghost crystal that hung around Sonya's neck. Light flared in its depths, a ruddy glow that made the stone seem darker than ever. Power hummed in the stones. She grasped it, drew it in, tuned them to harmony.

Buoyed by the whirling crystal song, Lydia beat Sonya's will aside. Acquiescence settled in, and a swirling warmth that spread throughout the captive mind. It wouldn't last long, but hopefully, long enough. It had to.

"Don't worry," she said, stroking one finger down the curve of Sonya's cheek. "I'm not going to make you do anything you didn't already want to do."

Reaching deep into the faceted heart of the stone, Lydia spun along the black vortex of Suldris's power. There, she touched the thread linking her to Elizabeth. Even unawakened, the vampire hung like a dark sun in Lydia's consciousness. Her power and her need lurked just below the surface, requiring only the darkness to be free again.

Sister, Lydia thought. She delved deep into the vampire's blank, sleeping mind, dug through shrouding layers of oblivion to touch the place where Suldris had laid his hand on Elizabeth's psyche. He'd intended to control her. Lydia lacked his power, but she could use Elizabeth in a way that would never have occurred to any man.

Lydia took the essence of what had been Elizabeth Garry, things the vampire had lost the ability to remember. She took them, drew them deep into her crystal, then passed them through to Sonya's.

The crystals lay warm in her hands. In another time, in another world, it might have felt like a benediction. She rubbed her thumbs along the angled faces of the stones, frustrated by the lack of sensation in her fingertips.

Drawing her breath in with a hiss, she let the crystals fall. They pulsed with a light the color of old blood.

She looked up at the house. The western windows reflected the sunset in a blind, carmine gaze, and the trees laid slats of shadows across the pale walls. Somewhere in there, Alex lay sleeping.

"You want Elizabeth?" She clenched her hands into fists she couldn't quite feel. "I'll give her to you."

Oblivion released Alex into Blood-Hunger. It surged through him, a hot-acid wash through his veins, and brought him to his feet. His need was an almost palpable force, hovering like a black ghost in a room that was no longer a haven.

He went upstairs, knowing he couldn't outrun what lurked inside him. He'd never been able to outrun it; never would, until the day he walked out to meet the sun.

Sensuality closed around him, thickening with every step he took. It drew him out of his bedroom and out into the hall. His revenant senses arrowed straight toward the suite where Justin and Kelli had set up housekeeping.

Aha, he thought, shaking off the foreboding that had begun to claim him. Young love, passionate enough to spill out over those who ought to be too old and too wise for it. And far too old to be standing here, looking in on something that was none of his business.

He returned to his room, shedding clothes as he went. A shower was just what he needed; cleansing the body, cleansing the mind. Ah, to be young again! The joy of their lovemaking sparkled in the air, sent bright little darts through his belly. He'd possessed that joy twice in his long existence. Once with Catherine, once with Elizabeth. But how brief those times seemed now, with only an empty future stretching ahead of him.

He let the hot water beat his skin into warmth. Blood-Hunger drummed a tattoo in his head, counterpoint to the simple human need to hold and be held. Steam rose around him, enclosing him in a hot, private well. He half closed his eyes, searching for visions of Elizabeth. There, over to the left, a swirl of mist echoed the way her hair lifted in the wind. And there, to the right, another swirl suggested the slim, graceful curve of her hip and thigh.

He squeezed his eyes shut, unable to bear the exquisite torture of memory even as his body reacted powerfully to it. Even now, he could remember the way she felt under his hands; the softness of her skin, the resilience of the flesh and muscle below, the heat of her as she accepted him. He ached for her, body, mind, and soul.

Water streamed out of his hair and down his face. It felt like tears, like the gaping emptiness inside him that no one could fill. Impaled on Blood-Hunger and yearning, he held out his arms.

"Elizabeth," he said.

If need alone could call a person back from the grave, he'd have her.

He swallowed, trying to ease the tightness enough to speak again. "Elizabeth. Oh, God. If there is mercy in this world or the next, let her know that I love her."

Suddenly he sensed another presence in the shower with him. Lost in his memories of Elizabeth, he reached out and gathered it in. And found it real. Human. Female. Naked.

Staggered, he opened his eyes. For a single, breath-stopping moment he thought Elizabeth had answered his call. But then he realized that the woman's honey-colored hair was really blond, only darkened by water.

"Sonya," he said, his voice harsh with disappointment. He released her, stepping back as far as the confines of the stall allowed.

"Hello, Alex."

"You shouldn't be here."

"You can't go any farther," she said. "Why so shy all of a sudden? It's not like you're . . ." Glancing down, she smiled. "Disinterested."

"That?" He shrugged. "An anatomical anomaly peculiar to men, and not always an accurate barometer of interest. Women have always overestimated the importance of such things."

"Do we?" Her hair lay sleekly against her head, emphasizing the delicate structure of her face. Water sluiced down the front of her body. It glistened on the crystal that lay between her small, high breasts, ran in curving rivulets down the length of her legs, and beaded in the pale thatch of pubic hair. The scent of skin and perfume and arousal filled the shower stall.

"What are you doing here?" he asked.

"I had to come," she said. "I couldn't help myself."

"Go away." But his body wanted her to stay—and his Blood-Hunger.

"I can't. And you don't want me to. Anatomical anomalies notwithstanding."

She moved toward him. Beautiful, exotic as a white orchid. The scent of her rose with the steam, filling the room, filling his senses until his mind spun helplessly. A jolt of mingled Blood-Hunger and desire went through him. Revenant and man, man and revenant, he wanted her.

"Don't you feel it?" she asked, laying her hands on his shoulders. "Tonight's *our* night."

"It's a bad idea," he said. "You and I—"

"Shhh." She put her hand over his mouth. "I know. We're unsuited and unsuitable, we're fighting over everything from money to Justin. But right now, here, none of it matters." Smiling into his eyes, she took one more step forward so that their bodies touched. Shoulders, breasts, hips . . . Alex felt as though he'd been dipped in fire.

She took her hand from his mouth. Slowly, as though ready to replace it if he protested again. But he'd passed beyond protest, beyond anything but touching her. He spread his hands out across her back, feeling the warm, fragile humanity of her.

"Kiss me," she said.

He slid her upward along his water-slick skin until her face was level with his. Then he kissed her. She tasted of mint and heat and woman, and for a moment he thought the world had taken a half turn around him. Blood-Hunger amplified her heartbeat, made it thunder along his nerves and settle deep in his belly.

He tore his mouth from hers, kissed his way along her jaw and down her throat to the spot where her pulse hammered beneath the skin. He hovered there for a moment, tormenting himself. So rich, he thought. Bursting with life. A thousand years of being revenant seemed to coalesce inside him, focusing on this one pulse point of temptation.

She moaned. A sound rife with anticipation. A human sound. It saved her, saved him. Wrenched from the summit of Blood-Hunger, he slid away from her throat.

He moved lower, tasting her as a man would taste her, limiting himself to a man's sensations. She caught his face between her hands, bent to kiss him with unrestrained violence. It sparked a matching surge in him, a bestiality that for once was all human.

She raised her head to stare down at him. For a moment her eyes made a strange shift of color, changing from amber to green to amber again. A trick of the light, he told himself. He sank his hands into her hair, winding the wet silken strands around his fingers. If it were a shade or two darker, he might almost think . . . She kissed him again, and Alex forgot everything but what he could feel and taste and the wild sensuality spiraling through him.

It no longer mattered who she was—or wasn't. She was here. For this moment that would have to be enough.

He rose to his feet and lifted her to him. Her head fell back as she wrapped her legs around his hips, and the sight of that long, smooth expanse of throat almost sent him over the edge. The steam intensified the scent of her skin, her hair, the sweet, hot pulse of life just beneath the surface.

Water pounded his back, counterpoint to the rage of his Blood-Hunger. He ran his open mouth over the taut expanse of her throat. She sighed, sinking her hands into his hair. The pulse of her life throbbed so close, so invitingly, that he couldn't keep from sampling it. Sweet and hot, it spiraled through him. He wanted to take all of her, take and take until she filled that clamoring emptiness inside him.

Do it, it seemed to say. *Take me, and you'll feel like a human again.*

Until the next time. And the next. He'd become at last the very thing he abhorred.

With an effort of will that made his legs shake, he tore his mouth away from her throat. A single drop of blood clung to her skin, hovered for a single, trembling moment, then slid down to dissipate in the water flowing between her breasts.

"Please," she gasped.

Pleasure. That, he dared give her. And himself. But there was something about her that called to him powerfully, something that urged him to hurl himself into the hurricane-tossed sea of Blood-Hunger. Poised on a tightrope of self-control, he gazed down into the roiling active volcano of his own need.

Take her.

As a man. Only as a man.

The water beat down upon their straining bodies, steam rose to envelop them in a shroud of heat. Alex sank into a sort of haze, born of exquisite pleasure and the even more exquisite torment of withholding his raging Blood-Hunger. She clung to him, sliding up his body to deepen the sensations for them both. Her eyes changed color as she shifted position. Blue. Amber. Green. Amber.

Elizabeth.

Someone cried out. Alex wasn't sure if it had been he or Sonya, or both. And then it didn't matter; helplessly he fell into a well of release so deep he didn't think he'd ever climb out again.

But reality returned, as it always does. He looked down into her eyes and found them only blue.

"I've got to put you down," he said. "We're running out of hot water."

"I don't think I can stand up yet."

He set her on her feet, keeping his arm around her waist while he turned the water off. Then he picked her up again and carried her out of the shower.

"We shouldn't have done that," he said.

"Probably not." She wound her arms around his neck. "But it was a lot of fun, wasn't it?"

He considered erasing it from her memory then and there. But Sonya had come back from France an enigma, and tonight might be his only chance of solving it. For Justin's sake.

Who are you trying to kid? His cynical revenant voice edged through his mind, bringing mingled amusement and self-deprecation. He wasn't doing this for Justin. *He* needed a woman in his life, if only Sonya, and only for tonight. Tomorrow he'd do the expedient thing: rape her of the memory of these hours with him.

"Why did you come in here?" he asked. "You had to know what would happen."

"I didn't *know*," she said. "But it's nice to find out that you're human after all."

Caught by the irony of it, he smiled. Alex Danilov hadn't been human for a long, long time; but then, in some ways, perhaps he was all too human.

"You realize," she murmured, tracing his lips with her fingertip, "that we're still at odds on nearly everything."

"So this is only a truce?"

"Truce is too strong a word. Let's call it an interlude in the battle."

"If you like." Her blunt cynicism excited him; he'd always enjoyed a challenge. Desire hummed in his veins, spread through his flesh in a sweeping rush. He set her down, but slowly, letting her slide along his reawakening body.

"Mmmm," she said. "I see you're still feeling friendly."

"Interludes are never to be wasted."

She spread her fingers out over his shoulder, a greedy, possessive gesture. "You sound as though you've done this sort of thing before."

"Once or twice." Or a hundred. Blondes, brunettes, redheads—all exquisite, all as deadly as a good rapier.

"Do you enjoy it?"

"Always."

Her lids drifted to half-mast. "Is it dangerous?"

"Always."

He kicked the door open and carried her into the bedroom. Starlight lay in pale bars upon the floor. He watched her eyes change as they passed through alternating light and dark. France had changed her. She'd left here a woman bruised and uncertain, returned able to fight even him to get what she wanted.

"What *is* it you really want from me?" he asked, laying her on the bed.

She reached up to pull him down. "Just this," she murmured. "For starters."

13

Lydia floated in the reflected heat of Sonya's pleasure, a vicarious participant in hers and Alex's lovemaking. It began as an intriguing experiment, but had quickly become pure torture.

Making love to Sonya, Alex was . . . well, Alex. Skilled, sensual, with a dangerousness to him that was like nothing else in the world. Lydia remembered what it had been like. Oh, yes, she remembered. And she, who'd sent Sonya into his arms, would have killed just now to be there herself.

She could feel his Blood-Hunger, feel his desire. He rode the edge, walking a tightrope between the two. One slip, and Sonya would be dead. Consumed. Fed to the flames of the vampire's need, human sacrifice to the eternity of Alex's life.

"Do it," Lydia muttered. Gripping the crystal until it cut into her hand, she tried to force him over the edge. She needed him to kill Sonya; that death would give her access to him, to his thousand-year-old power.

She wanted it. Needed it. Immortality had to wait until she'd handled the more immediate crisis of her crumbling body; who'd want to live forever like *this*?

So, voyeur, she hovered at the fringes of his passion. Hung on the edge of eternity, she cursed him, shouted for him to take Sonya on the long slide into hell. But he didn't. Something hard and pure and impenetrable sprang to life inside him, enclosing and controlling the Blood-Hunger. Setting him free.

Heaviness settled in Lydia's body as Alex fed Sonya's arousal until it burned to immoderate heights, then stoked it even higher. She wanted to be there. She wanted to be the one being loved, the one touching him, the one . . .

"Oh, God!" she muttered. "It should be me. Damn you, Alex! Damn you, damn you, *damn* you!"

Swamped by waves of heat, she wrapped her arms around her knees and strove to endure what she'd begun. No, to take advantage of it. There had to be something here she could use.

She snatched bits and pieces of his power, using the camouflage of the skyrocketing sexuality. Bits and pieces; dregs. Even in climax, he still managed to hold something of himself back. Something important. Something, Lydia realized, she wanted very much.

"Don't you ever let yourself go?" she asked.

Sure. With Elizabeth. Sonya had been a pale substitute, acceptable only because his Blood-Hunger had felt a little like loneliness.

As you were. The thought was unwelcome; the limitation even more so. She chopped at the air with her hand, dismissing them both.

"*I've* got Elizabeth," she said.

She felt him delve into Sonya's mind, his usual vampire sleight of hand with another person's memory. Hastily she disengaged; she didn't think he could sense her, but with Alex, you never knew.

"Go ahead, make her forget," she said. "But I'm not going to forget, and I'm going to make your life *hell* until I get what I want."

It took her a few moments to recover, a few moments more to realize that youth had returned to her skin. She held her hands out, letting the moonlight play over her skin. Nice. It should have pleased her more. But she knew she'd been cheated. Reaching up, she clasped the crystal again. It throbbed gently in her palm, surfeited with what she'd fed it.

"And now," she murmured. "Elizabeth."

She pushed herself to her feet and headed down the corridor. Her stride had regained its grace, her body nearly all its sensation.

There'd be more.

As she neared the room where the vampire slept, a sense of wrongness settled in the pit of her stomach. She broke into a run. Turning the corner into the doorway, she faced her greatest fear: an empty room.

Elizabeth had gone to hunt. Lydia pounded her fist on the doorjamb. Not now. *Not* now. Alex had no doubt sensed the flare of Blood-Hunger. As soon as he could get to Savannah, he'd be on the vampire's trail. And without Lydia to protect her, he'd find her.

Using the crystal, she found the thread of Suldris's power that bound her to the vampire. Found it and followed it. Raging. God*damn* Elizabeth for doing this now!

"She's mine," she panted as she ran. "You're going to give me what I want, Alex *darling,* and then I'll let you have her. Or what's left of her."

Alex laid Sonya on her own bed. She was deeply asleep now, her lashes lying in crescent fans upon her cheeks. Caught on a spike of momentary tenderness, he brushed a stray lock of hair back from her face.

He felt drained in body and spirit, as though he'd engaged in a battle rather than simple lovemaking. But then, nothing seemed to be simple for him, least of all making love.

"Adieu," he murmured, turning away from the bed.

He found Justin waiting for him in the hallway. The young man leaned one shoulder against the wall, his expressionless face betraying little of the emotions churning below.

"Hi, Alex," he said.

"I—"

"Don't deny it. I saw you carry her out of your room."

Guilt settled heavily on Alex's shoulders. He'd made love to many women in many times, many settings; other men's wives, sisters, daughters. But he'd never been caught at it. Now, facing his lover's son, he found he had no better way of explaining himself than any man. So he merely spread his hands, accepting the accusation in the young man's eyes.

"I know you feel—"

"Betrayed?" Justin's smile was a bit lopsided, but seemed genuine enough. A man's smile, rife with cynicism. "Why should I? My mother screwed everyone else she came into contact with. Why not you?"

"She didn't betray you. *I* did."

"I'm glad you understand the difference."

"You expected me to be perfect."

"No!" With an obvious effort, Justin brought his voice under control. "I expected you to do your sinning somewhere else."

Alex didn't answer. There *was* no answer.

"Look. . . ." With a sharp exhalation, Justin pushed away from the wall. "If screwing you makes her willing to back off about my marriage, I say go for it."

"I doubt you really mean that."

"I mean it. Just be sure you get your money's worth."

Crossing his arms over his chest, Alex regarded this young man who carried all of House Danilov on his shoulders. An angry man just now, frustrated by his elders' weakness and his own inability to fight society. "Justin—"

"Why did you do it?"

"It just . . . happened." Alex damned the Blood-Hunger, damned his own weakness. "At the time I didn't seem to have much choice."

"No choice!" Justin snorted. "And they say teenagers don't know how to control themselves."

"Everyone has weaknesses. Even those who pontificate."

"Sex being yours?"

Alex sighed. He couldn't explain the urges that had driven him to make love to Sonya. Not to Justin, not even to himself. Somehow she'd touched the burning loneliness that Elizabeth had left behind. He didn't know why or how, and that frightened him more than his own lack of control.

"I'm sorry," he said.

"Yeah. Everybody's sorry. Everybody's always sorry."

Alex pulled the door closed and leaned his back against it. "I made a mistake tonight. You know it, I know it. Your mother probably knows it."

Justin grimaced. "She doesn't care, as long as she gets what she wants. It's you that bothers me. What's with you? You've been twanging off the walls lately, and now this. It's not like you, Alex."

He's too perceptive. Always has been. "I never twang."

"Don't patronize me!"

"Fine," Alex said. "I won't. But you're intruding on things that aren't any of your business, and you have no right to an answer."

Turning on his heel, Justin stalked away. Alex started after him, but stopped as a sudden surge of Blood-Hunger scraped along his bones. The other revenant had begun the hunt.

Soon someone would die.

Alex disdained the car; man's means was too slow tonight. Instead he opened the nearest window and leapt out, shifting from one moment to the next. His wings cupped the wind, caught the moonlight in a flurry of white feathers. He arrowed out over the marsh.

He flew over the quiet water, the small seas of nodding grass, the mysterious dark islands that had resisted the touch of man since the beginning of time. There were times when his shadow paced him, times when it was swallowed by the marsh to be spewed out later at Wildwood's whim.

Here, he was no different from the grass, the trees, the frogs, and myriad insects that populated Wildwood. The marsh accepted them all, briefly, then swallowed them all with the same lack of prejudice with which it had harbored them. An interesting notion, to a revenant.

He left it behind, winged out over the places humankind had settled and changed. Ahead, Savannah lay like a dusting of stars upon the horizon. Blood-Hunger rose like a dark specter above it, leeching the magic from the moonlight. It seemed to stretch toward him. Beckoning. It would draw him into the realm of the revenant, where the bits and pieces of humanity he still possessed were a handicap, where the law was kill or be killed, and everyone prey.

So be it. Tonight, I'll be only revenant. On to the hunt, my kindred. You, too, are prey.

He glided down on the arms of Blood-Hunger. It entwined with his until he wasn't sure where his ended and the other's began. The city lay sleeping around him, lush, beautiful, dangerous.

The scent of the other hung on the air like raw meat, the stench of unrestrained Hunger. He flew just above the treetops, owl senses and revenant senses tuned high. Close, so very close.

Fluttering down to a perch high in the branches of a great old oak, he blocked out the pall of the surrounding humanity, searching for the monstrous. Menace lay all around. He breathed it in, tasting it for some sign of his quarry.

Catching a flicker of movement in the shadows at the end of the street, he held his breath and waited for more. The night seemed to congeal round him.

Where are you?

Nothing answered his silent summons. But the other's presence raged at him, scraped like a rusty blade along his nerves. And then he touched it.

His senses reeled with the power of its Hunger and the torment of Blood-Hunger so fierce it could never be controlled. Pain. The gut-clenching, brain-twisting burn of need, the howling emptiness of spirit that only human lives could fill.

"You feel me, too," he muttered.

A dark shape detached itself from the shadows and moved away, swifter than any human being could have moved. He launched himself after it in a smooth glide.

Light burst all around him, the sudden, incandescent glare of headlights. He cupped air, striving frantically to rise above the great black shape of the onrushing truck. Its horn blared. He managed to miss the grille, bounced hard on the hood, then rolled up and off the windshield.

Dazed, he lost his hold on the owl form. He landed heavily on the asphalt. The truck's driver, having managed to wrestle his vehicle to a stop, came to stand over him.

"Hey, mister," the man panted. "You okay?"

"I . . . just had the wind knocked out of me," Alex said.

"Jesus, God, I swear I never saw you! This damned owl flew right into my windshield, and I—"

"It's all right," Alex said. He tested his right arm, found it broken. Holding it in place with his left hand, he climbed to his feet and started to follow the other revenant's swiftly fading trail.

"Hey!" the man called. "Hey, mister!"

He didn't look back, and the man's voice was soon lost behind him. Pain still twinged his arm; until it healed, he wasn't going to be doing any flying. But he'd gotten the scent again, and nothing was going to stop him from tracking the revenant down.

It moved toward the river in a sure, steady path that showed its familiarity with this territory. It had apparently forgotten him; its Blood-Hunger quested forward, not back.

"Hunting again," he murmured.

His arm healed as he made his way down Drayton Street. He flexed it cautiously, then less so. Ahead, he spotted a dark shape moving swiftly toward the river. He followed, running across one of the metal bridges connecting the buildings to Bay Street. His shadow moved across the corrugated shapes on the paving stones of the level just below. Factors Walk. A new term, one he wasn't comfortable with.

The revenant seemed to be moving faster now, and with more purpose. Alex's nostrils flared as he caught the blood scent of a human being.

Time had run out.

He leapt down the twenty-odd feet to the lower level, landing in a crouch amid the graceful, crosshatched shadow of the bridge. Slowly he straightened. Blood-Hunger rose on the air, stark and powerful, overwhelming the scent of its human quarry. Cursing, Alex ran along the line of buildings.

He found them in the courtyard of a converted warehouse; the man lying upon the ground, the revenant, a slim, pale shape in the moonlight, crouched above him.

Alex scaled the slatted wooden gate and dropped down on the other side.

He stalked forward as the other rose slowly, reluctant to leave its meal. And then he froze.

Elizabeth.

Elizabeth.

Her gaze met his. In the space between one breath and the next, he sank into those dark amber eyes, sank deep. And found nothing. No recognition, no joy, no awareness of him as anything but an enemy. He recoiled, fleeing back to the safety of his own mind.

She stood watching him, hands at her sides. Her hair lifted on the wind, and the moonlight shattered on the paler strands. The blood of her kill stained her mouth, her chin, the front of her dress. Guiltless in the face of murder. Revenant, drinker of human blood, swallower of souls. His Elizabeth. Monster.

He couldn't move, couldn't think, couldn't believe. She was more beautiful than he'd remembered, even in his dreams; more terrible than any of his nightmares.

"Elizabeth," he whispered, forcing her name through a throat gone tight with pain.

She bared her teeth at him. Her body tensed, and for a moment he thought she was about to spring at him, to rip his throat out as an animal would. He wasn't sure he wouldn't let her. Then something touched the air, something hard and evil, and Elizabeth raised her head. Her nostrils flared.

Then, so suddenly that Alex was taken by surprise, she leapt to the top of the adjoining wall. She crouched there for a moment, as tawny and deadly as a lioness, and as beautiful. He started after her.

A cloud of dark power rose up in front of him, reaching out to gather him in. He fought it savagely. It dragged at his legs, twined around his arms, sank into his nose and mouth as though trying to suffocate him.

He managed one step, then another. As he struggled for a third, Elizabeth disappeared down the other side of the wall. His breath rasped as he strained to follow.

As suddenly as it had come, the clinging web of power vanished. Alex leapt up to the top of the wall. But Elizabeth had gone. Whisked away, into the arms of that rank evil.

He sank to his knees. "Elizabeth." His voice rose to a scream as his pain broke free. "God, Elizabeth!"

Uncaring, the wind took his cry and cast it away.

14

Floodlights bloomed in the courtyard. The searing illumination brought the scene into stark, cruel focus: the trees, every leaf cut with knife-edged shadows, seeming to nod in startlement; the slatted gate barred like a prison door; the sprawled body of the man, his eyes open in horrified surprise as the thickening dregs of his blood filled the mortared spaces of the brick pavement.

And Alex, crouched atop the wall, pinned in the light like a butterfly on a board. He flung himself backward, landing on hands and knees on the far side. Brushing himself off, he ran up Factors Walk to Bay Street as sirens shrieked to life in the distance.

For the police, this would be another baffling murder. For Alex, it had shattered his world, reconstructing a very different one in its place.

Elizabeth. His Elizabeth. Her intelligence gone, replaced by the most basic and base revenant instinct: Blood-Hunger. Her independence taken from her, leaving her the tool of whoever had helped her escape. Her salvation, stolen.

He'd killed her to keep her from this.

Rage burned in him, and outrage. The joy and gener-osity of spirit that had been Elizabeth had been made into something that existed only to kill. Had *he* created her, all unknowing? Had he abandoned her to mindlessness in his blind certainty that he'd saved her soul?

How else? Who else? "Why, Lord?" he asked. "Of all the punishments in the world, why this one?"

He strode up one street and down the next, unfurling his revenant senses in a great, spreading net. But she was lost to him. Her "protector" had spirited her away, a subtle shifting of reality's cards; first you see it, now you don't, and the hand is always quicker than the eye.

Finally he stopped beneath the fringed canopy of a mimosa tree. It took an effort of will; instinct screamed at him to continue searching, to tear the city apart if that was what it took to find Elizabeth.

Stop. Think. Look beyond the facts . . . find the source.

He headed toward Colonial Cemetery, where he'd left her so many months ago. A faint drifting of mist made the hoary old burial ground seem a magical place. Alex walked noiselessly through the dew-sparkled grass, not wanting to break the silence with even the sound of a breath.

Mist softened the harsh edges of the Danilov vault. Alex found the shattered lock, ran his fingertips lightly over it. This had been done from outside. Which meant that Elizabeth's protector had gone into the vault to get her.

He pushed the door open and stepped inside. The moonlight pooled at his back as though reluctant to enter the tiny chamber. For the fourth time, he tasted the psychic residue of evil. First, in the cathedral; second, in the house where Roger Essler had died; third, in the courtyard tonight; and now, finally, in the place where his heart had been entombed with Elizabeth. It tasted the same each time: dark, full of malice, and edged with triumph.

He turned in a slow circle, closing his eyes to better concentrate on his other senses. He could hear the slough of branches as they moved in the wind, the chirp of a cricket, the faint *scritch* of a mouse's claws in the grass outside. But those were natural things. He shifted focus, concentrating on the unnatural.

The memory of lavender hung in the vault, although dissipated by the passage of years. It surprised him. But perhaps some vestige of Catherine would always remain in this place, caught, like her, in the dark area beyond reality. Here, too, he tasted the shadow of Elizabeth's Blood-Hunger. She had lain unawakened, her need growing and deepening until someone had come to set it free.

He let his breath out in a harsh sigh. She'd been summoned to a Hunger that had been unsatiated far too long. Then she'd been sent out into the city to hunt. Mindlessly. Brutally. Seventeen lives had been lost because of it—no, eighteen. And there would be more. She wouldn't stop. Couldn't.

"I have to fix this," he said.

The vault swallowed his words, turned them cold; the only way to fix this was to destroy Elizabeth and her protector.

His gaze lifted to the plaque that bore Catherine's name. It drew him. The scent of lavender grew stronger, perhaps from the mummified flowers in the nearby urn. Perhaps it was only his imagination providing what the world could not. He ran his fingers lightly over the brass. The metal felt warm, like silk on a woman's body. Startled, he snatched his hand back. Then he reached out again, spreading his fingers out over the plate. Yes, it *was* warm. And smooth as her skin had been that night long ago when he'd first made love to her.

"Catherine?"

The name seemed to slide around the vault before settling deep in his chest. Temptation came to sit on his shoulder. *Look,* it whispered into the aching void of his loneliness. *In your heart, you've always wondered if she's really there.*

"Of course she's there," he said.

Why not? You never saw her body.

"No." He closed his eyes, fighting the lash of his need. "I know she died."

You loved her for many years. Who knows what effect those years with you had on her physical self? If her body is intact, and you pull her soul out of the Abyss someday . . . You can have her back.

He drew a deep breath, almost ready to pull Catherine's coffin out of its slot. Then he felt the evil close around him. Eager. Black with malice. Waiting to feed on his pain.

Slowly he pushed away from the stone. "No," he said. "I'll walk out to greet the dawn first."

He'd been so close, so close to doing it. Catherine had died an old woman. Her body had lain in its coffin for more than a hundred years; no amount of magic would have preserved anything he'd recognize. He closed his eyes, imagining himself opening her coffin to find a pile of bones and crumbling fabric. And that black evil tittering off, pleased to have ripped his heart out.

"Begone," he said. "You've taken Elizabeth. Catherine is mine, here"—he tapped his chest—"and always will be."

He turned to go. Something in the far corner caught the moonlight, casting it back in a smooth flare of color that had been familiar to him for nearly a thousand years. The griffin medallion.

His shoes grated on dust as he strode across the chamber. Crouching, he retrieved the medallion. The chain had

been squashed into an unusable mass; he tore it free and
cast it aside. But the medallion itself was unharmed, and
the cabochon winkled at him in greeting.

"And so you should," he said, gently wiping the dust
away.

He tilted it, letting the ruby catch the light in a crimson
whirl. It was the only link he had to the man he'd been,
oh, so many years ago. His humanity. He'd given it to
Elizabeth, then buried it with her.

"I'm sorry, love," he murmured, slipping the medallion
into his pocket.

Rising, he walked straight through the aura of evil. It
clung to his skin like a thin coating of mist, and felt as
greedy and malevolent as it smelled. But once outside,
the wind sloughed the evil from him, tore it, and tossed
the shreds into the sky.

He glanced at his watch, frowning in surprise as he
realized daybreak was a scant half hour away.

"Well, Charles, it seems that I'll have to take advantage
of your hospitality," he said.

He walked the few blocks to Charles McGinnis's house.
The windows were dark and blind, the house unten-
anted by anything but the lawyer and his loneliness.
Alex smiled a bit crookedly; it was a fitting place for
them both. Once inside, he took a business card out
of his pocket and dropped it on the table beside the
door.

Charles would understand.

The smell of frying bacon led Alex upward out of
Oblivion. He sat up, sniffing the air. Delicious. Night
dweller that he was, he still missed the simple human
experience of eating breakfast. He followed the scent
downstairs to the kitchen and found Charles hard at
work over the stove. With its wrapping of well-worn
maple cabinetry, the room echoed the shabby gentility

of the rest of the house. Most of the equipment was years old, left untouched when Charles's wife died.

The lawyer pointed to a chair with his spatula. "Have a seat."

"Thanks. That smells wonderful."

"Grab yourself a plate, then."

"I don't eat," Alex said with more than a little regret.

"My sympathies. Will it be uncomfortable if I eat in front of you?" Charles patted the soft bulge of his stomach. "As you can see, *I* haven't given up food."

Alex smiled. "I've been watching my friends eat for a number of years now."

"Centuries, you mean."

Alex sat down at the kitchen table, placing his hands flat on the top. It had been polished recently, although no amount of buffing could have overcome the effects of feeding children: the layer-upon-layer accumulation of rings left by wet glasses, the burned spot at one corner, the place where someone had begun to carve his name.

A family had lived around this table, eating, fighting, growing up. Loneliness crashed over Alex, a tidal wave of regret for what had been lost and what could never be.

"How many children did you and Meg have?" he asked.

Charles loaded a plate with bacon, eggs, and french fries and came to sit down. "Three. Two boys and a girl. They've been gone awhile now. Sam's an environmental engineer out in California, Dave's teaching English in New Mexico, and Julie's in Houston finishing up the last year of her residency." He dropped a ruby mound of jelly onto his toast, spreading it with too intense concentration. "We would've liked to have had a half dozen more, but God knows I was blessed with what I had."

"It's never enough, though, is it?"

"Not until it's gone," Charles said. "I got a visit today from Lieutenant Rhudwyn."

"Oh?"

Charles shot him a glance. "A blond man was spotted leaving the scene of last night's murder."

"That was me."

"You came close, then."

"Yes," Alex said. "I came close."

"I saw your card on the table, so I knew you'd come here," Charles said. "I told Rhudwyn you were out of town today, but that I expected to see you again tonight. After dark. I expect he'll be back."

"I'm sure he will."

"There's a key on the counter there. I have a little cabin a few miles outside Eden—"

"How apropos."

"—that I get away to once or twice a year. There's no TV, no telephone, and no newspaper. And especially no neighbors."

"And no witnesses to place me there."

"But I gave you the key, remember?"

Alex picked the key up and held it to the light. "I remember. Thank you, Charles."

"We don't need any complications right now."

"Any *more,* you mean."

Charles twitched the pan off the burner. "Last night . . . Did you see the murderer?"

"Yes."

"Ah."

"It was Elizabeth."

Charles's face settled into creases, making him look years older. "Oh, my God. She's . . ."

"Revenant. Yes."

"I'm sorry, Alex."

Discovering that his throat had become too tight for speech, Alex merely gestured his acceptance. Charles poured a cup of coffee, and brought it to him. Steam rose from the hot, dark liquid.

"Here," he said, thrusting it into Alex's hands. "Take it for comfort, if not sustenance."

Alex obeyed. Strangely enough, it steadied him. With the hot porcelain cupped in his hands, he told Charles the story.

"I don't . . ." The lawyer exhaled sharply and pushed away from the table. Propping his hands on the counter, he stared out the window. "She has no memory of her previous life?"

"How could she, and still kill?"

"I didn't know Elizabeth Garry."

"I did," Alex said. "And she begged me to kill her rather than let her become what she is now."

"Which you did."

"Yes." The memory of that night lay like a black weight on his shoulders. He'd given up everything in that brief, shattered moment. And only to save her immortal soul.

If I had made her revenant then . . . I would still have her. The hot-acid wash of bitterness sluiced through him.

"Alex, look at me," Charles said.

Reluctantly he obeyed. The lawyer had turned back around, his arms crossed, his hips propped against the counter behind him. Although he hadn't begun to touch Alex's experience, there was something patriarchal about him that was oddly steadying.

"There are things beyond a man's control," he said.

"Not mine."

"Yes, even yours."

Feeling his shoulders hunch, Alex forced himself to relax. "Suldris set me up. He made it so Elizabeth would become revenant whether or not I killed her."

"You're sure *he's* dead?"

"Quite."

Charles glanced away, and Alex realized he'd let too much of his grim anger show. And maybe just a little of his inhumanity.

"Someone went into the vault," he said. "Went in, and woke Elizabeth."

"Who?"

Alex spread his hands. "How many candidates can there be?"

"I'd say you're a better judge of that than I. But Lydia's body was never found, you know."

"Yes," Alex said. "There's Lydia. But if so, why now? What was she doing for the past year?"

"You've got me. What *do*, ah, what . . ."

"Suldris made her a zombie. A slave. Soulless, lifeless . . . a piece of clay held together only by its master's will."

"And when he was destroyed?"

"Animation should have left her body."

Charles cocked his head, considering that. "Lydia never played by anyone else's rules."

"Do *you* believe she's responsible for this?"

"I believe," the lawyer said, "that whoever's doing this wants to hurt you as much as possible. And what better weapon to use than Elizabeth?"

"And what of the man whose youth was stolen?"

"Could a zombie—"

"A zombie is merely a dead body that is manipulated by the person who created it. When I first encountered Roger Essler, I thought he'd been killed by a succubus."

"Huh?"

"A demon lover. To my knowledge, a legend only."

Charles sighed. "So are revenants."

"True." Alex smiled, felt his lips twist with cynical humor. "But I think I have more experience with legends than most."

Charles opened his mouth to reply, then closed it again as the doorbell chimed. "What do you want to bet that's the lieutenant?"

"Never bet with a revenant, Charles. I already know who's waiting outside the door."

"Can you predict the stock market?"

"Unfortunately, no. My expertise is in long-term investments."

The doorbell chimed again. Charles went out, returned a few moments later with Lieutenant Rhudwyn. The detective sat down in the chair opposite Alex's, his yellow-brown gaze direct and challenging.

"I've been looking for you all day," he said.

"Coffee?" Charles asked.

"No, thanks." Rhudwyn didn't look away from Alex.

"I was at the murder scene last night," Alex said, rising to keep the detective from noticing the swift dart of surprise on Charles's face.

"And how did you end up there?"

Alex spread his hands. "Accident. I happened to be heading for the riverfront—"

"At midnight?"

"I have trouble sleeping at night," Alex said. "Sometimes a nice, long walk along the river relaxes me."

"Do you do this often?"

"More times than I care to admit."

"I see," Rhudwyn said, his voice harsh with disbelief. "So, you were walking along the riverfront—"

"Hadn't reached it yet. I was walking down Bay Street."

"Fine," Rhudwyn snarled. "Whatever."

Alex almost smiled. "I was walking along Bay Street and happened to notice movement in one of the courtyards below. When I got a little closer, I realized that the killer had just taken another victim."

"Did you see the killer?"

"Sorry. He was up and over the wall so fast I only saw this black, leaping shadow. I tried to follow him, but then someone turned those floodlights on, completely blinding me."

"You said *he*."

Alex raised his brows. "I did, didn't I? Maybe it was the way he moved. Some sort of subliminal impression, I suppose."

"I suppose. Where did you go today?"

"Out for a nice, long drive out into the country. I needed to think, needed to be alone to do it."

"Did anyone see you?"

"No."

"Give it a rest, Lieutenant," Charles interjected. "With Sonya suing him for everything he's ever owned and Justin about ready to tear the walls down with his teeth, the Arbor isn't much of a haven these days. Can you blame the man for wanting to get away?"

Rhudwyn glanced at the lawyer, then returned his attention to Alex. "What about last night? Were you with anyone then?"

"I was alone. From the time I hit Bay Street to the moment your witness saw me on top of the wall, I didn't see another human being—except for the killer and his victim, of course."

"The shadow."

"Yes."

"Was it dark in the courtyard?"

"Very. I could only see shapes and movement. Do you think I killed the man, Martin?"

Rhudwyn sighed, raking his hand through his hair. "No. If for no other reason than if you had, you're way too smart to have let yourself be seen."

"Thank you for the confidence," Alex said.

"Tell me you weren't really searching for this killer on your own."

"I wasn't searching for the killer on my own."

"Liar." Rhudwyn stood up, a sharp movement that betrayed his frustration. "Look, this guy is dangerous. What do you think is going to happen if you corner him somewhere?"

Alex smiled. "Then you'll have Francine 'reading' the scene of my murder."

"That's not funny."

"Humor depends on one's point of view," Alex said. "Doesn't it?"

With a muttered curse, Rhudwyn stalked out. The sound of the front door slamming echoed through the house.

"Good God, Alex!" Charles cried. "Why didn't you just tell him you were at my damned cabin?"

"Because it's a lie. And lies seem to grow with time, and get more and more tangled as they do." Sliding back into his chair, Alex traced the faint scar of the carved initials. "I should know."

"Then why didn't you tell him about Elizabeth?"

"You've got to be kidding," Alex drawled. "You see, Detective, I used to be in love with this woman, but then I had to kill her to keep her from becoming a vampire. But she became one anyway, and now she's running through the city sucking people's blood. Now, *that* would go over very well."

"That's not why you lied to him, and you know it."

Alex studied the lawyer from beneath his lashes. "Oh?"

"Oh. You're not fooling me, Alex. You didn't plan to protect her; but when the chips were down, you did."

"Nonsense!" Alex shouted, grabbing a handful of the man's shirtfront.

"Be honest with *yourself*!" Charles shouted back. "How are you going to destroy her? You still love her!"

Truth. Look at it. See it. Taking a deep, shuddering breath, Alex relaxed his hold on Charles's shirt and smoothed the wrinkled fabric. The lawyer's heart beat beneath his hand, fragile and human. This life was a mere flicker in the long path of the revenant's existence.

But however fragile, however ephemeral, Charles had pierced the dross and arrowed straight to the core. Alex sighed. Could he destroy Elizabeth, even knowing what she'd become?

Could he not?

"I don't know," he said, more to himself than to his companion. "I just don't know."

15

Lydia sat on the sun-swept grass of Forsyth Park. The melody of the fountain chimed in the hot air, a pleasant underscoring of the shrieks of children playing nearby.

"Ahhh, this feels good," she murmured, closing her eyes and tilting her face up to the sun.

Last night had been a good night despite a rocky beginning. Ah, sweet vengeance! She'd caught up with Elizabeth a moment before Alex, just in time to watch his face as he realized what had become of his sweetheart. And then she'd snatched Elizabeth out from under his nose.

It had cost her, though. She twitched her skirt down to hide the purple-black splotches on her shins. Decay, not bruises.

"Lydia?"

The voice was female and shocked. No less than Lydia. She opened her eyes to see a woman standing a few feet away. Slim, brunette, somewhere in her late twenties or early thirties . . . pretty, anyway.

"Lydia?" the woman asked again. "Lydia Danilov?"

Panic raced in shrilling waves through Lydia's brain. Had they been somewhere more private, Lydia would have killed her. Instead she merely said, "Do I know you?"

"I'm Jennifer Caulfield. Sonya and I are . . . were members of the Ladies' Charity Club. You and I met at a luncheon at the Arbor, oh, a couple of years ago. I'm so surprised to see you here—the newspapers said you'd disappeared."

Lydia considered denying everything. But recognition hung with such certainty in the woman's eyes that she didn't dare. "I . . . went to Europe for a while. A nervous breakdown. The family knew."

"Oh, I see," the woman said, although it was obvious she didn't. "But the newspapers—"

"Speculation. If they can't find information, they'll make it up."

Jennifer nodded. "I hope you're feeling better."

"Oh, I am. Much."

The woman's face showed too much of her thoughts; she'd compared the old Lydia with the new, and found the difference shocking.

Lydia sighed. A year ago she wouldn't have envied this woman for anything. But now, looking at the clean, healthy glow of her skin, the serenity of eyes that had seen only human things, Lydia felt a white-hot stab of jealousy.

Reaching up, she closed her hand around the crystal. It pulsed sluggishly in her hand, as though reluctant to use any more of its energy. Lydia touched the fringes of the woman's mind, then readied herself to go deeper. Frustration raked her. If only she could stay! But she'd be lucky to hold the woman's consciousness away long enough to snatch the memory marked *Lydia Danilov*.

"Mom!"

A child's voice, pure and sweet, slashed her concentration. She let her breath out in a sharp exhalation as a girl ran up to join them. The child seemed to be nine or ten, and was as dark and pretty as her mother. Her skin glowed from the exertion of running. The sight sent a shaft of jealousy shooting through Lydia.

"This is my daughter, Karen," Jennifer said, reaching out to gather the girl against her side. "This is Miss Danilov, Karen."

"Hi," Karen said.

"Hi," Lydia replied, sinking straight into the child's mind.

Inhabiting this mind was like walking through a stained-glass window. Sensations flashed at her with all the intensity of childhood; the colors more vivid, the sights and sounds and smells so clear, each ringing true like a brass bell. Joy rose above it all like a big white bird, the innocent assumption that the world was a fine and safe place.

I could do this forever.

Lydia looked down at herself with the child's eyes. She saw the faded red of her hair, the lines radiating from beneath the sunglasses, the sagging skin of her upper arms. Ugly. Old. It wouldn't have been so bad if the shadows of the beauty that had been Lydia Danilov hadn't remained in her face.

She nudged at the child's consciousness, seeking room to settle in. And found resistance. However innocent, the girl's psyche was fully formed. Lydia wanted that body, craved its youth and freshness and the bright burn of its life. But doing so would drain the crystal completely. She'd be trapped forever in that mind, locked in battle with its rightful owner. And if she lost . . . There'd be no way back to the crystal, no way back to her own body— even if there was anything left of it.

Death.

She wasn't about to die. Not now, not ever.

Enough power remained in the crystal to do what needed to be done. She delved into those minds, found the threads of memory marked *Lydia Danilov* and pulled them. It took a shuddering, gut-clenching act of will to return to her own body. A wail rose in her mind. Her own skin was a shroud, her body a collection of limbs that were becoming harder and harder to command. Going back was like stepping off the edge of heaven and landing straight in hell.

She looked up at the woman and child who stood staring blankly at her. "You don't know how lucky you are," she said.

The breeze blew a lock of straight, dark hair across the child's face. Like satin on silk, Lydia thought, and all kissed by the sun. She shuddered, not wanting to let it go.

You have to. They'll be missed. Between you and Elizabeth, there've been too many bodies showing up lately.

She set the woman and child free. Jennifer blinked, then looked down at her with no recognition in her eyes.

"Excuse me, ma'am," she said. "Did you say something?"

"Yes," Lydia replied. "I just told you what a pretty little girl you have."

"Why, thank you." Jennifer glanced at her watch. "Oh, no, look at the time! Sorry, but we've got to run. Come on, sweetheart, we've got to get to the grocery store before Daddy gets home."

Lydia closed her eyes, unable to bear watching them walk away. So close, so close. She could all but taste it. A little more time, and a lot more power, and then she'd have it. Youth, immortality, revenge.

"And all from you, Alex darling," she murmured.

Alex. From the beginning he'd been her prize and her downfall. The selfish bastard. He had so much! The accumulated power of a thousand-year-old vampire, the grace and charm of a man with a millennium's worth of experience—everything she wanted. No, needed. And he was too damn stiff-necked to see beyond the bounds of his rigid ethics.

"At least *my* prison was not of my choosing," she muttered.

She rose to her feet, lurching as her legs refused to work properly. Almost sobbing in disgust and frustration, she forced them to obey. She needed power, and fast.

Maybe she'd pick up one of those pretty little boys who sold themselves to the highest bidder. Warmth ran through her veins at the thought. No one was going to miss a prostitute. No one ever did. And she could do a bit of experimenting at the same time. It might be that the little dark-haired girl had been an especially strong personality; another sort of child might be more accessible. Some drugs, the distraction of sex . . . It might be worth a try.

Smiling, Lydia squinted up into the sun. She had three or four hours to play before night fell. Long enough to go through one boy, or maybe a couple.

And then . . . Alex.

Pain. A red cloud of it enveloped Alex the moment he woke, white-hot lancets of it stabbing through his mind, racing along every pathway of his body. No gentle awakening, this, but a plunge into a dark, flaming sea of Blood-Hunger. It permeated the very air, turning the silent underground room from haven to torture chamber.

He flung himself off the bed. Blood-Hunger wrapped him like a cloak, and he carried it up the stairs with him. The eyes of Catherine's portrait seemed to move with him, her gaze as serene and compassionate as it had been in life. It couldn't touch him, however; he'd been armored with an iron cloak of revenant need.

Was it his, or Elizabeth's, or both, their souls inextricably entwined after death as they'd been in life?

Will destroying her destroy me as well?

It didn't matter. Elizabeth, with her vibrancy, her generosity, her caring for others . . . Soulless, mindless, a monster driven to consume human lives, a walking thirst for human blood. If she'd known what she'd become, she would have begged him to end it.

He'd created her. He was the only one who could stop her. Lost in the wild, violent tide of his own inhuman thirst, he went out into the night.

Gibbous clouds plied the sky, moving like plump matrons upon the arm of the wind. They revealed, then concealed the moon, turning the land below from pale, crystalline radiance to a place where shadow hung thick and deep beneath the trees, and bushes stood like dark sentinels along the garden pathways.

Alex drew in a lungful of the thick, humid air. It would rain soon; the night was charged with the skin-pricking awareness of an approaching storm. But the heavy, prescient feeling was not all nature. Old powers lay just beneath the threshold of reality tonight; a touch, an ill-timed call, and they'd break free.

Wildwood knew. A hushed stillness hung over the quaking sea of grass, a vast, inhuman anticipation of what might be. The marsh had helped him once before. But perhaps not again; it was more akin to those ancient powers than to him.

"What do you say, my old friend?" he murmured. "Could this be your chance to rid yourself of the clinging parasite known as man?"

He turned as another presence came into the garden with him. Sonya. She filled his senses like a flame, the scent of her skin more fragrant than the perfume of the roses and jasmine around her. Her skin, set off by the rich blue of her dress, almost seemed to glow with a light of its own. His Blood-Hunger focused on the fresh, rapid beat of a human life. It rooted him to the spot when good sense urged him to flee.

As if drawn by her own brand of Hunger, she made her way unerringly through the darkness. She came to a stop in front of him, her eyes as knowing and tender as if she'd loved him for a thousand years. It rocked him. *She remembers*, he thought, wishing he could take back the lovemaking that had occurred between them. And yes, wishing he could do it all over again.

"Hello, Alex," she said.

Loneliness stretched the fabric of his heart, the pain of a man who'd had to give up everything he'd ever wanted. "Hello, Sonya. And good-bye; I'm on my way to Savannah."

"Will you walk with me? I want to talk to you."

"Sonya, I've got urgent business—"

"It's about Justin." She put her hand on his arm. "Please. This is important, Alex."

Alex would have liked to think that concern for Justin prompted his decision. But he knew it was the contact of her hand, the scent of her flesh and warm, pulsing blood that made him nod in acceptance and walk deeper into the garden.

"Have you decided to drop your custody suit?" he asked.

"Not at all," she said. "As I told you before, our . . . time together doesn't impact on other aspects of our lives." She didn't take her hand from his arm, and he didn't ask her to. "The issue tonight is Justin's opinion of you and me. He jumped all over me at breakfast today."

Alex nodded. "He saw me coming out of your room."

"Caught red-handed, hmmm?"

"I expect he'd been watching for something like that. You haven't been exactly subtle, you know."

She cocked her head, making her hair swirl like pale silk across her shoulders. It was an indolent, cynical gesture. He didn't like it, and wasn't sure he liked her.

But his hands itched with the desire to touch her.

"I think he's more upset on your account than mine," she said.

"How so?"

"He's more territorial about you than me. I may be his mother, but you're his hero. You're not supposed to be human, just heroic. So it's easier to blame me than you. He feels that I trespassed on a relationship that was his and his alone."

"Sonya—"

"He told me he felt I'd deliberately seduced you to blur the issue."

"It did blur the issue. It blurred everything."

"Are you claiming innocence in the matter?"

"No," he said. "I haven't been innocent in a very long time."

She smiled. The moon peeked out as though to illuminate it, and turned that simple upcurving of lips into something as magical and mysterious as Woman herself. Goddess, demon, saint . . . For all his years and experience, he was as much in thrall to that magic as any green boy.

Blood-Hunger and desire flooded through him in a hot tide, too much to hold, too much to let go. He looked into her eyes, saw both reflected there. *Both.* He stopped, grasping her by the shoulders to pull her around to face him.

Clouds buried the moon once more, and the disquieting image faded. A trick of the light, perhaps. Opening his hands with an effort, he let her go.

"What's the matter?" she asked.

"Nothing," he said, turning away. "Nothing. Look, I've got to go. I'll have another talk with Justin when he's had a day or two to think things through."

"Do you ever feel so alone that you think you're going to die from it?"

That stopped him, brought him around to look at her. Her eyes had gone heavy-lidded, and her skin radiated a warmth he could feel even here. Her pulse thundered in his head, his chest, rocketed through his veins until he was sure it was his.

She walked toward him. Against him. All that softness, all that perfume and sweet, pulsing womanhood. Everything in him that was a man, and everything that was revenant, responded. His mind seemed to float off in a cloud of arousal as his hands spread out over her back.

"Don't go," she whispered.

"I can't help myself," he said, his breath stirring the fine hairs at her temple.

"Neither can I."

She sank her hands into his hair, hard enough to hurt. But the small pain lost itself in the raging maelstrom of arousal and Blood-Hunger, and he accepted it as part of the skyrocketing sensations he was feeling.

Her mouth was as hungry as her hands, and drew him deep, deep. He pulled her skirt upward, slid his hand over smooth, bare skin, and discovered that she wore nothing beneath. An alligator bellowed out in the marsh, a vast, primal sound that fed the fire roaring in his brain. Her dress tore in his hands, drifted to the path unnoticed.

"This is crazy," he said.

"Everything's crazy," she whispered against his mouth. "At least this feels good."

He laid her upon a nearby marble bench. Her skin was as pale as the stone, but much hotter. She yanked his shirt down his arms, sending buttons flying everywhere, and he tore the sleeves getting it the rest of the way off.

His need for her was immoderate, tumultuous, a wild, surging storm that overwhelmed mind and body and submerged the spirit. Her mouth tasted like wine, her blood like the hammering pulse of life he'd regretted a thousand years.

She matched his need with abandon, his Blood-Hunger with the greedy demands of desire. Beckoning him on, offering him things he hadn't dared take for many years. Too many years. He clung to the ragged edges of control, hanging on to a lifeline becoming more tenuous by the moment. One slip, one scant inch, and he'd take her over the threshold.

In the end it was her own violence that gave him the strength to contain his Blood-Hunger. He looked down into her eyes, saw only a blind whirlpool of desire. She frightened him—both with her mindless need, and her ability to tap so powerfully the darkness within him.

"Sonya," he said.

She shook her head from side to side, her nails digging into his back.

"Sonya!" He grabbed her wrists before she could break the skin, then pinned her hands over her head.

Reason flooded into her eyes. "What's the matter?"

"Take it easy."

"Easy?"

"You're falling over the edge, and you're taking me with you."

"I don't care," she whispered. "I'm going to die if you don't finish what you started."

He closed his eyes against the flooding temptation of it. *You're going to die if I do.* He knew he should go. He even tensed his muscles to get up. But she was so beautiful, so very warm and eager, that he hesitated. Blood-Hunger sidled up to his conscience, whispering things he knew, things he knew better than to do. But he'd walked this tightrope for a thousand years; sex for power, for a subtle lessening of the torment that raked his body and his soul.

Catherine had been dead a hundred years. Elizabeth had died in his arms a year ago. By his hand. She'd become revenant, and mindless. Again, by his hand. He needed power to undo what had been done. As far as his guilt went, no power in the world—or beyond it—could help him. There was no absolution for him, only closure.

In her fragile humanity, Sonya held the power he needed: blood. The barest slaking of the thirst that racked him, but enough. Now that he'd regained his control, he dared take that power.

"I won't let you die," he murmured.

Afterward, when she lay sleeping, he gathered her into his arms and carried her upstairs into her room. He stood for a moment looking down at her. Such cool beauty, with that pale hair and skin, the long-limbed, languid grace that was so characteristic of her. He wished he could feel tenderness for her.

"I'm sorry," he murmured.

She stirred. The crystal pendant slid over her chest, coming to rest finally upon the small, red mark at the base of her throat. His mark. It would be gone tomorrow—a lesser bruising than that of his conscience. With a sigh, he pulled the covers over her.

A wave of terror hit him the moment he stepped into the hallway. It was an unconscious kind of fear, born of blackness and the smell of the pit, creeping dark things and the screaming well of night.

"Justin," Alex breathed, breaking into a run.

He raced down the hallway to the west wing, tore through the door of Justin's apartment. Kelli appeared in the bedroom doorway in a swirl of white nightgown.

"Alex!" she gasped. "Hurry!"

He picked her up with one arm to keep her from impeding him as he went past. Justin lay on the bed in a tangle of sheets, his eyes closed, arms and legs flailing as he fought against whatever had entered his dreams.

"I can't wake him up," Kelli said. "What is it? What's going on?"

Alex set her down beside the bed. "A nightmare," he said. "Justin! Justin, can you hear me?"

No answer. Justin's head swiveled from side to side, and he arched as though in pain.

"Help him." Kelli clutched at Alex, her hands surprisingly strong. "Alex, help him!"

He nodded. "Don't be afraid. No matter what you hear, no matter what you see."

"Help him!"

Pinning Justin's shoulders to the mattress, Alex reached in the dark and frantic place that was the young man's mind. Terror closed around him. He felt the soul of the man Justin had become, and the soul of the boy he'd been. It writhed in the grip of things that raked and tore and slavered. Talons grasped that struggling consciousness, tearing bloody gobbets of it, and dragged it toward the yawning emptiness of the Abyss.

"Justin!" Alex called.

The boy reached out to him. He flung himself after, found himself caught in a whirlwind of memory. Sight/smell/sound. Clear and precise, as though it had happened yesterday. As though it was happening now. The scrape of the Hellspawn's feet on the floor of the sanctuary, the feel of the cold chitin beneath his hands as he fought to live. The velvety blackness of the Abyss waiting for him.

And Catherine. What he wouldn't give to see her again, to clasp her hand one more time . . .

Justin's soul called to him. Despairing, as it was dragged toward the blackness and Oblivion.

All I have to do is reach out . . . Catherine.

Justin. The one price he wouldn't pay.

Alex turned his back on the Abyss. Launched himself toward Justin, wrapped him up, tore him away from the dark evil. It roared and gibbered behind him, wanting Justin. Wanting *him* more. *You can't have me. Or this boy.* Outrage propelled him upward, toward the light.

And broke through, gasping, to find himself and Justin on the floor beside the bed.

Kelli fell to her knees beside them. Her right hand cupped Justin's cheek, her left the gentle swell just beginning to curve her belly. Protecting them both. "Justin," she said, the calmness of her voice belying the concern in her eyes. "Wake up. Justin, talk to me."

His eyes opened. For a moment only terror filled them, a razor edge of memories no human should have. Then he focused on Kelli. Slowly the stiffness drained out of his body.

"It's all right, Kel," he said. "I'm back."

I'm back, Alex thought in shock. To him, the journey had been real. He glanced away as Justin's fathomless dark gaze fastened on his. He felt stripped bare, turned inside out and vulnerable.

"It was all true," Justin said. "It happened."

"Justin—"

"You're the one who pulled me out."

Alex released the young man's shoulders, knowing the mark of his grip would remain for weeks. He sat back on his heels and sighed, wishing this time hadn't come so soon. Justin wasn't ready.

"No," he said. "It was a dream." There was danger in the lie, even more danger in the truth.

Shock slackened the line of Justin's mouth. "What?"

"A dream, Justin. A nightmare. Don't make more of it than what's there."

"The blackness, the things with fangs and claws—"

"They're not real."

"The old church—"

"What church?"

"Don't lie to me!"

"Justin, have I ever lied to you?" Alex asked, each word scraping like sharp, rusty iron in his throat.

"No."

"Then believe me when I say those things are not real. They never happened, they never *will* happen."

Vaguely Alex was aware of Kelli watching him. But most of his attention remained focused on Justin, and the task of nudging that tough and independent mind away from things that could swallow it up.

"It felt so real," Justin said.

"It must have," Kelli said, "the way you were fighting it. I thought you were going to punch me when I tried to shake you awake."

"God, I'm sorry, Kel."

"You almost punched me, too," Alex said.

Justin's mouth thinned. "Gee, that's too bad. Maybe I should try again."

Alex knew the moment of intimacy had ended; Sonya had stepped between them again. Or, to lay the blame where it belonged, his own indiscretion. "I've got to go," he said, rising to his feet.

"Yeah, I bet," Justin snarled. "Your nights have been pretty busy lately, haven't they?"

At another time Alex might have been amused by the irony of Justin's statement. But not now. He'd forfeited Justin's trust, first with Sonya, and again with the lie.

At least this is one punishment you don't have to inflict on yourself. He pushed the cynical thought away.

"Where *are* you going to sleep tonight?" Justin asked, his voice harsh.

"Don't be like that," Kelli said.

He didn't look away from Alex. "I can smell her on you."

"I'm sorry it's come between us," Alex said.

"And I'm sorry you ever came here."

Alex turned to go. Distrust lay too thickly between them right now, and he didn't have the resources to tear it down.

"Of all the women in the world, why her?" Justin asked.

Slowly Alex turned to look at him. Pain lay in the depths of those dark eyes, the pain of trust betrayed. "I don't know," he said. "I wish I did."

"I don't understand you," Justin said. "You say you care about me, then you do something like *that*."

"I do care."

"Then why are you screwing my mother?"

"Justin, stop." Kelli put her hand on his chest, a gesture evidently meant to comfort as well as restrain. "You called his name when you were caught in that nightmare. I couldn't help you, but he did."

His eyes turned cold and hard, and for a moment Alex saw his father in them. "But it was only a *dream*, Kelli. Remember?"

Temptation plucked at Alex. *Tell him the truth. Absolve yourself with that.* And place a burden on Justin he didn't yet have the strength to carry. No.

Turning on his heel, he left the room.

"I'm not finished with you!" Justin shouted.

Yes, you are.

"Alex!"

He strode downstairs, leaving Justin's voice behind—if not his anger. Wrenching the front door open, he stepped out into the night.

16

The storm hit at midnight. Alex, flying in owl form above Savannah's rain-slashed streets, was forced to take shelter beneath the canopy of a great live oak.

There had been no sign of Elizabeth.

No sign of her protector.

No trace of Blood-Hunger, other than his own.

But nothing could mask the taint of power that hung over the city. It felt . . . familiar. Perhaps it had become colored with Elizabeth, whom it protected. Then again, perhaps it was the source of power itself that touched his memory. A faint touch, however, too fragile to be held.

He felt oddly tired, his wings heavy from more than rain. It felt as though something dragged at him, body and spirit.

Perhaps it's the knowledge that you may have to destroy your beloved tonight.

A cynical thought, cold in its hopelessness.

Lightning crashed overhead, drawing his gaze. A good old southern summer storm, he thought, the kind Catherine used to say swept the air clean of everything but Sallee's singing. And that, they all knew, came straight from heaven.

They'd had such innocence then. Even he. Somehow things had been clearer, the separation between good and evil easier to discern. Now there were more shades of gray than ever before, truth subject to variances he'd never expected.

He had to kill Elizabeth. Once, he'd done it to save her immortal soul; that had been his reason and his consolation for an act he would have cut his arms off to avoid. This time there was no soul to save. Only the killing.

So much blood on his hands. A thousand years' worth of it, and all shed so he could survive. But he'd thought he'd left the killing behind.

A taxi turned the corner and came toward him, moving slowly against the driving rain. Its headlights speared twin golden arcs on the glistening asphalt. Alex flew down into the patch of shadow beneath the tree, becoming a man before his feet hit the ground.

"Charles, my friend, I hope you're in the mood for company," he murmured as he ran to flag the car down.

A few blocks from the lawyer's house, Alex sensed the brightness that was Francine Dey. Almost, he told the cabbie to drive past. Then he felt the psychic's mind touch his and knew the moment for flight had passed.

Charles answered the door, his face turning surprised when he saw Alex on his doorstep. "Hello, Alex," he said, opening the door wider. "Come on in. It's a hell of a night to be out."

"It's a hell of a night, period."

The lawyer's eyes turned grave and questioning. Because he didn't ask, Alex chose to tell him.

"I didn't find her," he said. "Couldn't."

"I'm sorry." With an abrupt lift of his head, Charles shifted to another subject. "There's someone here to see you. A Mrs. Dey. But I suppose you knew that?"

"Mrs. Dey is easy to pick out, even in a crowd."

"Is she for real?"

Alex inclined his head. "Very real. It's a shame Rhudwyn refuses to understand what he has in her."

"Maybe it's a good thing he doesn't."

A good thing for you. The lawyer's unspoken thought seemed to hang in the air between them.

"She's trouble," Charles said. "As your attorney and a prudent man, I advise you to walk out that door."

"She already knows I'm here."

"So I'll tell her you didn't want to see her."

"But I do."

Charles shrugged. "It's your funeral." There was no indifference in his eyes, however. "She seems to need to talk to you rather urgently, said she'd wait all night if she had to."

"Did she say why?"

"Not to me."

Alex followed the lawyer into the study, where Francine sat in the easy chair in front of the window. Someone had opened the curtain, framing the storm. Echoes of lightning limned the woman's silver hair against the blackness outside.

"I'll leave you alone," Charles murmured. "As the poets would say, watch your hind end."

He went out, closing the double doors behind him. Alex stood for a moment, looking into the psychic's bottomless green eyes. Then, moved by some inner prompting he neither questioned nor resisted, he strode across the room and bent over her hand.

"Hello, Francine," he said. "Such a prosaic name for such an unusual lady."

She smiled. "It's the name I was born with. Should I have taken something more . . . psychical, say, Sabrina or Serena?"

"Pandora, perhaps," he murmured.

"Ah. What dangerous thing do you accuse me of opening?"

"My life."

"What life?"

"You see?" He grinned, letting go of her hand. "You've already peered into my box of tricks."

"I've hardly begun."

"That sounds suspiciously like a threat."

She cocked her head to one side. "Sit down, Alex, and stop obscuring the issue with clever repartee. Where did you learn such sly obfuscation, anyway?"

"In a hundred courts, a thousand drawing rooms. And there was a time when conversation was considered a skill."

"Tonight, however, it's a crock."

"Touché," he said. "So, let's get down to business. Why did you come looking for me?"

"You're in danger."

He raised his brows. "Ah, has Martin decided to arrest me at last?"

"Not yet."

"Did he send you here?"

"No. Not that he wasn't curious when I called to see if there was some way of contacting you. He gave me this address *very* grudgingly. I don't think he liked letting his trained psychic off the leash. Particularly with you."

"If he can control it, he can understand it."

"Are you so different?"

"Are you?"

"I think so," she said. "It's men who grasp, who hold, who rearrange the world to suit their vision."

He inclined his head, accepting the charge. "And women mold the men."

With a graceful movement that should have belonged to a much younger woman, she rose to her feet and came to stand in front of him. The touch of her mind deepened, became as deep and vital as the night. "There's a darkness gathering around you."

"You're mistaken," he said softly. "The darkness is inside me."

"No. It's wrapping itself around you, as though attracted by something you have. Something you are. You shine like a beacon within it. But"—she reached up and placed her fingertips against his temple, drew them down his cheek—"even the brightest of lights can be extinguished."

Gently he took her hand from him. "Can you tell the source?"

"I don't know enough about you."

"I'd think you needed to know more about *it*."

"You're the key," she said. "I think you always have been. Is that such a surprise, Alex?"

"I'm a drifter, a dilettante. I touch the human world only lightly."

"A being such as yourself, so full of pain and power, moving through human lives and not touching them? No, Alex. You pass through the world like a hurricane, leaving eddies and currents in your wake. Things are forever changed."

"If I accept that, then I must accept the charge that everything I touch, I destroy."

"You already think that. And it might be true." Her eyes almost seemed luminous. "If you take responsibility for that much, why not the rest?"

He turned away, toward the window. The storm raged outside, hurling rain down so hard it almost seemed as though the drops bounced when they hit the ground. Vehicles groped like blind insects through the downpour, wheels sending up parallel waves in the ankle-deep water. Alex welcomed the violence, took it as a mirror of what raged in his soul.

"Hold tight to your anger," Francine drawled. "It feeds the darkness."

"Sarcasm doesn't become you."

"This . . . force didn't just appear overnight. It's tied to what you are and what you've done. Something happened to trigger this, and you've got to know what it is. I want in, Alex."

With his forefinger, he traced the path of a raindrop as it wiggled its way down the window. "This is a dangerous time for me. I can't afford to let you—or anyone—complicate it with your interference."

"You don't dare, you mean?"

"You see too much."

"It's been a problem all my life. Let me help."

"Why?"

"Because I think I can help you stop the killing."

He turned to face her. Behind him, the wind pressed against the window. "Some people might call you arrogant for assuming you could step into my world and come out again unscathed."

"You should know about arrogance." She tilted her head back, meeting his gaze levelly. "And I never said I assumed to come out unscathed. But if I, mere human that I am, am willing to give it a try, why shouldn't you?"

"I don't want your life on my hands."

"My life is my own," she said. "You have no right to it."

"You're absolving me of responsibility ahead of time?"

"Yes."

A crash of thunder brought their gazes to the window. Lightning spread incandescent fingers across the sky, for a moment turning all the world to flame. Each raindrop hung gilded in the searing light, as though turned to stone by the sheer power of the storm.

Alex turned back to the woman, knowing his eyes would look less than human in this light.

He smiled. "And they say there's no God."

• • •

Lydia knelt above the boy. Sunlight from the single filthy window played over his soft, beautiful features, caught flickering gleams on his mahogany skin.

"How old are you?" she asked.

"Fourteen. Goin' on a hundred. You promised me fifty."

She dropped a wad of bills on his bare chest. "Pretty young, to do what you do."

"Old enough to know a good deal when I see one."

Lydia glanced down at her naked body, at the wrinkles and sagging breasts and mottled skin. She put her hand on his stomach, studying the contrast between her skin and his.

Frustration gnawed at her. And desperation. She'd snatched half a night's youth from Alex's coupling with Sonya, a couple of hours from each of the two young prostitutes she'd taken yesterday.

And this one? He'd give her another hour of youth and free movement before her body shut down around her again. She'd found only respite, not an escape from the body that was crumbling around her.

She slid her hand across the boy's chest to his ribs. An almost man, he had the beginnings of adult musculature beneath the skin. Beautiful. All but useless, because he wasn't the right one. Neither were the other two, or the child in the park. But she knew, bones and blood and soul, that she'd hit the right path. Somewhere out there, a child waited. Boy, girl, black, white, pretty or not, it held her salvation in its hands. All she had to do was find it.

"Time to get dressed," the boy said. "I got work to do."

"Do you do it with men, too?" she asked.

"It's the money, lady, not who's carrying it." He rolled

over, retrieving her clothes from the floor, then tossed them to her. "Come on."

Lydia didn't try to catch them. She looked around at the shabby little room, the stained wallpaper and filthy floor, the rust stains in the sink and toilet visible in the bathroom doorway. "Don't rush me."

"You want to buy my time, I won't rush you."

"What's my name?"

His face went blank. "You never told me."

"I did," she said. Excitement rode hard in the depths of her belly. "You must have forgotten."

"Must have." Indifferently.

"It's Lydia. Say, 'You're beautiful, Lydia.' "

"Pay me."

"Say it."

His face turned ugly. "You fucking old bitch! You ain't beautiful. You *stink* like something rotten. If you wasn't paying me, I wouldn't fucking *touch* you!"

"Say it."

He opened his mouth to scream at her again. Lydia stopped him. She wielded her power with delicacy, not wanting to bruise that marvelous skin of his. His eyes rounded in fear as she made him lie back upon the pillow.

"Say it," she said.

"You're beautiful, Lydia." The voice wasn't quite natural, but good enough.

"Say, 'I want you, Lydia,' " she murmured.

The tendons in his throat stood out clearly. "I want you, Lydia," he rasped.

His penis swelled and stiffened, impelled by the crystal's power. He shook his head. A frantic gesture, and a useless one. Lydia smiled.

"You see?" she said. "I'm not so bad once you get to know me."

Leaning down, she fastened her mouth on his. Drained

him, wriggling in voluptuous ecstasy as his vitality poured through her in a crashing wave of sensation. She might not be able to take his body, but this . . . this was enough. For now. She looked into his eyes as she sucked him dry of everything he had, and pretended they were gray, not brown, and that she'd be able to keep this incredible feeling forever.

Alex.

The young man died silently, and quickly. She raised her head and looked down into his now sunken eyes, the skin that had become as wrinkled and lusterless as hers had been. *Fourteen going on a hundred,* he'd said.

He hadn't known how right he was.

There was little left of the Garry house, a few fire-blackened bricks, the rectangular traces left in the earth by the foundation, the garden that had swiftly become overgrown. But Alex could see much more in that empty lot; worlds of loss, of disillusionment, the tearing memories of the night Elizabeth died.

"Oh, Alex," Francine whispered. "So much pain."

He swallowed convulsively. "I haven't been back . . . since it happened."

"Tell me."

"What's to tell?" he asked, hating the too revealing bitterness in his voice. "I fell in love with a woman, and I killed her."

Francine swung around to face him, reaching to touch his face. He caught her hand, holding it away from him, and she reached up with her free hand to grasp his wrist. It would have been easy to fling her away. But caught in a struggle much deeper than physical, he didn't. Couldn't. She wrenched her hand free, raised it to his face.

"You fought for her." Strain aged the psychic's face as she delved into the past that had been etched into this place. "He . . . *he* killed her, not you."

"No. I did. Of my own free will."

Alex forced that memory onto her and watched her eyes as she visibly groped for understanding. He sighed. Perhaps no one living could truly understand the choice he'd had to make that night; somehow the implicit faith in the human soul went wanting in these cynical modern times. Heaven had become too remote a reward for goodness; nirvana was held in the here and now.

"How little you value us," she said.

"Does that mean you accept the choice I made?"

"It was an unnatural choice, forced on you by unnatural circumstances. I find I don't have the ability to judge you."

"An admirable quality."

"Then why do you presume to judge me?"

"I presume everything," he said. "It's the prerogative of the old and powerful. And after all, it *is* my past."

"Your past caught up with you here, didn't it?"

"And stole my future."

Suddenly her face closed, and withdrawal darkened her eyes. "You cloud everything around you," she said. "Your pain overwhelms the events that took place here, and I can't see past it. Can you damp it down?"

"Let go of me," he said.

She obeyed, disengaging both physically and mentally. He drew in, rolled himself up like a carpet, and tucked it all away. After a moment she nodded.

"Terrible things happened that night," she said, walking through the spot where the house had stood. "Something powerful and . . . twisted walked here—"

"Suldris," Alex said. "A specter from my past. Created by me without my knowledge."

She closed her eyes. "I feel the echoes of his power, and yours. But there's a closure to it, an ending. And I can sense . . . Elizabeth. She stands out clear and bright . . . a purity of soul." Her eyes opened, locked with his. "Is that her, or are your perceptions of her bleeding in?"

"That was her," he said.

"That's why you loved her."

"Yes." He had to force his voice to work.

She nodded. Relief flooded through Alex when her eyes drifted closed again; her understanding flayed him, making him feel naked, vulnerable.

"Something else was here that night," she said. "Its touch is oddly distorted, as though it was, ah, reflected in a flawed mirror. A female touch."

"Lydia," Alex said.

"There were powerful ties between you."

Inevitability settled on his shoulders; he wasn't surprised to find it so heavy. "Yes."

"You wanted her."

"It wasn't a comfortable desire," he said. "Or a very manageable one."

"It still isn't."

Alex closed his eyes, trying, like her, to *see* the darkness around him. But Blood-Hunger blinded him to it. "So she's still . . . alive."

"The darkness is hers. Or her."

"Can you tell me how to free myself?"

"Not without getting closer. You'll have to let me in, Alex."

"How far?"

"As far as necessary."

He took a step backward. "I've never let a stranger have . . . that kind of access."

"Who, then?"

"Only Catherine, my first love, and Elizabeth, my second."

"Two in a thousand years?"

"I was fortunate."

She drew in her breath sharply. "Yes, you were. How lucky you are to realize it."

It was that statement—not trust, not logic, not the hope that she could help him—that made his decision. He would allow this woman in and, by doing so, would give her the power to destroy him if she chose. Reckless, perhaps. But there was little left for him *but* recklessness.

"Very well," he said.

He felt the brightness of her mind as it delved into his. It sank deep, deeper still, and opened to him like a flower. The duality of her humanity staggered him. On one hand, it was as fragile as the finest blown glass; on the other, it shone like the sun, vital, enduring, courageous. He could have shattered her with a touch, but he could never have taken that glorious spirit from her.

He gave her more than he would have believed possible. After a moment she disengaged and stepped back, her eyes dazzled as though she, too, had looked too long into the sun.

"Thank you," she said. "You won't regret it."

"Don't make promises you can't keep."

She nodded, apparently accepting the distinction. "Lydia's very warped."

"What happened to her would warp anyone."

"Be careful of making too many excuses for her," she said. "Or of taking the blame. She'll suck you dry if you let her."

Ah. Understanding sat like a hot spike in his brain. "Roger Essler."

"And the priest."

"What's she looking for? What does she want?"

"You."

He shook his head. "Once, she did. But she's no longer the woman I knew—and almost loved. She's no longer a woman at all, but a zombie, Suldris's soulless creation."

"Men are so stupid," Francine said. "You always assume a woman wants *you*. But many women are attracted to power rather than to the man himself—"

"And Lydia was uniquely equipped to sense power."

Francine touched his arm. "To find her, you're going to have to touch your Blood-Hunger. It's your tie to her."

"Why the caution, Francine? Blood-Hunger has been my companion for a millennium."

"No. You've *fought* it for a millennium. You've held yourself apart from it, gave it only limited access. Now you have to take it in hand. Use it."

He turned away, striding to the faint rectangle that marked the spot where the kitchen had been. "I'm not sure I can do that . . . and retain myself."

"You have to," she said.

He wasn't sure. Damn it, he wasn't sure. To give in to the Blood-Hunger, even for good reason . . .

"Alex," Francine said.

He sensed her coming closer, sensed her reaching out, then dropping her hand without touching him. Silence stretched between them. He could hear her heartbeat, smell the mint-bourbon scent on her breath on the heavy air.

Her voice was harsh when she spoke at last. "Answer me a question, Alex."

"Of course."

"Do you intend to die with Elizabeth this time?"

And there it was. Stark, naked, unanswerable. Turning on his heel, Alex walked away.

17

Moonlight filled the hallway outside Sonya's door. The big mimosa sent lacy shadow patterns fanning over the pale walls, a sensual image, like black lace on a woman's skin. Alex stood still, letting the shadows pass like a caress over him.

It's only Blood-Hunger.

Only. It was the part of him he feared the most, the one thing he couldn't control, couldn't leave behind. The mark of the beast.

It also represented his ticket to Lydia—and Elizabeth. He raised his fist, knocked softly on Sonya's door.

"Who is it?" she called.

"Alex."

The door opened, framing her against a flood of golden light. Her robe hung open, revealing a wisp of a bra and a handspan of silk panties. It was much more effective than mere nudity would have been.

"Come in," she said, stepping back to give him room. "It's only ten o'clock; have you decided to spend a night at home for a change?"

"I was on my way out, actually."

"Is there anything I can do to convince you to stay?"

"Not tonight."

"Are you sure?" She moved closer. The robe whispered against her skin, and the scent of perfume mixed with the musk of her arousal. His Blood-Hunger sharpened, sending hot darts of need shooting through his body.

"You're very beautiful," he said, reaching out to run his fingertip along the chain she wore.

"Then you'll stay?"

Gently he clasped her throat, feeling her pulse hammer against his palm. He narrowed his eyes against the rush of sensation. The tide of her life—so sweet, so fragile, so beckoning. She sighed as he eased the robe open further. So did he. Her nipples stood out clearly beneath the lace of her bra.

"I want you," she said.

He looked into her eyes, knowing she didn't understand the risks, or the consequences. *To find Lydia, you have to touch the Blood-Hunger,* Francine had said. Very well, tonight he would be all revenant. But not with Sonya; in this, she was an innocent.

"Do you ever wonder what happened to Lydia?" he asked.

"Lately," she murmured, "I've been having trouble thinking at all."

"So have I."

He kissed her with a tenderness that surprised him, and felt her spirit flutter like an injured bird. He raised his head to look at her. Her eyes were closed, her chest rising and falling with ragged, irregular breaths.

Reaching out, he slid his hand beneath the crystal, lifted it away from her chest. "Hello, Lydia," he murmured, closing his fist around the stone.

He let his awareness sink into the faceted depths. No song lightened this crystal's dark heart, no inner light played along the arches and smooth stone walls. A bleak and empty place, Alex thought. Faintly he could hear the pain of the great quartz crystal from which this had been torn, but the song was lost in the malice of Lydia's shattered soul.

Did you enjoy watching us?

A sharper edge honed Lydia's touch. It tasted of triumph and unholy greed, and was shadowed with desperation.

Don't you wish it had been you? After what we shared, I can't imagine you willingly sending another woman to me. Does it bother you, Lydia?

Her anger thrummed through the crystal. Hate dripped from every angle, ran in rivulets down the smooth, dark walls to pool around him. It hurt the spirit, that hatred, burned along the mind's pathways, leaving bands of desolation behind.

But desolation had been his companion since the moment he'd become revenant; the sum of his existence. He opened himself to it. His Blood-Hunger quested forward like a famished wolf, surging through the dark, angled world of the crystal. He let it carry him toward the source of the hate.

His grip on the crystal tightened. Sonya's back arched as though a sudden pain had gripped her. Heat pulsed through his palm, a stigmata of dark intent. Images raced through his mind. Fleeting pictures of the world Lydia now inhabited. He grabbed at them frantically, hoping to hold one long enough to track her down. A large room, showing signs of long neglect, the bleat of tugboat horns from the river nearby . . . The river. Flesh and blood of the city, its source and its sustenance from the moment James Oglethorpe stood on Yamacraw Bluff and saw the future. He could almost smell the water.

His breath caught as Elizabeth's face appeared. The whorl of images stopped, focused. So beautiful, he thought, looking into the echoing emptiness of those dark amber eyes. She'd become a vessel for Blood-Hunger, a tool driven only by revenant need. A killing machine. And yet, strangely innocent.

"Elizabeth," he whispered, reaching out to her with everything he was or had ever been.

He saw her nostrils flare, saw her raise her head as though she'd heard his call. Blood-Hunger shrieked through the caverns of his soul, a raw, jagged knifepoint of need that could never be quenched. His need. Elizabeth's. Entwined, powerful, linked somehow.

Then sudden darkness swept over his vision, like a hand over a camera lens. Lydia, he thought. She'd found a way to block him.

The crystal cooled against his hand. He let it go, and it fell like a drop of old blood upon Sonya's chest. Light roiled in its depths, a sullen dark glimmering that looked like no illumination born of this world. Alex held his hand over it, felt malice radiating from it.

With a suddenness that took him by surprise, the stone disintegrated. A sifting of black dust hung for a moment in the air, then winked out of existence.

Sonya sagged. Alex caught her and swung her gently onto the bed. Although she'd fallen deeply unconscious, her heartbeat was steady, her breathing regular.

"You're free," he said. "At least for now. I'll do my best to keep it that way."

He covered her, then turned toward the door. He'd touched Elizabeth, felt the rage of her Blood-Hunger. She'd hunt tonight. And tonight, with his Blood-Hunger so finely tuned to hers, he held his best chance of finding her.

Perhaps his only chance.

The weather changed in the short time it took Alex to reach Savannah. Clouds piled upon the horizon, stacked by a thick summer wind. Then fog came to creep along

Savannah's streets. Reality turned inside out; vehicles groped through the misted dimness like blind, lumbering beasts, traffic lights burned like cyclops' eyes in the misted dimness.

Alex moved through the fog, nostrils flaring at the scent of marsh air. A breath of Wildwood had come to Savannah, faint, but definitely there. Perhaps it, too, had been drawn by Blood-Hunger and the taste of Lydia's hate.

"Have you come to help, or merely to claim the loser?" he asked.

The marsh scent faded. Alex shrugged, then walked down to the riverfront. To his right, Factors Row stretched five stories over his head. To his left, the Savannah River stretched like a ribbon of molten lead. Mist swirled over the dark water. The vast, lumbering shape of a barge pierced it, swept through like some unlikely sea monster, and then was gone.

Anticipation ran in icy spurts along his nerves as he walked down the esplanade. He could almost taste Elizabeth on the slow, heavy breeze. Close. So close, in fact, that he whirled, almost expecting to see her walk out of the fog behind him.

She'd begun to hunt. Alex could feel his own Blood-Hunger deepen as she followed her prey. The fog thickened, shrouding the old-fashioned streetlights until they looked like candles in cotton. But Blood-Hunger transcended the blindness of his sight, focusing finally on the level above River Street.

"There you are," he murmured.

He made his way to the nearest staircase, built long ago of ballast stones from the ships that had come to the port. Moisture glistened like tears on the rock, ran in slick beads on the metal handrail.

The urgency of her need increased until it sang along his nerves. He drew in the scent of fresh blood, heard the quick patter of human heartbeats, and for a moment wasn't sure if it was his perception or hers.

Footsteps grated above him. He registered two humans, male. They fumbled about for a moment, then moved into sight on the landing above. The smell of beer preceded them as they started down the narrow stairs.

"Goddamn fog," one of them snarled. "Can't see your fucking hand in front of your face."

Alex watched astonishment spread over their faces as he came into their view. They stopped, young, brash, and drunk, and blocked his path.

The men grinned. "Hey, mister," one said. "You're in our way."

"Yes," he said. "I am."

He could have taken them. Blood-Hunger clamored for him to do it—his and Elizabeth's. Close, so close. He could feel the pump of blood through their veins, almost taste their lives pouring into him. Almost . . . With a sudden swift dart of shock, he realized *they* were her quarry.

And there she was, standing at the top of the stairs. The fog wreathed her legs, wrapped around her like a lover. Inhuman need raged in her eyes as she stared down at the two men. Even here, even now, she held something of the sun in her gold-shot hair and tawny eyes. She should never have been bound to the night.

"Elizabeth," Alex murmured.

She looked at him then, and it was like falling down a well. Dark need, dark desire. A spiraling hell of appetite. He spun downward slowly, fighting what he was, what she'd become. His gaze locked with hers. Those dark amber eyes gave him nothing to hold on to, however; she was more lost than he.

"Hey, man, I'm talking to you," the larger man said, jabbing two fingers into Alex's chest. He started to jab again.

Without taking his gaze from Elizabeth, Alex caught the man's wrist before those fingers touched him again. Bones grated as he bore down.

"Christ," the man whined. "You're hurting me!"

"Hey, leave him alone," his companion said, taking a wild swing.

Alex caught the fist in his open hand, immobilizing it. Something black and malicious fluttered in his mind, and he tightened his grip until both men sagged to their knees in pain. Then Elizabeth smiled. It wasn't her smile at all, but another he knew almost as well. Lydia's. Stunning and cruel, blazing bright and dark with malice, just like the woman herself.

Shocked back to his senses, he let his hands fall. "Go," he said. "While you still can."

The two men eased past him, their backs pressed to the rough stone wall. He could hear their footsteps fade as they ran down the esplanade. Elizabeth started down the stairs, as graceful a revenant as she'd been a woman.

Alex moved to block her. "No," he said. "They're not for you."

He expected her to shape-shift and readied himself to follow her lead. To his surprise, she stopped. Then he realized she didn't know her abilities, didn't know anything but the killing. Lydia, in her ignorance, had failed to utilize the full power of the being she'd enthralled.

Elizabeth's lips lifted in a snarl. An animal's expression. The sight made his spirit clench in agony. *Ah, Elizabeth, to see you come to this!*

His resolve firmed. If Elizabeth could have seen herself, she would have begged him to destroy her. He took a step upward. She retreated. It wasn't fear; he could feel something bleak and powerful move between them, urging her back.

Not tonight. Lydia wasn't going to steal her away from him again.

"She's mine, Lydia," he said. "She always was."

Malice filled the night, spread like cancer through the pale, grasping tendrils of fog. Alex moved against it, into it. A man would have shuddered. But he welcomed it. He embraced the pure, cold hatred that was Lydia. He let it sink deep, twine with his Blood-Hunger.

And cast it forth, a blind, furious blast of revenant power. Lydia's spell shriveled and died, sucked as dry as a man would have been. He could feel her astonishment. She wasn't beaten, but she'd had her claws clipped for a while.

He looked at Elizabeth, hoping that her mindlessness had been Lydia's doing. But her eyes remained empty. He searched within her, found only the stark wasteland of Blood-Hunger. Blood caked her slim fingers and spotted the front of her blouse. He could smell the killing on her.

He took another step upward. Her gaze never left his, but her bare feet shifted on the stair.

"It's Alex, love," he said. "Don't you remember me?"

She doesn't even remember being human. Do you expect her to fall into your arms? You came here to destroy her, so get it done.

Yes. Now, before he lost the chance.

He sprang at her. She spun out of his grasp, kicking at him with an animal's ferocity, a revenant's strength. Her foot connected with his knee, sending him reeling against the rail behind him. In that moment's grace, she leapt to the top of the wall and raced away. He leapt up after her, only he didn't come to ground again. His pale wings blurred into invisibility in the fog.

The mist parted from time to time, giving him glimpses of her. Had he been blind and deaf, however, her Blood-Hunger would have led him after her as she ran into the shrouded depths of Emmett Park.

He caught the breeze beneath his wings and canted

down after her. She glanced over her shoulder, obviously as aware of him as he was of her. He scented no fear, no anger, only the tang of thwarted Blood-Hunger. If he lost her now, she'd immediately begin the hunt.

So don't lose her.

She dodged. He cupped air, wheeled with her. She shifted direction again, and once again. Alex, more maneuverable than she, stayed with her. When she turned to head into the trees, he arrowed down in a raptor's plunge.

He landed on her shoulders, shifting instantly to man-form to bring her down with his weight. As she went down she snarled, a low, ugly sound. Impact dislodged him; she turned on him with teeth and nails and raging Blood-Hunger. Revenant against revenant. But he was older, more powerful, and strengthened by outrage. He struck at her with everything he had, his fist smashing into her temple even as his mind drove in on hers.

She went down beneath the double attack, unconscious before she hit the ground. Head bent, Alex crouched beside her. Something cool ran over his upper lip. Thinking it was tears, he touched it. His fingers came away red.

Do it. Do it now.

Rising, he went to the nearest tree and ripped a branch off. She lay motionless, her lashes fanned across her cheeks, her hair spread out over the dew-wet grass. He drew in his breath sharply. She'd looked just this way the night he'd buried his heart with her. So beautiful, so still.

Do it.

He placed the raw end of the branch against her chest and readied himself for the thrust. His arms trembled, resisted. Logic hammered at him, telling him things he'd told himself a hundred times. This wasn't Elizabeth. This was something evil and twisted, something that would kill and kill until it was stopped. A monster.

Made by him. And best destroyed by him.

"Forgive me," he said.

18

Alex tensed, ready for the thrust.

The fog swirled around him, bringing the smell of marsh with it. Suddenly it seemed as though the world had taken a half turn sideways; the sounds of the city vanished, replaced by a nature gone mad. Cicadas sang hard and fast, crickets chirped, and for one insane moment he thought he heard the full-throated *gronk* of a bull alligator.

"Wait!"

Justin's voice. Astonished, Alex turned to see the young man step out of the roiling wall of fog. His eyes had the dark, fey look they'd held so often lately. Old power surrounded him. Finally Alex understood why Wildwood had come to Savannah tonight. Not for him, not for Lydia. For Justin.

"What the hell are you doing, Alex?" he demanded.

"How long have you been following me?"

"Long enough. What are you doing?"

Alex looked down at Elizabeth. Her face that would haunt his dreams forever, frozen in this moment of impending death. "I'm ridding the world of a monster."

"Don't."

"She looks like a woman, Justin. But she's not."

"And you're not a man."

Alex sighed. Justin had come into his legacy, ready or not. "No. I'm not a man."

Justin moved closer to study Elizabeth's face. "I remember her." His gaze lifted to Alex. "I remember a lot of things now. And killing her will be the biggest mistake you've ever made."

"That's saying a lot," Alex said. "How do you know?"

"I don't understand, but I *know*." Wildwood swirled in his eyes, ancient, powerful, implacable.

Alex sighed. "Ah, Justin. I wouldn't have wished this on you."

"Is that why you messed with my memory?"

"I wanted you to have a normal life. Because once you step into this world"—Alex swept his hands to indicate the mist all around them—"you can never truly step out again."

With an abrupt gesture, Justin turned away. "Come on. I've got the car parked nearby."

Bending, Alex lifted Elizabeth into his arms. Justin strode into the fog, as surefootedly as if he were walking in broad daylight. Alex was struck by the unconscious certainty of it. Certain abilities cropped up from time to time in the Danilovs; his own daughter Chloe had had an uncanny rapport with horses. Then there'd been great-niece Alexandra, born blind, yet able to "see" colors with her fingertips, and Munroe, Margaret's cousin once removed, whose skill in finding things under the ground—water, oil, natural gas—had greatly swelled the family coffers. And of course, Lydia.

Wind stirred the fog, parting it long enough for Alex to spot the BMW a short distance away. The car seemed an anachronism in this mist-shrouded world. He wouldn't have been surprised if it had sprouted legs and stalked off down the street.

Justin unlocked the passenger door and swung it open. "Do you want to put her in the back?"

"I'd rather hold on to her," Alex said. "Just in case."

Justin nodded. He slid behind the wheel and eased the car forward, driving with the same sureness with which he'd walked. Alex let his head fall back against the headrest.

"You still love her, don't you?" Justin asked.

"Yes."

"What is she?"

The time for lying had passed. "A revenant. Ah, you'll be more familiar with the term *vampire*."

"For real?"

"You don't believe me?"

The young man's large, bony hands shifted on the steering wheel. "I saw you change into an owl and back again. Right now, I'd believe just about anything."

Alex shook his head. "I wish you hadn't come tonight."

"You've been real weird lately, Alex. I knew something was wrong. And tonight you looked like a man who had—"

"Had to destroy the woman he loved for the second time."

"Je-sus."

"Don't blaspheme."

"Shit, then. What the hell happened that night?"

Alex gave him the story. All of it. Justin took it without flinching, the only betrayal of emotion the restless tic of a muscle in his jaw. When Alex finished, silence fell. A strand of Elizabeth's hair drifted down over her face, and he brushed it gently back.

"Why did you stop me back there?" he asked.

Justin shrugged. "You looked like something was tearing you apart, and it just . . . felt wrong. Are you sure she can't be fixed?"

"Fixed?"

"She used to be Elizabeth. Maybe she can be Elizabeth again."

"Elizabeth is dead."

"And as the story goes," Justin said, "so were you."

"It's impossible. It's always been impossible. Some revenants simply awaken without mind or memory; the only way to deal with them is to destroy them."

"Yeah? Who's the expert on it?"

Alex drew in a breath, exhaled it in something that might have been a laugh if it hadn't hurt so much. "I am, I suppose."

"So, why did you stop?"

"Because you asked me to." He smoothed Elizabeth's hair again. "Because I wanted to."

Justin sighed. "Aunt Margaret knew, didn't she?"

"She was one of the trusted few. Or maybe unlucky. How did you guess?"

"You know how people are when they've danced together for a long time? They know each other's rhythm, slide into each other's moves without thinking about it. That's how you and Aunt Margaret were."

"Dead on, as always, my young friend," Alex murmured. "Margaret and I knew each other for a very long time."

"How long?"

"I helped bring her into the world. I raised her, as much as her parents did."

"Oh, man."

"You wanted the truth."

"Stupid me. Exactly where do you fit into the family?"

"Catherine Danilov was my wife. I built the Arbor for her, and for our children. But the Danilovs are an old family, older by far than this country. My ancestor, Valsarian, held Kiev together during the rule of Prince Igor. Or perhaps I should say despite Igor."

"History wasn't my best subject," Justin said.

"My father served St. Vladimir himself—"

"Whoa! I remember reading about *that*." Justin looked away from the road long enough to make Alex nervous. "We're talking a thousand years ago."

"Almost, yes."

"Your father."

"I was a knight to Iroslav, Vladimir's son," Alex said, as though it meant nothing. "He didn't have his father's greatness."

"This is nuts!"

"I can take your memories away again, if you like."

"No, you can't," Justin said. "Not anymore."

Alex watched the young man's hands as he steered the car with utter surety through a featureless, trackless plain of fog. Anyone else would have been lost. Anyone.

"You know exactly where you are, don't you?" he asked.

"Yeah."

"It's a gift. A talent. We Danilovs seem to run to that sort of thing."

"Your legacy to us?"

"Catherine's."

Justin's head bobbed, a noncommittal gesture. "So, what does it feel like to be a vampire?"

"I prefer the term *revenant*."

"Answer the question."

"To use a modern term, Justin, it sucks."

"Freudian slip."

"If it barks, it's a dog."

Justin snorted. "She's killed a lot of people."

"Yes," Alex said, looking down at Elizabeth. "It shouldn't have happened. None of it should have happened."

"*You* don't kill."

"Why do you assume that?"

Shock slackened the young man's jaw for a moment. "I . . . don't know."

"I don't kill for *that*," Alex said, taking pity on him. "But I've lived long enough to have killed many people for many other reasons."

Justin fell silent, obviously having difficulty digesting that. Alex gave him time. This was the dangerous moment; he might lose the young man forever. The prospect hurt more than he would have expected.

Inertia pulled him to one side as the car turned, and a moment later he heard the unmistakable sound of crushed oyster shell beneath the wheels. They'd reached home. The Arbor came into view, seeming to float in the sea of mist. Lights burned golden on her flanks.

Justin parked in front. Without a word, he got out and strode into the house. He left the door open behind him, laying a spill of light across the porch and down the steps. Alex levered himself and Elizabeth out of the car and followed.

To his surprise, he found Justin sitting on the bottom stair. His shadow, distorted by the angles of the stairs, stretched far up behind him.

"Why my mother?" he asked.

Alex sighed. "Shall I assign blame? Your mother came to me because she had no choice, and I allowed it to happen because I didn't have the wisdom to stop."

"Say it in English this time."

"I—" Alex broke off, feeling something strange on the air. It was elusive, fleeting, and he lost it before he could pin it down.

"What's the matter?"

"I don't know. Something touched me for a moment, but slipped away before I could get a fix on it. Wait," he said, stiffening as that fragile sensation shivered the air again. Briefly, and so intangibly—it shouldn't have felt imperative at all. But it did, somehow.

Justin got to his feet. Wildwood had come into his eyes again. "I'm going to check on Kelli."

"I'll check Sonya."

At the top of the stairs, Alex turned right, toward the section where Sonya's room was located. The sensation was stronger here. The hairs lifted on the back of his neck as he finally recognized the thrum of crystal song. The voices had skewed, becoming sly and stealthy, insidious as Satan himself. Danger shrilled along Alex's nerves.

Justin. He trusted Wildwood to deliver the summons.

The air lay thick and stifling in the hallway. Alex strode through it, his alarm rocketing upward when he saw that Sonya's room was empty. She should have slept all night.

He laid Elizabeth on the bed, then moved down the hall to the room that had been Lydia's. The hum of crystal voices grew louder as he neared it, the aura of danger more imperative.

He found the door locked. With a wrench, he tore the whole thing free—lock, hinges, and all—and stepped into the room. Sonya lay on the floor, curled around herself as though in pain. Kelli, holding the big quartz crystal in both hands, stood over her. The girl's eyes were dark with things that shouldn't have existed in this time and place.

"Ah, Lord," Alex murmured. "Why is it always the innocents?"

He went to Kelli and cupped her hands in his. He plunged into the roiling dark sea of Lydia's emotions, a vast, bleeding squall of hate and fear and desperation. And most of all, greed. It buffeted him, sent dagger thrusts of pain as intense as Blood-Hunger.

He could feel Kelli's spirit struggling, caught in a current too strong for it. And there was something else with her, something as clear and pure as spring water.

Too young, too unformed yet to protect itself, it curled in the lee of its mother's soul as she tried to shield it.

Alex fought to move against the stormwind of Lydia's hate. Around him, the crystal wailed for its stolen heart, adding its cry to the whirl of power. He breasted the current to reach Kelli and the child.

Vaguely he registered Justin's hands on his shoulders, the moldy, fecund scent of the marsh. Both gave him a grounding in the real world, and the strength to pull Kelli and the child out of Lydia's grasp.

The crystal fell to the floor with a thump. Alex caught Kelli by the elbows as she started to fall, holding her long enough for Justin to come around and ease her to a sitting position. Color slowly came back into her face.

"Are you okay, Kel?" Justin demanded.

"I . . . think so." She brushed the tumbled hair back from her face, looking not at him, but at Alex. "Sonya . . . is she all right?"

He nodded. "How did she get here?"

"I don't know," she said. "I was downstairs getting something to eat, and I heard this . . . singing."

Justin's brows went up. "Singing?"

"Crystals have voices—at least to those who are equipped to hear them," Alex said. He glanced down at the big stone, which still wailed its pain out at the world. It set the teeth on edge and made the spirit ache. "Some are sweeter than others, however."

"Okay." Justin turned back to Kelli. "So you came up here to see where the voices were coming from."

"The door was open, so I came in. Sonya was standing with that crystal in her hands. Her eyes were closed, and she didn't answer me when I spoke to her. It was like she was sleepwalking."

Lydia, Alex thought. She'd reached into his home, into the circle of his protection, and tried to pull Sonya back under her control. He didn't want to think about where she'd gotten that kind of power—or who'd had to die to provide it.

"I took the stone from her," Kelli continued, "but the minute I touched it, I got . . . sucked in." She wrapped her arms around herself. "It was horrible. I was holding on as tight as I could, because I knew that if I let go, even for a second, I'd get swept away and never come back."

Justin looked up at Alex. "I thought you locked that door."

"I did."

"Sonya must have had a key," Kelli said.

"Sure," Justin said. "She must have had a key." He didn't look away from Alex. A hardness had come into his eyes, the outrage of a man whose life had been violated.

And still the crystal cried. Justin couldn't hear it, obviously. But Kelli could.

"Why doesn't it stop?" she asked, a rising edge of hysteria in her voice. But she controlled it well, and Alex was proud of her.

"Because it can't," he said. "Something important was taken from it, and it can't stop crying until it gets it back."

Alex glanced down at the crystal. It reflected the lamplight in a smooth, golden glow. So innocent looking. But it was a trap, a one-way ticket to the hell that was Lydia's spirit.

"In a way, it's so sad," Kelli said. "But scary. Really, really scary. There's something dark and awful in there, something that grabs you and sucks you down."

"That's someone else's nightmare," Justin said, surprising Alex with the skillful half lie. "My aunt Lydia had a definite talent for crystals, Kel. She always said that stones reflect the person, and that if you knew how to talk to them properly, you could make them work for you. Maybe she was right; when she died, something happened to this crystal. It got . . . sick. And that's what you touched."

Bending, he picked the crystal up and hefted it in one hand. "I'm getting rid of this thing. Throw it as far out in the marsh as I can get it."

"I'm not sure that's a good idea," Alex said.

Justin swung around to stare at him. "You've got to be kidding! What makes you say that?"

"It's a link. To the past, and maybe to the future. We may need it before this is all over."

"Can you guarantee it won't be a danger to Kelli again?"

Lie. It's best. "No," he said. "I can't guarantee it."

"Well, I'd rather be wrong, and Kelli safe."

Alex turned to look at her. She met his gaze levelly, but he could see her decision reflected in her eyes. Her child had been at risk with her; for her, there was no choice.

Nor for Alex. He spread his arms, acquiescing.

"Come on, Kel," the young man said, reaching down to lift her to her feet. "Let's go for a walk."

Alex watched from the window. The fog had turned the garden into a magical place—but a blind one. Wildwood's hand lay heavily upon it. Justin led Kelli toward the marsh with the same surety he'd shown on the drive here.

Interesting, Alex thought, that Justin's first impulse was to entrust the crystal to Wildwood. Or was it *Justin's* impulse? A sobering thought, that.

He lost sight of them when they moved into the trees at the edge of the garden. The marsh lay just beyond. Mist coiled across the quiet dark water, whipped from time to time by the wind into fog wraiths that danced provocatively through the nodding grass. Wildwood: primeval, mysterious. Ancient and vastly powerful. Its motives not measurable in human terms.

Alex pressed his fingertips against the glass. "Don't trust what you cannot understand, my young friend," he murmured.

He saw the flash of reflected light as the crystal arced out over the marsh. Its voice spun in a paean of loss until the water closed over it.

A chill raced up his spine. He had the strongest feeling that he'd just made a terrible mistake in allowing Justin to discard the stone.

With a sigh, he banished it. Foreboding seemed everywhere now, and mistakes too numerous to count. Whatever the outcome, the crystal belonged to Wildwood now.

And Elizabeth was waiting for him.

19

Alex carried Elizabeth down into his underground sanctuary. She'd begun to stir, throwing off his restraints little by little. Perhaps he didn't hold them as tightly as he could have; he wanted to look into her eyes again, empty though they were.

He laid her on the bed. Bracing one hand on the post, he studied her. Revenant. Killer. Stalker in the night. She didn't look like any of them. No, she looked like Liz Garry, who'd carried the sun in her eyes.

A lifetime ago she'd loved him.

"I should have done it back there in the park," he said, reaching out to run one finger down the curve of her cheek.

She caught his wrist in a grasp that grated bones together. He watched her eyes open, saw the void within. A ravening sweep of Blood-Hunger shot through him, stabbing white-hot needles of agony deep into his brain. He took a step backward. She came up with him, still holding his wrist.

"Elizabeth," he said. "Do you even remember your name?"

Only the Blood-Hunger answered. She let go of him

suddenly, taking him by surprise, and leapt for the stairs. He caught her halfway up. She turned on him, biting, scratching—revenant strength without the regulator of self-preservation.

He lost his footing. But he did manage to grab her ankle and bring her with him as he bumped painfully down the stairs. She slashed at him with her nails, raking bloody furrows down his cheek. He caught her hand, pulled it away from him before she could do still more damage. Something red and inhuman sparked in her eyes. His own rage matched it, surpassed it, and he flung her into the center of the room.

He rose to his feet and stalked her, staying between her and the stairs even as he wondered what to do with her. Killing her would have been easy; controlling her was something else entirely.

"Do you ever wonder how you came to be, Elizabeth?" he asked.

Her eyes held only the need to hunt. Blood-Hunger. Hers, his, theirs, spiraling higher than anything he'd ever known before. It staggered him, overwhelmed him, sent him reeling in a thick, dark sea of revenant power. His field of view narrowed to those endless dark amber eyes. His world narrowed to her, and only her. The killing didn't matter. Her mindlessness didn't matter. Only the need. Only the Hunger. His soul quaked with a wash of desire so primal, so fierce that it swept everything else away. Ten thousand years of existence couldn't have prepared him for this.

"Elizabeth," he said, and his voice didn't sound human at all.

He sprang at her. She grappled with him, but it was not to fight. They fell to the floor, straining, entwining, mouths locked on each other's flesh. Alex closed his eyes in unbearable, exquisite pleasure as her blood spurted into the back of his throat; God help him, she tasted like Elizabeth still.

Desire roared in his mind. He lay impaled on it, pinned on a spike of a need so powerful it made even his fingernails ache. *She* felt it, too. He could tell by the way her hands moved on his back, the unconscious shifting of her body beneath him. Blood-Hunger still coursed through his veins, but like a beast whose kill already lay before it, it had lost some of its mad urgency.

He raised his head and found her staring at him. Beautiful, inhuman, her eyes paled to molten gold by the need coursing in her. His heart twisted at what had been lost. Sun-woman who would never again see the sun, the generous spirit who had once loved a revenant but now had forgotten that love existed . . . Elizabeth.

Suldris had set his trap well; this was indeed a particularly sharp-edged kind of torture. She looked like Liz Garry, felt and tasted like her, but Liz no longer occupied the lovely shell. And still he was compelled to look at her, taste her, bury himself in her, all the while waiting in vain for something of Elizabeth to return.

Pleasure and pain, pain and pleasure. The pain was made worse by the memory of a time when he'd had the woman, when love had been pure and as uncomplicated as his nature allowed.

Her hips moved beneath him. Voluptuously. And yet, a bittersweet innocence clung to her, a killer without conscience or therefore guilt, a drinker of blood, stealer of lives, a creature of knife-edged sensuality who didn't even understand what her body wanted. The world seemed to tilt around him, as though someone had torn it from its moorings and cast it adrift in chaos. Gazing into her heavy-lidded eyes, he knew that she was his destiny. The past thousand years no longer mattered, nor did the next thousand; tonight there was only her.

"You feel it, too," he said. "It's our fate, Liz Garry.

We'll have to go to hell together, you and I."

The edges of her teeth gleamed white as she pulled him down. Alex led the way, drawing her with him into the searing sensuality only the revenant can know. For the first time since he'd left his homeland, he let himself go; he could hurt her no longer. A thousand years of self-denial went up in flames. Blood-Hunger twined with Blood-Hunger, passion with passion, and both hotter than hell itself.

They touched each other recklessly, tasted and stroked, drank deeply. Alex knew her desire and response was only a reflection of his, knew the only intimacy they could share was sex and Blood-Hunger. He didn't care. If someone had plunged a stake into his heart, or if the world itself were coming apart around him, he couldn't have stopped.

She matched him caress for caress, even her taking of his blood a sweeping rush of pleasure. He shuddered as he plunged into her, body and spirit, seeking to fill the emptiness inside her with his own longing, his own loneliness.

"Elizabeth," he groaned.

Elizabeth had gone forever, leaving only this beautiful revenant who held him so tightly and who knew neither him nor herself. But the passion was real. And the Blood-Hunger. Always the Blood-Hunger. It fountained high and hot, as though it realized it would finally be allowed satiation.

Her hands closed over his buttocks, pulling him deeper, closer. He sank his hands into her hair. His flesh was so sensitized that he could feel each separate strand as it slid across his skin, feel the flicker of her eyelashes against his throat as she took another draft. Gasping, he brought her wrist to his mouth, tasted her sweetness yet again. It was exquisite, too compelling, essence of Elizabeth distilled into a revenant's power. He disengaged, pulled her up to kiss her. He tasted his own blood on her lips, and passion.

She wasn't Elizabeth, not anymore. But oh, God, just now she was close! Most men would have called the fire in her dark amber eyes love. Caught in the grip of something too powerful to deny, he accepted the illusion. He had to.

A thousand years of restraint fell away, and he plunged into a star-shot sea of sensation. Locked in an embrace that death couldn't have parted, she went with him.

The aftershocks ebbed. And although he still held her in his arms, he felt her slip away from him. The void within her, no longer filled with passion, echoed emptily. He held her tightly, his spirit wailing down those unpeopled corridors. Seeking the woman that had been. Seeking, in this trembling moment, even the illusion.

"Elizabeth," he whispered. "Talk to me. Tell me there's something left inside you so that I can keep you."

She only looked at him. There was no consciousness in her eyes, no humanity. He might as well have taken a leopard in his arms and tried to turn it into a woman.

And then, magically, he felt her soften, watched her eyes turn molten as she reached up to pull him down. It began all over again. Desire, need, the spiraling ache of sensuality and sheer, voracious greed of Blood-Hunger caught him up. It wasn't real. *She* wasn't real. But as the night moved inevitably toward dawn Alex found that for now, it was enough.

Something unfurled deep within him, something that had been tightly bound for so many centuries that he'd forgotten it was there. There was nothing of humanity about it; dark as a storm-tossed night, implacable as death, it arrowed straight to the core of his revenant power. He dared to set it free. Revenant that she was, she accepted it, drew it deep, then sent it back to him in a sweeping tide of desire and power.

Gasping, whirling like a leaf in forces more powerful than anything he'd ever known, he touched the stars once again. And again. He lost track of time, lost track of any reality except this coupling. It might have been made in heaven, perhaps in hell, but for tonight it was everything he wanted.

Oblivion caught him there in her arms. He hung on as long as he could, watching her eyes dim and the heat fade from her face. It felt a little like dying. He let himself slide toward the edge of consciousness, his cynical revenant's mind framing a last thought to take him over.

It's a good thing you're already damned.

Lydia screamed as she was flung out of the fragile web of crystal power. Sensation faded as she returned to the crumbling husk of her own body. She found herself on hands and knees in the center of the fog-shrouded causeway, her numb flesh only vaguely registering the dampness of the concrete.

Air rushed into her lungs with a sound that started as a sigh and ended as a thin wail. She'd been *this* close to paradise, one heartbeat away from freedom. He'd taken Elizabeth and Sonya from her, and now, tonight, the biggest prize of all.

The child. Her savior, the key to her prison. Lydia had felt that touch once before, but it had been so faint and fleeting that she hadn't recognized it for what it was. Oh, God, it couldn't have been more perfect if she'd placed an order. It had an affinity for crystals—her affinity. And it was too young and unformed to protect itself. If she could get to it . . .

Headlights bloomed at the end of the causeway. They moved toward her slowly, hesitantly, as though feeling their way through the mist. As they came nearer, the fog turned them into an amorphous, shrouded glow. She stared, caught like a moth in a candle flame.

Get up or be squashed, you idiot.

That small, sane voice got her up and moving. She lurched toward the side of the roadway as the car passed. The mist spun in whorls behind it, then closed in. The causeway returned to silence.

Lydia peered toward the spot where the Arbor lay. She could feel Alex even here; the breeze carried siftings of his power, slid them over her skin like the memory of lovemaking. Her hand closed on the rail beside her. The concrete grated, and a sifting of dust fell into the marsh below. Her hand grated, too, bones overtaxed by the pressure. But there was no pain—at least no physical pain.

Ah, but inside . . .

"I've got to have it, Alex," she said. "And you're not going to stop me."

A new life, a new body. And it hadn't come any too soon. She lifted her hand and examined the spreading purple-black splotch marking the palm. Corruption. She could smell it on herself, feel it spreading through her flesh.

"I'll be a Danilov," she said, closing her fingers into a fist. "And I'll grow up in your house, dear, doting Uncle Alex. Fifteen, sixteen years, and I'll be ready for you again. You won't know what hit you."

But she needed power to rip the child's fragile persona from its moorings. A little luck, and a lot of power. A *lot* of power. She knew exactly where to begin; that big quartz crystal Justin had thrown into the marsh. Fool kid, to waste it.

She walked to the end of the causeway, then clambered down the embankment and made her way toward the spot where Justin had thrown the stone into the water. Cautiously she tested the boundaries of Alex's power; treading the fringes was all right, but he'd sense her if she stepped too far in.

Her crystal began to pulse with heat. It spread through her, a smooth coil that slid like hot wine through her veins and settled deep in her belly. Sex and Blood-Hunger, Blood-Hunger and sex. Damned Alex was at it again. With Elizabeth; even the reflection of that lovemaking was almost enough to set the air aflame.

"I don't care," she said, reaching up to grip the crystal.

But she did. She did. Moisture slid like tears down her face as she limped along the edge of the water. Closing her eyes, she let herself sink into the surging wave of sensuality. It reeked of power. She moved along the edges of it, seeking entrance, but it remained impenetrable to her. A closed loop: Alex and Elizabeth, Elizabeth and Alex.

Denied access, she turned her attention to the marsh. The ghost crystal vibrated in her hand as it sought the stone from which it had been taken. Another, deeper vibration echoed it from beneath the dark, sullen water about thirty yards out.

"There you are," she said. Luckily it seemed to have fallen in shallow water.

She edged down the embankment, leading with her good leg. A cloud of mosquitoes rose up from the edge of the water. Disdaining her, they whined off toward the house. Lydia laughed, but it sounded more like a sob. She swallowed it quickly.

"Hell," she said. "I wouldn't want me, either."

She stepped into the water. Muck closed around her ankles, rose up her calves. It felt warm, grasping . . . almost alive. She forced herself to move forward.

Step, *squelch*. Pick up one foot, let it sink again into the mud. Step, *squelch*. Harder this time, her bad leg not wanting to obey. Again.

The fog wrapped tightly around her, seeming to pluck at her hair and skin with curious fingers. She struggled forward, fighting the muck that seemed deeper and more clinging with every step. The ghost crystal throbbed against her chest.

Warning her. She stopped, only then realizing her danger. The marsh was a trap. If she kept going, it would swallow her up. Her nerves singing with sudden terror, she backed slowly toward shore. The mud sucked at her legs as though reluctant to give her up.

The rasp of her breath seemed overloud in the white-shrouded quiet. She glanced at the shore over her shoulder, where trees stood like ghostly sentinels. Just a few more yards. The mist closed even more thickly around her, trying to hold her back. It smelled hot and primordial, as though some enormous beast had opened its mouth and sighed. Its breath was redolent with fish and rotting vegetation, earth and water and the teeming life that inhabited it.

Almost there. She grasped an overhanging branch, used it to pull herself toward dry land. The mud gave her up with a sudden, sucking lurch, sending her sprawling awkwardly onto the embankment.

"What are you?" she muttered,

The fog remained thick and silent. A fish broached the surface of the water, returned with a plop. Such a quiet and innocuous scene, but underneath . . . She shook her head, unwilling to believe what had happened, equally unwilling to walk back out there to see if it would happen again; the crystal was one source of power, but there were others.

The ghost crystal shivered, radiating the ebb and flow of Alex's Blood-Hunger. It had a new flavor to it, as though it had blended with Elizabeth's to make something entirely new. Lydia hated it.

"Stop it," she said, beating her fists against the damp ground. "Stop it, stop it, stop it!"

But it didn't stop. It went on and on, higher and higher. A bonfire of the body and the soul. And she, cast out of the circle of firelight like a disobedient dog, hovering at the fringes. She should have left. But she didn't. Couldn't.

It should have been me.

It must be torture for Alex to make love to Elizabeth's body, knowing that her mind no longer occupied it. Did he call her name? Lydia already knew how sharp the pleasure was; she could feel the echoes of it all the way out here. Damn him.

It should have been me.

She took comfort in the knowledge that he'd have to betray Elizabeth in the end. Alex and his damned, outmoded code of honor—he'd have to destroy her to protect the world. Our savior. Beautiful, crystal-eyed, thousand-year-old vampire. A bigger, older monster than any of them.

Lydia drew her knees up to her chest, hugging them as though to press away the burning frustration in her heart. He held her salvation in his hands. Eternity in a drop of blood. How could she hate one man so fiercely and still want so much from him?

"Alex," she whispered, resting her chin on her knees.

Dawn was near. An air of hushed waiting settled over the marsh, stilling even the background hum of insect voices. Light sparked in the eastern sky. The fog seemed to catch it, cast it wide like a scattering of wildfire, and then the whole marsh turned to gold.

She drew in a deep breath, let it out slowly. At least Alex would never have this.

The gilding of light faded into true morning light. Lydia struggled to her feet, tapping into the ghost crystal's stored power to keep her bad leg from buckling under her. She had a day's grace; might as well take advantage of it.

How many lives would it take, she wondered, to give her the power she needed? Then she shrugged; one or a thousand, she'd take as many as she had to. Before anyone had a chance to figure out what was going on, she'd been safely tucked away in a nice, cozy womb.

"What the hell," she said. "Maybe the city will give me a medal or something for solving its homeless problem."

Those Bible-thumping Christians had nothing on her. Born again? Yes, indeed.

20

A sense of urgency pulled Alex up through Oblivion. He could feel Elizabeth returning to consciousness with him, the two of them rising like twinned bubbles through the void.

He opened his eyes to the dark amber chaos of hers. "Hello, Elizabeth," he said.

He let her go, needing distance to think. She didn't try to run. Why should she? he thought with a depth of bitterness that surprised him. Everything she needed was right here: Blood-Hunger and more Blood-Hunger, a coupling with a being as powerful and destructive as she.

"What am I going to do with you?" he asked. "I can't keep you here forever." Gazing into her blank, beautiful eyes, he felt his heart stretch painfully. "And I can't let you go."

She rose to her knees. Her hair fell in loops and whorls across her naked shoulders, spun gold on ivory. Sun-woman. He reached out to clasp her neck.

"I should do it now, no matter what Justin feels," he said, exerting pressure.

Heat spread from that point of contact, spurted along his veins to settle deep in his belly. His Blood-Hunger roared. Of their own volition, his hands dropped to her shoulders and spread out over the smooth curve.

She turned her head and pressed her mouth to the inside of his wrist. He felt a surge, as though every cell in his body had concentrated on that one spot. Blood-Hunger pounded a heavy rhythm in his mind, beating like far-off drums. Danger within danger, twined as surely as their Blood-Hunger; hers, because he couldn't afford to let her live, and his, because he'd already begun to doubt his ability to exist after he destroyed her.

She released his wrist, gazing up at him with heavy-lidded eyes. He slid his hand up the curve of her neck to her cheek. Her head went back, exposing the smooth, pale length of her throat. Compliant, he thought. Utterly compliant. A slave to sensuality and to Blood-Hunger. His slave, because he was the one who could give her both.

Nothing else could have so thoroughly underscored how alien she was to Elizabeth, who'd never been compliant. It gave him the strength to let her go.

"No," he said. "Not this time."

She knelt at his feet, naked and seductive. He wanted her. He wanted her with an intensity that made his spirit ache. But that was the beast in him. The man wanted more. He wanted Elizabeth, craved the fire of her spirit, the love that was at once human and divine. With a low sound that might have been a groan or a sob, he turned away. He braced his hands on the table and bowed his head.

"I know you don't understand," he said. "But I still have to say it. From the moment I became revenant, I've struggled to keep the little humanity left to me. The one who made me revenant couldn't take it; I left her, in all her power and glory, and found another way. But you . . ." He faltered for a moment, and swallowed to clear his throat. "You tempt me beyond all others, shadow of Elizabeth. Your emptiness calls to mine, and until now, I didn't know how empty I was. Nor how much I feared it."

His gaze fell on the medallion he'd given Liz Garry at a time of happiness that seemed very long ago. The griffin glared back at him with its single ruby eye, clutching the perfect pearl that had been its possession for more than a thousand years.

He picked it up, his thumb caressing the raised contours, then closed it in his fist. Turning, he looked at her. She blazed like the sun against the gray flagstone floor, a creature of tawny hair and eyes of molten gold. An almost palpable aura of heat rose from her skin. He felt an echoing heat bloom in his chest and rush out along his limbs.

He closed his eyes. It would always be like this. Every time he looked at her, touched her, breathed the fragrance of her skin, he'd lose himself. And he'd pour himself into that dark void within her, over and over again until there was nothing left. For she was revenant, and only revenant. Bringing her here had been a mistake, sparing her an even bigger one.

"I can't keep you," he said. Because he wanted to so badly.

Slowly he walked to the metal-banded chest that sat at the foot of the bed. He hadn't opened it in many, many years; it held too many memories to be comfortable. The nightgown Catherine had worn on their wedding night, gossamer thin and edged with fine Provençal lace; the diamond-studded earrings he'd given to Mireille Labourdeaux, his lover in the court of Louis XIV; the gold cup given him by Ivan, the magnificent madman who had become Terrible. Layers of his past, lives outlived and left behind. At the very bottom lay a sword. The chasings on its hilt were pitted and tarnished. But the blade, made of fine Damascus steel and consecrated to God, remained unblemished.

He drew it out, slid it out of the sheath. It lay in his hand like an old lover, remembered in his flesh for a thousand years. For a moment his mind filled with the chant of the Mass, the mind-numbing scent of incense, the glitter of gold and jewels and the whorl of color from stained-glass windows. He'd been a man then. How many times had he carried this blade into battle, unafraid of dying because his soul had been pledged to God.

He turned to her, steeling himself to see the revenant and not the woman. Her gaze fell from his eyes to the crossed hilt of the sword.

"Don't be afraid," he said. "Elizabeth would have wanted it this way."

She rose, a graceful swirl of ivory skin and gold-streaked hair. As she walked toward him he saw that her attention was focused not on him, but on the sword. His breath came quick and shallow; something had sprung to life in her eyes, something that made his chest tighten with a terrible kind of hope. Terrible, because he knew it was impossible.

"What is it?" he whispered.

She traced the cross-shaped hilt with her fingertips; he trembled, remembering that Liz Garry had been raised a Catholic. Then she trailed her hand up his arm, leaving goose bumps behind. His Blood-Hunger surged. But there was something different about this encounter, for her touch seemed more questing than sensual.

Her fingertips explored his face, traced the curve of his mouth and angle of his jaw, then moved down along his other arm. With a sudden, startling movement, she grasped his wrist and pulled. The sword fell to the floor. The clang of metal on stone seemed to echo through his blood and bones like the trumpets of heaven itself.

Lost in inevitability, he opened his hand, revealing the medallion. She reached out and placed her hand over his, trapping the medallion between their palms. Ruby light bloomed in that cup of flesh, spilled over to stain the walls and ceiling crimson. Her eyes closed. Alex felt a powerful rush of sensation, and then she cried out in a voice full of pain and triumph.

She sank to her knees, then slowly tilted onto her side on the floor. He stared down at her, unable to move, unable, at this moment, even to think.

"I'm cold," she said.

His breath went out in a gasp. He sank to his knees beside her, wanting to touch, but not daring to, lest this, too, prove to be an illusion.

"Elizabeth?" he whispered. "How . . . ?"

He looked into her eyes, saw his love there. Reason came flooding back. And joy. It blinded him, but put his hands in motion; he snatched her into his arms as though she might escape him. She clung to him, shuddering, her hands as frantic as his.

"I was lost," she sobbed. "I was walking down corridors of red glass, going first this way and then another, but never finding my way out. There were times when I could hear you calling me, but I couldn't find you, couldn't reach you—"

"Shhh," he murmured, not questioning the miracle. He picked the medallion up from the floor where it had fallen, unnoticed. "I think an old friend preserved you for me."

Reaching out, she touched the ruby. He watched the realization come into her eyes.

"The ruby? Is that possible?"

"There are times when anything is possible," he said.

She looked down at herself. "I'm naked, and so are you. What have you been doing, Alex? Up to tricks while I left my body unattended?"

"Liz, I—"

"Shut up," she said. "I was teasing."

Suddenly she frowned, reaching to touch the marks she'd left on his wrist. With a swift, graceful movement, she pushed away from him and got to her feet. Alex watched her, his heart aching for the pain she would have to bear.

"There aren't any lights in here," she murmured. "But I can see."

"Yes."

"Did I . . . do that to your wrist?"

"Yes."

"Who . . . ?" Her voice faltered, but he knew what she needed to know.

"It was Suldris."

She placed her palms against her cheeks as though to hold herself in. He wanted to put his arms around her. He wanted to take reality away and make things the way they'd been before. She started to pace the room, her hair swinging like spun daylight with every pace. He knew that bright mind of hers was assessing the situation. And he saw her come to the conclusion not by logic, but by the taste and power of her own Blood-Hunger.

Suddenly she crouched in front of him. Her eyes were haunted by the things she only suspected, and Alex dreaded the truth she'd demand.

"Have you had my body here with you the whole time?" she asked.

Tell her a lie. "No," he said. "I only found you last night."

"What have I done?"

"Liz—"

"What have I done?"

"*You* have done nothing."

"But my body did."

"It had only instinct, with you gone."

"I . . . killed someone."

He gripped her shoulders, hard. "It's the revenant's nature to kill. The true sustenance is death, the taking of blood the means to that end."

"How many?"

"Does it matter?" he asked. "One or a hundred—you'll still feel the guilt."

"Why should I feel guilty? It was my body, not me, right? Do you know if they were men, women, or children?"

"Don't do this to yourself, Elizabeth."

"Did they suffer? Did they scream?" She laughed, a wild note of hysteria edging her voice. "Do they fight when you drain them, or do they just sit there and let you do it to them?"

"Stop it!"

"You say it was my body, and not me. But you had sex with that empty body."

"Yes," he rasped. "I did."

"What was it like? Did you enjoy it?"

"It was like dying and like being reborn. I learned things about myself I'd rather not know, things I've avoided for a thousand years. And yes, I enjoyed it. Loved it and hated it and wanted to do it all over again."

"And I thought you such a moral man," she cried, lashing out, punishing herself and him. "I thought you knew the difference between right and wrong."

"There is no right and wrong between us," he said.

"I killed people! I drank their blood, and I killed them. How could you let that happen to me?"

Anger flooded high, a searing outrage that went far beyond the stark fact of her accusation. "You dare ask me that? I *killed* you to protect you from that. I laid my heart to rest in that tomb with you, and my only comfort was knowing that I'd spared you my fate!"

"I can't do this." She beat her fists on his chest. "I can't *be* this!"

He rose to his feet, pulling her up with him roughly. She hung unresisting between his hands. Tears slid out from beneath her closed lids and ran down her face.

"Look at me," he commanded.

"I can't."

He shook her. "Look at me!"

She obeyed. Her eyes held such pain that all the violence went out of him. He took a deep breath, trying to find a way out of the agony for her. "Long ago, when we first became lovers, you couldn't understand why I was so sad. Remember, Liz?"

"I remember."

"Now you know. Immortality is both a gift and a burden. A lot of sinning can be done in eternity, and revenants are no more immune from sin than humans. For those of us with a conscience, guilt is the price. The real challenge is continuing to live with it."

"I don't know if I can," she whispered.

Fear hammered at him. If she was to survive, she'd have to accept what she'd become.

Like you did? You ran from yourself for nearly a thousand years, and it took a human woman to finally show you the way.

He pushed the cynical little voice out of his mind. "Come on," he said. "Let's find you something to wear."

She shook her head.

"You can't stay down here forever."

"No," she said. "Only until dawn."

He let go of her, and she sank to her knees. Her hair fell forward over her face. Despair flowed out of her in dark waves until it filled the room. Filled him. But he'd lived with despair for too long to be overwhelmed.

"Get up, Liz. We have work to do."

She shook her hair back to look at him. "Work?"

"There's Lydia. She's the one who woke you."

"So what? She didn't *make* me."

"But she's the one who taught you what you were, and nothing else. She's the one who sent you out into the city to kill. And now she's begun killing on her own. I need to stop her, and I need your help to do it."

For a moment Elizabeth didn't move. Then she rose to her feet. "Is this how you do it? Focus on revenge?"

"Just tasks, love. Some are big, some little, but they give you a reason to live when there doesn't seem to be anything else. One day at a time; that's how you survive."

"One night at a time, you mean."

"The night can be very beautiful," he said, holding out his hand.

He was asking for more than her hand; he wanted her trust. If she could give him that much, he'd preserve her life until she found a reason to care.

Slowly she reached out and placed her hand in his. He let his breath out in a sigh; it was a small first step, but it healed something raw and painful within him.

The last magenta streaks of sunset were fading from the sky as Lydia drove toward Delano. She'd acquired a new car today, and a whole lot of power. It surged in her like a great, dark storm cloud, curbed but fighting to break free.

She'd become beautiful again. And she could feel. She slid her hands on the steering wheel, glorying in the smoothness of the vinyl, the touch of coolness from the air-conditioning vent. It had taken eight lives, one after the other, to give her this. It was worth a hundred.

But it wouldn't last. She had to spend it, strike hard and fast before Alex tracked her down, and hide in a place he'd never think to look for her: his future.

She parked in front of the Hamlen house and got out of the car, wrinkling her nose at the sheer suburban mediocrity of it. The ghost crystal pulsed darkly against her chest as she rang the bell.

A man opened the door. He looked her over, his eyes appreciative but cautious. Amusement sparked in her; even a beautiful stranger was still a stranger. "May I help you?" he asked.

"My name is Lydia Danilov. It's very important that I talk to you."

"Come in." The overhead light gleamed on his bald head as he stepped back and swung the door open wider. "My wife is in the kitchen," he said. "If you'd like to wait in the living room—"

"I love kitchens."

"Follow me, then."

He led her toward the back of the house. Lydia was a bit disappointed that he seemed so perfectly at ease; she'd expected him to be a little gauche and uncomfortable with the Danilovs.

"Mr. Hamlen—"

"Just Phil."

"Phil." She smiled at him, saw it register. Men were men, always. God, it felt good to be beautiful again! She was never, ever going back to anything else.

He paused, letting her enter the kitchen ahead of him. Mrs. Hamlen stood at the sink, washing dishes. She glanced over her shoulder, then turned the water off and swung around. Lydia dismissed her: aging, bourgeois, pretty in a bovine sort of way.

"Susan, this is Lydia Danilov," her husband said, moving to put his arm around her waist.

"Hi, Susan." Lydia smiled, amused by the picture they made. So cozy, so charmingly middle-class. Grandma and Grandpa.

"Nice to meet—" Suddenly the woman broke off, frowning. "Wait a minute. Aren't you the one who disappeared a year or so ago?"

"Yes," Lydia said, reaching up to clasp the crystal. She swept into Susan's mind. The woman swayed, fighting with surprising tenacity.

"Susan?" the man asked, alarm edging his voice. "What's the matter?"

"She . . . wants me to . . ." The woman fell to her knees.

He tried to lift her, then straightened and strode toward Lydia. "Whatever you're doing, you'd better—"

She backhanded him carelessly, sending him crashing into the wall with enough force to crack the plaster. Blood streamed from his ruined mouth and nose as he slid to the floor.

"And now," Lydia said, bearing down on the woman's faltering will, "do what I told you."

Moving with jerky, uncoordinated movements, Susan Hamlen rose to her feet. Lydia dialed the Arbor's number and held the receiver out to her.

"You know what to say, don't you, Susan?"

She nodded.

Lydia took the few seconds' grace to consolidate her hold on Susan; the woman's movements became smoother, her eye blinks more regular. By the time someone answered the phone, her voice sounded almost normal.

"Is that you, Kelli?" she asked. "Hi, darling. Are you feeling all right today? Oh, I'm glad." She paused while Kelli spoke. Impatient, Lydia made a chopping gesture with her hand.

"Why don't you come here and tell me?" Susan said, breaking in. "Your father and I are dying to have you to ourselves, just for a few minutes. You will? Aren't we lucky to have tagged up on a night when Justin's busy?

It'll make your father so happy to see you, sweetheart. See you in a few minutes."

"She's on the way?" Lydia asked.

Mrs. Hamlen nodded.

"Thank you, Susan," Lydia said, taking the phone from the woman's suddenly lax hand. "Thank you very much."

21

Alex returned to his room to find Elizabeth tearing a sheet from his fax machine.

"It's from Charles McGinnis," she said without turning around. "He says the psychic came to his house looking for you and is now on the way here." She swung around to look at him, eyebrows raised. "Psychics?"

"Only one, love," he said, holding out the clothes he'd found for her. Although it was a shame to cover that smooth ivory skin.

"Thanks." She shook the dress out and held it up in front of her. "Looks like it'll fit. Whose is it?"

"Sonya's."

"Which one is she?"

"Justin's mother. The blonde."

"I don't remember her."

"It was a long time ago," he agreed. "A lifetime."

"I can feel the people in this house," she said. "A man and a woman there." She pointed down, toward the living room, then shifted her finger toward the back of the house. "Another woman there."

"That will be Eve, in the kitchen. The other two are

Justin and Sonya. I can't sense Kelli anywhere in the house or grounds."

"Who's Kelli?"

"Justin's fiancée."

"Fiancée! When I met him last year, his voice had barely finished changing."

"She's pregnant."

"Good Lord, Alex. Is this sort of trouble a hereditary thing with you Danilovs?"

"I have never gone around impregnating teenage girls," he said with dignity.

She opened her mouth to say something, then closed it again and took the clothes into the bathroom. "You'd better fill me in on what's going on. All of it."

He took a deep breath and began. Just as he got to the part about Sonya, Liz came out of the bathroom, looking like a queen with her sun-shot hair brushed into a neat coil at the back of her head.

"Really, Alex," she said. And that was all.

A wise man, Alex took forgiveness when it was offered and passed on to the rest of his story. When he'd finished, she sat down on the edge of the bed. He watched her clasp her hands in her lap like a prim and proper lady, and wanted to make love to her all over again.

Suddenly she looked up at him. "I know what you're thinking," she said.

"Didn't you always?"

"Well, now, I *feel* what you're thinking."

"It's the Blood-Hunger," he said, unable to give her anything but the truth. "Mine calling to yours, yours to mine."

"Is that all it is?"

"Do you need to ask?"

"Apparently."

He clenched his hands into fists. Man and revenant, revenant and man, and both wanted her more than life itself. He could feel the Blood-Hunger surge in a great soaring loop between them, and see the fear it brought to her eyes.

With a sigh, he damped the sweeping tide of emotion. "Blood-Hunger is a terrifying thing," he said. "But you'll get used to it in time."

"Will it always be like this?"

"Always. The trick is in learning to control it, instead of letting it control you."

She wrapped her arms around herself. "I feel as though I've been trapped in a nightmare, and I'm never going to wake up."

"Yes," he said. "I know."

"I suppose you do."

She rose from the bed in a swift, fluid movement and walked to the window. Her feet made no sound on the bare oak floor. Nor did her face reflect in the dark glass. Alex saw her knuckles whiten as she pulled the curtains closed again.

"This . . . situation is a continuance of the night I died, isn't it?" she asked, head bowed.

"Yes."

"What does Lydia want?"

"Ah, the sixty-four-thousand-dollar question. What would you want, if you were in her place?"

She turned to face him. "To live again," she said.

"Yes, indeed."

"How?"

"I wish I knew. But she's been taking lives this way and that, as though experimenting. And that's what frightens me the most; for all his ferocity, Suldris did less damage simply because he knew what he was doing."

"So Lydia's undisciplined and"—Elizabeth shot him a glance—"completely amoral."

"Yes," he said.

"I can feel her, just a little." She closed her eyes.

"There's a link between us, faint but very dark."

"Suldris made you both."

"It's ugly."

This, too, was something he'd forgotten. He reached deep inside himself, searching for the traces of Darija, who'd made him revenant so many centuries ago. Finding it at last, he touched it and found it still raw. Yes, it was ugly.

"I should have been the one to wake you," he said. "It was my right. If I had known—"

"Alex." Elizabeth raised her head, her nostrils flaring. "Someone just came in the house. A woman. Is that your psychic?"

He shifted focus, registering the new presence. "Yes," he said, shuttering himself and Elizabeth against Francine's probing mind.

"I can feel her," Liz said. "Her mind glows."

"That's a glow that can burn you," he said. "She's helping Lieutenant Rhudwyn investigate the recent murders. I can't stress just how dangerous she is; she knew what I was the moment she set eyes on me. And she knows about you."

"But you like her."

He nodded. "She likes me, too. But that doesn't mean she won't betray me if she thinks it's the right thing to do. To save the world, you know."

"As you were prepared to destroy me?"

"Touché."

"I can't wait to meet her. Just let me get some shoes on—"

"You can't. She'll tell Rhudwyn, and he'll be out here asking questions for which there are no answers."

"Do you expect me to live in a cave?"

"Be reasonable, Liz. What are you going to tell him when he asks you what happened the night your parents died? What are you going to tell him when he asks where you've been all this time?"

She met his gaze levelly. "You'll just have to trust me."

"To be as good a liar as I am?"

"I didn't say that."

He smiled. "But you thought it, didn't you?"

"I'm sure you have to weave one very tangled web just to survive in human society."

"Oh, no," he said. "You only lie about the really big things, like who you are and what you do. When you outlive that identity, you move and begin the process all over again. The only things you need are a good imagination and a lot of money."

"You, however, keep cropping up as Alex Danilov."

"It's an old family name."

"Well?"

He bowed, accepting both her judgment and the inevitable. "Lie well, then. This will be a crash course in survival."

"So what's new?" She bent to slip Sonya's sandals on her feet, then stood up and smoothed her skirt. After a moment's hesitation she slipped the medallion on over her head. Gently she touched the chain. "It's lovely. It seems quite old."

"I keep a few things, selected more for memories than value. Reminders of lives lived."

"Which life was this?"

"Renaissance Italy."

"And the woman?"

"Gianetta Torannetto. Her father served the great Lorenzo himself."

Elizabeth ran her fingertips along the chain, as though feeling for an echo of Gianetta, then dropped her hand to her side. "How do I look?"

"Like a beautiful woman."

"I don't feel like a woman."

"Liz Garry is still there, inside you. She won't leave unless you let her go."

He offered her his arm. She placed her hand on his forearm, that curiously archaic gesture of hers that had so struck him before. His heart ached with the desire to hold her. But this was not the time; she needed to find herself before she could let him love her again.

He led her toward the stairway. Their shadows slithered down the steps ahead of them as they went down, then vanished beneath the foyer light.

"I hope that's not an omen," Liz murmured.

"There are no omens. Only bad luck."

"No good luck?"

"I'm a pessimist by nature," he said. "Be careful now, Liz. Justin can be trusted, Sonya cannot. She's been controlled once by Lydia, and will remain vulnerable to her. And no matter how much you like Francine, remember that she'll betray you if she feels it's necessary. Martin Rhudwyn is a bulldog; once he gets his teeth in something, he never lets go. And I don't want that something to be you."

"Was that what they call a Freudian slip?"

He blinked. "At least you haven't lost your sense of humor."

"I'm not smiling, Alex."

He wanted to say more, but the time had passed for explanation or warnings. It was up to her now.

They walked into the living room. Alex absorbed the scene in one encompassing glance: Justin playing solitaire at the desk, snapping the cards with crisp motions that betrayed his agitation. Francine and Sonya sat together on the sofa, the former serene, the latter pale and drawn.

"Hello, everyone," Alex said.

Justin looked up, his gaze inquiring. Alex shook his head slightly and turned to introduce Elizabeth to the women.

"Elizabeth Garry?" Sonya's astonishment was obvious. "But I thought—"

"You thought I was dead." Liz smiled. "I suppose I was, in a way. You see, I woke up in an Atlanta alley a few days ago, feeling as though half my life had been taken from me. I have no idea how I got there or what I'd been doing."

Excellent, Alex thought. And perhaps the only way to explain the incredible. Martin wouldn't believe it for a moment; but neither could he prove her wrong. If Elizabeth had the guts to brazen it out, she'd be all right.

"She called me last night," he said. "And I drove to Atlanta to fetch her back."

Francine met his gaze with a basilisk stare, then turned to Sonya. "You look tired, dear. Wouldn't you like to lie down?"

"Yes . . . I suppose so." She rose to her feet. Silently, like a pale spirit, she left the room.

"She's very suggestible just now," Francine said. "I've never experienced anything quite like this; her psyche has been brutally controlled, and I got the impression someone tried to literally tear her mind away from her body."

Justin pushed away from the desk. "She doesn't remember anything from the time she got here. I hated her. I *told* her I hated her." He smacked his right fist into his left hand. "Damn Lydia!"

"She doesn't remember what you told her," Francine said. She got to her feet and walked slowly around Alex and Elizabeth. "Martin will never buy that story, you know."

"He doesn't have to," Alex said.

The psychic stopped in front of Liz. There was something fey in those vivid green eyes tonight, something dangerous. Alex smelled bourbon on her breath, and knew the clamor in her mind must be riding high.

"I can *see* you," she said. "You can't hide like Alex does, not when we're this close."

"So, look," Liz replied, serene and reckless.

Alex made a gesture of protest. Both women ignored him, their gazes locked in a silent communication from which he was barred. Finally Francine took a step backward.

"I wish I could help you," she said.

Elizabeth smiled. "No one can help me. As Alex says, I just have to learn to live with it."

For a moment Francine looked very old. Then she sighed, and became merely a plump, middle-aged woman again. "Martin Rhudwyn is looking for me, Alex. And he's looking for you."

"Why?"

"They dumped eight new murders in his lap today."

"Eight?" Alex repeated. "Did they all die today?"

She nodded. "And they all died like the priest."

Letting his breath out in a sharp sigh, he turned away and went to look out the window. Outside, the mist swirled like a live thing, obscuring his view of the marsh.

"What does it mean, Alex?" Justin demanded.

"Lydia's got two objectives, two methods of killing to reach those objectives. One is to seduce the man before killing him, taking his vitality to rebuild her beauty—"

"Vanity, thy name is woman," Francine murmured.

". . . And if she kills them ah, ritualistically, then she's looking for power."

"What does she need power for?"

Alex spread his hands. "Nothing good."

"God, I need a drink." Francine went to the sideboard and started searching through the liquor.

"Bourbon's third from left," Justin said.

She poured a stiff one, took a long drink. "Thanks."

"Wait a minute," Elizabeth said. "If she can get power from her own killings, what did she need *me* for?"

"Perhaps to learn from."

"Dear God in heaven!" The note of hysteria had come back into her voice, and Alex strode to her. "All those lives . . . all the pain and suffering, just for that?"

"Apparently," he said, "she learned very well."

The sound of breaking glass brought them all around to stare at Francine. The psychic's eyes glittered like green glass in a face gone the color of putty.

"Don't you see?" she whispered.

Justin made a sharp gesture of impatience. "See what?"

"The darkness. It's her. She's very strong now, and gathering more strength all the time. You're in danger. All of you are in danger."

All of you. An ice-water flood of dread rushed through Alex's veins. He knew, as surely as if it had been written in fire on his brain: to live again. A new life. A *new* life. "Justin, where's Kelli?"

"She went to visit her parents—" He leapt for the phone. A moment later he glanced up, his face grim. "There's no answer."

"Take the others in the car with you," Alex said. "I'll go on alone."

"Be waiting at the door or get left behind," Justin said, taking off at a run.

"Alex—" Elizabeth began.

"You don't have this skill yet, and I don't have time to teach you."

"Don't go alone!" she cried. "Alex!"

He slung the window open, not caring that he broke glass when he did. A moment later he was winging his way toward Delano.

22

Alex's nostrils flared in disgust at the reek of Lydia's power. It twisted the quiet, unassuming air of the Hamlen house, twisting the family home into a black, stinking den of evil.

The door had been closed, but not latched. He pushed it open. The stench rolled out the opening, too sweet, almost overpowering. Ignoring the instincts that shrieked against it, he stepped inside.

He found Susan Hamlen in the living room, her body sprawled like a broken doll's. Her neck had been broken. An easy death, compared with that of Lydia's other victims. The zombie must be seething with power, so much so that she hadn't needed Susan's life to feed it.

He closed the woman's wide-open eyes, anger coiling hot in his chest. She'd been cast aside with utter carelessness, like a piece of paper crumpled and discarded. Such casual taking of life . . . He drew his breath in sharply. He, who'd taken many lives for many reasons, had never been casual about it.

"I'm sorry," he said.

His revenant senses caught a trace of live human scent. He followed it into the kitchen, where he found Philip

Hamlen on the floor, blood seeping from his shattered lower face. Shockingly the man's eyes were open and aware.

"Philip!" Alex went down on his knees beside him, wanting to help but knowing the injuries were far beyond his skills.

The man's mouth moved, a shifting of flesh and ruined teeth. "Ssssee . . . took . . . Kkkk . . . Kkkel . . ."

"Kelli? Did she say where?"

"No . . ." A gasp, a trickling of blood, as Hamlen forced the words out. "My . . . girl . . . help."

"Let's get you an ambulance." Alex laid his hand on the man's shoulder for a moment, then got to his feet and called 911.

Ignoring the dispatcher's request for his name, he gave the Hamlens' address and then hung up. Philip Hamlen grunted imperatively, and Alex returned to his side.

"Help is on the way," he soothed. "Take it easy."

Then he stiffened, realizing that Hamlen's eyes burned not with pain, but with a terrible rage. And he wanted something. A feeling of inevitability settled on Alex's shoulders as he leaned close.

"Yes, Philip?"

"Ssssee . . . sssiled."

She smiled. Alex clenched his fists. "I understand. I'll find her. You have my word."

Ah, rashness! The cynical revenant voice dripped ice water into his mind. But the gratitude in Philip Hamlen's eyes made it worthwhile.

Tires squealed outside, heralding the others' arrival. A moment later Justin plunged into the room. His breath came in short, sharp rasps.

"I saw . . . Mr. Hamlen," he said, bending over the injured man. "Oh, God, I'm sorry." He glanced up at Alex, his face congealing like fast-setting concrete. "Did you find Kelli?"

"No. Lydia took her."

"Where?"

"I don't know." *She smiled.* Alex locked gazes with Hamlen again, reaffirming the promise. Hearing sirens in the distance, he rose to his feet. "Let's get out of here before we spend the rest of the night answering questions at the police station."

Hamlen's eyes said, go, go, go. The wail of the sirens grew louder, closer.

Alex turned, found Elizabeth standing in the doorway. Her face had gone pale, and her hand trembled as she braced herself against the doorjamb. He had no time to comfort her; taking her by the arm, he spun her around and marched her toward the front of the house. Justin followed close behind, his impatience almost seeming to push them faster.

"Where's Francine?" Alex asked.

Liz's chignon had come loose; she pushed her hair away from her face with her free hand. "She couldn't come in. *I* almost couldn't come in. God, Alex, how could Lydia have come to this?"

"By wanting more than anyone should have," he said.

They reached fresh air at last. Alex took a deep breath, clearing the miasma of evil from his lungs. Suddenly he became aware of the sound of retching nearby. He followed it, and found Francine on hands and knees in the driveway, quietly vomiting onto the concrete.

"It's like swimming in a cesspool," she moaned.

Alex plucked her off the ground and carried her toward the car. "It's going to get worse, Francine."

"I don't want to do this."

He bared his teeth in an almost smile. "But you will. Don't you wonder why you were compelled to visit the Danilovs tonight? You've become entwined in our destiny, and the game must be played out to the end."

"I need a drink," she said.

Justin had already started the car. Alex slid the woman into the backseat beside Elizabeth, then climbed into the passenger seat.

"Go back to the Arbor," he said.

Justin's hands tightened on the wheel. "That's the one place we know she *didn't* take Kelli."

"Move."

His head snapped back as Justin slammed the accelerator to the floor.

"I'm moving," Justin snarled. "Now talk. I want to get to Kelli before that . . . nut hurts her."

Elizabeth reached over the back of the seat and laid her hand on Alex's shoulder. He clasped her fingers, feeling the surge of emotion within her. She'd guessed, then.

"Kelli is quite safe," he said.

"Safe! Lydia's been killing people right and left, including Kelli's mother and maybe her father. Now she's taken Kelli somewhere to do God knows what to her, and you're telling me she's safe? You've got to be . . . Shit!" The car slewed dangerously as his hands clenched spasmodically on the wheel. "Oh, God," he said. "Oh, God."

"Look out!" Francine shrieked as the BMW strayed over the yellow line, straight toward the lofty headlights of an oncoming truck.

With a curse, Justin wrenched the wheel, pulling them out of danger just in time. The blare of the truck's horn followed them down the road.

Francine's breathing seemed abnormally loud. "Okay, now that we're going to live, I'd appreciate hearing this fact that everyone but me seems to know."

"Lydia doesn't want Kelli," Alex said, turning to look at the psychic. "She wants the child."

"That's crazy! What does she want with a two-month-old fetus?"

Elizabeth's eyes were stark and beautiful. "She wants to live again."

"It took me a while to figure out," Alex said. "Kelli never had an affinity to crystals, even when exposed to her girlfriends' stones. What factor had changed when she came to the Arbor? She'd become pregnant. And you told us yourself that Lydia had tried to rip Sonya's psyche away. Why? Because she's trapped in a body that will fall apart around her, and she needs a new one."

"But the child?" The psychic groped for the door handle, latching onto it as though it was her only anchor in a world gone mad.

"She tried for Sonya, and failed. The baby is a much easier target." Alex slammed his fist into the back of the seat. "Damn her! The child's psyche is still fragile, and because of its affinity for crystals, wide-open. And Lydia's got all the power she needs."

"The eight killings," Francine whispered.

"She didn't bother with the Hamlens," Justin said. "She just threw them away."

Alex looked at him. His face had the dark predatory beauty of a hawk, and nothing youthful or soft remained in those sharp features.

"There's still time, Justin." Elizabeth said. "There has to be."

"We don't even know where they went."

"But we have a compass," Alex said. "If we can find a way to use it."

The young man glanced at him, a flash of seething black eyes. "The crystal."

"Yes."

"I threw it into the marsh."

"So we'll get it back."

"Do you think it will work?" Liz asked.

Alex spread his hands. "Lydia wears its heart around her neck. It cries to be whole again."

"If she could reach Kelli—the baby—through the crystal, then maybe we can make the thing work the other way," Justin said.

"I don't like crystals." Francine's voice was too loud.

Understanding bloomed in Alex's mind. He turned to look at her, noting that she still gripped the door handle. "But you hear them, don't you, Francine?"

She seemed to fold in on herself, growing smaller and older right before his eyes. "You're going to make me do this, aren't you?"

"I have no choice."

"And I don't have the guts for this."

Alex nodded. "A human soul is at stake. Not a personality, not a fetus, not a collection of cells, but a soul. Can you walk away and still live with yourself?"

"This is . . ." She drew a deep breath, let it out again in a shaky sigh. "I've helped out in crime scenes, I've walked into a murderer's mind and tasted all the things people do to one another. But they've been *human* things."

"Destiny, too, is a human thing."

"Damn destiny," she said. "I need a drink."

Justin stopped the car at the mainland side of the causeway. Alex looked up, saw that fog had claimed the Isle of Palms. It swirled in a solid-looking wall just a few feet from the car's grille, occasional tendrils licking out as though to taste the intruders. Old power permeated the air, lay on the tongue like thick syrup.

"Do you feel that?" Justin asked.

Alex nodded. How could he not? Blood-Hunger speared through his body, clenched iron fingers in his brain, as though responding to the ancient power Wildwood had cast over the land.

"What is it?" Elizabeth asked, her eyes dark with need and pain—the stinging lash of Blood-Hunger.

"I think Wildwood has its own agenda tonight," Alex said. "And one that may not be compatible with ours. Go on, Justin. You're the only person who might be able to find a way through this stuff."

The planes of the young man's face sharpened. He eased the car onto the causeway, moving slowly and steadily into the shroud of white.

"What's Wildwood?" Francine asked.

Alex turned to look at her. "Wildwood Marsh. A man's name for something much older than mankind. Do you feel that tingling in the air, that feeling along your skin that tells you something huge and powerful is watching you?"

"Yes." The psychic spoke with obvious reluctance; her eyes showed the fear that the admission would cost her more than she wanted to give.

"Wildwood is very old," he said with more gentleness than he expected. "It remembers the time when the earth ruled and man lived on sufferance upon her back. Then came a new power—the god named technology—that gave mankind the power to remake the world. The earth forgot what she once was, except for a few places like Wildwood. *They* remember. They're rare and precious— and very frightening when they begin to stir."

Francine closed her eyes. "It feels as though everything's coming apart. Like a piece of fabric unraveling and being rewoven into a different pattern."

"Perhaps it is," he said. "Lydia has upset the balance."

"And you don't?"

He spread his hands. "The revenant holds unique powers. But these merely exist, functions of the being. A sort of natural order, albeit not a human one. You yourself possess abilities beyond that of most men; do you use them to make the world conform to your needs?"

"I wouldn't know how. If I did . . . I'm not sure I wouldn't at least try." She took a deep breath, and pain lay heavily in her eyes. "The world presses too closely. There are times when I'd do a lot to silence it."

A rapid-fire tattoo of bumps brought Alex swinging around. He realized that Justin could no longer see, and had chosen to navigate by keeping the car's right tires on the reflectors that lined the road. Another bump signaled the change from causeway to land.

The trunks of the tall palms could be dimly seen on either side of the street. Their tops looked like plumed specters in the mist. Justin turned the car onto the Arbor's drive. Out of the corner of his eye, Alex watched Francine flinch away from the crunch of oyster shell beneath the wheels. He'd have to watch her carefully; she, more than any of them, was vulnerable to the power being wielded tonight.

The fog seemed thinner here, as though Wildwood had tried to put a barrier between the Isle of Palms and the rest of the world. Not a comforting thought. As Justin made the turn that would bring them onto the sweep of drive that passed the front of the house, something dark and solid appeared out of the mist in front of them.

"Whoa!" Justin cried, slamming the brakes hard.

Shells sprayed out from under the wheels as the car rocked to a stop. The grille halted not a foot away from that shadowy figure. Alex didn't need to see its face to know its identity.

He sighed. "It's Martin Rhudwyn."

"Cripes," Justin snarled, slamming the car into park. "Not now!"

"That's the homicide detective?" Elizabeth asked.

"The very one. And with the fog like this, we can't very well just kick him off the property."

"I should've run him over when I had the chance," Justin muttered.

Alex's smile felt almost genuine as he swung his door open. "Elizabeth, my sweet, I suggest you slip out that door while I let the lieutenant in this one." He raised his voice. "Get in the car, Martin!"

He heard the rear door click open as he slid over to give the lieutenant room. Rhudwyn almost fell into the seat, his breath coming in harsh pants. "Thanks. Can't see a damned thing out there. That fog closed in so fast I didn't know what hit me." Propping his elbow on the back of the seat, he half turned to look at Francine. "What're you doing out here?"

This is the time, if she's going to betray Elizabeth.

"I'm visiting, Lieutenant," the psychic said.

Alex let his breath out, surprised because he hadn't realized he'd been holding it. "And you, Martin? What brings you all the way out here on a lousy night like this?"

"It's a lousy night all over. Someone made a call to 911 from Delano a little while ago. The paramedics found a man semiconscious, in shock from a broken nose, cheekbone, and jaw. And his wife dead of a broken neck."

Justin's breath went in with a sharp hiss. Alex put his hand on the young man's shoulder and squeezed with enough pressure to keep him quiet.

"Delano is a little out of your jurisdiction, isn't it?" he asked.

"I happened to hear the dispatch on my radio. The name Hamlen rang a bell, so I came here to talk to you."

Justin slammed out of the car. The fog swallowed him up within just a few yards, and Alex felt the stirrings of unease.

"Where's he going?" Martin asked.

"Kelli's out with some friends. I expect he's going to try to track her down and tell her the news." Alex slid behind the wheel and slid the car back into gear. "You keep very good track of the Danilovs and those involved with us, Martin."

"Since so many of them seem to die violently, it's only natural."

"Sorry, but I've got an alibi." Alex parked in front of the house and turned the ignition off.

"Yeah, I know. Two witnesses. Is that right, Mrs. Dey?"

"Absolutely, Lieutenant. He's been with me all evening."

Alex tried to locate Justin, but so much power floated out there that he couldn't sense anything more than a few feet away. He swung his door open.

"Hey, I'm not through talking to you," Rhudwyn protested.

"I've got things to do," he said without turning around. "Francine, take him inside."

She laughed, but there was no humor in her voice. "Whatever you command, Sahib. Come on, Lieutenant; the bar's open."

Alex walked away. Wildwood hung in the air, its fecund, primitive scent overpowering even that of the nearby rosebushes. An owl hooted sharply in the distance.

"Justin," he called.

The fog seemed to absorb his voice, slowing it, letting it drop too soon. Spanish moss dragged chill fingers across his face; startled, he tore it off and flung it away.

"Justin," he called again.

Again, the sound died in the mist. Alex strode onward, fear beating a cold tattoo in his brain. Blinded by fog, his revenant senses unable to pierce the shield of ancient power, he still knew. God help him, he knew: Justin had gone into the marsh. Wildwood's chosen, going where no one else could have gone.

But even the chosen couldn't know the motives of an entity older than time. Or whether it would let him walk out again.

23

Silence. Thick, impenetrable, smothering. Alex pushed his way through it to the edge of the marsh.

"Justin!" he called, knowing it was futile.

He stripped off his shoes and socks and waded into the water. His feet sank into the mud below, a warm but unwelcoming touch. Wildwood didn't want him here. The mist swirled into his face, clutched at his shirt with grasping white fingers that seemed to have more substance than they should have. Oh, yes, the balance had been shifted.

Damn you, Lydia! Suldris would have had more sense.

Slowly he made his way forward. The water rose to his calves, his knees, inched up his thighs, deeper than it should be here. Glancing behind him, he saw that the traces of his passage disappeared too soon, as though a great hand smoothed the surface in his wake. Small things swirled around his legs: tadpoles, or perhaps fledgling fish. He passed through them, his skin twitching at their fluttering touch.

He could sense the crystal now. It cried its pain to the marsh, and Wildwood accepted it, absorbed it as it did everything else. The voice had spread through the substance of the marsh itself; Alex could feel it in the mud, in the water, a note of agony that scraped like sandpaper across his soul.

The mud thickened around his ankles, holding him back. He slogged through it, pulled by the fear that Justin would be lost if he didn't. One step at a time. Panting. Struggling, his thousand-year-old revenant's strength nothing against the power of the marsh. The crystal's voice coalesced, grew stronger and more tormented.

Alex pushed through chest-high water, knowing it was deeper than it should be, but also knowing the depth would be whatever Wildwood needed. A current, much too fast for any natural marsh, threatened to pull his legs out from under him. He braced himself against it, felt his strength streaming out like oil upon the water. Then realization hit, and he smiled.

"I'm too close, aren't I?" he murmured.

He arced forward in a smooth dive. The water closed over his head with a sense of finality. The crystal's voice was louder now, more vibration than actual song. Alex stroked toward it. Reeds waved a frantic dance before his hands, half-seen in the murky water.

He could feel Blood-Hunger coursing through his body, echoing the movement of the water along his skin. It responded to the old power that was Wildwood, driving spikes of pain into his being. For a moment it stopped him, pulled his limbs into a fetal curl, and sent him drifting down toward the muck.

The Alex of a week ago would have fought against it. Now, however, he knew better. Elizabeth the revenant had taught him to accept Blood-Hunger as a necessary part of his existence; Elizabeth the woman had given him faith enough to use it.

He shrugged off the paralysis and opened himself to the darkest aspect of his revenant nature. Darker, in fact, than Wildwood; there was nothing of innocence in Blood-Hunger, only need. He pulled it deep, deep into his center, then took that massive coil of revenant power and thrust it outward.

The current stuttered and slowed. Faintly, oh, so faintly, he heard the sound of a human heartbeat.

"You can't have him, old friend," he called into the mist. "He has work to do."

The fog swirled, eddies of white that seemed light-years thick. If he looked long enough, he could almost imagine faces in it, faces and shapes and grasping hands. . . . He tore his gaze away. Here, even fantasy could be dangerous, old power working to make the imagined real.

He pushed onward. The heart sound grew louder, nearer. Alex plunged both arms into the muck just below. His hands traced something hard and round. And human; he could feel the skull beneath the flesh and the slide of wet hair. He grasped, pulled. Justin came up, but slowly, as though the mud was trying to hold him back. Alex broached the surface, gasping, his left hand still gripping the young man's hair.

"You . . . can't . . . have . . . him!" he panted.

He got his feet under him somehow, shifting his hands beneath Justin's arms. But it gave him no purchase; every time he gained an inch with Justin, the movement drove his own feet deeper into the muck. Jagged red patches of exertion swam across his vision. Revenant power buoyed him, but not enough. He'd sunk nearly to his knees now; the water lapped at his chin, sometimes slapped at his mouth and nose.

Something caught him around the waist. "Have you got him?" Elizabeth asked, her breath fanning his ear like salvation.

"Yes."

He caught a mouthful of water, coughed it back out. Liz's arm tightened around him. Her Blood-Hunger touched his, sank deep in a blending of power that for the moment, at least, held even Wildwood at bay. Alex shook wet hair out of his eyes as his feet came up out of the mud inch by inch. Justin, too. He slid one arm around the young man's chest, freeing the other to work with Elizabeth.

"Go," he said. "And watch your footing. If we go under, I'm not sure we'll make it back out."

She pulled, he pulled. Strained with muscles and revenant power and sheer, human stubbornness. And then Justin came free, so suddenly that it sent them both floundering backward. Alex managed to keep his grip on the young man.

"Are you all right?" Liz asked, breast-stroking back to him. Her hair spread out over the water in a gold-shot fan, a memory of sun that defied the marsh's touch.

"Let's get out of here."

"You take one arm, I'll take the other. We'll tow him."

They started toward shore, swimming to keep from putting their feet into the mud again. Justin lolled between them, looking, with his coating of muck and algae and water plants, like something that had come from the dawn of time. The beat of his heart was faint and slow, his breathing imperceptible. Alex stroked through the dark, sullen water, unable even to see Liz in the smothering blanket of fog.

"How did you find me?" he asked.

"I just . . ." She paused to spit water out of her mouth. "I just followed my most regrettable tendencies, and there you were."

"Well, thanks. I'm surprised you made it that far in; I had to fight for every inch."

"*Fight* is the operative word. You always fight, Alex. Straight on and damn the torpedoes. So, while Wildwood was occupied with you, I sort of . . . made myself small and insignificant, and slipped right in."

"I should learn that trick."

"It's not your nature," she said. "And it's getting too shallow to swim."

Alex put one foot down and realized they'd reached the firmer ground near the shore. He stood up, reached down to lift Justin clear of the water. Wildwood gave him up with a little sucking sound, reluctant but without rancor. It knew it would claim him eventually; after all, it had all the time in the world.

Alex carried him toward dry land, moving through the mist more by instinct than by sight. "Liz?" he called.

"Here." She stepped out of the mist beside him. Water streamed from her hair and clothing, ran in rivulets down her pale skin. "Put him down, Alex. Let's take a look at him."

He obeyed. Justin's arms and legs flopped bonelessly. She tilted his head back, pinched his nose closed, and started mouth-to-mouth resuscitation. After a few moments he sucked for air on his own, then coughed up a gout of dark water.

His eyes opened. Wildwood swam in their depths, knowledge beyond what man had learned—or ever would. Panic clenched icy fingers in Alex's guts. Had he rescued Justin's body, only to leave the most important part behind?

"Justin!" Alex hissed.

The young man blinked, and his eyes became human again. He looked around, his face confused and frightened, then focused on Alex. "Am I alive?"

Alex exhaled, a long sigh. "By the hair on your chinny-chin-chin. What possessed you to walk out there like that?"

"Oh, man." Justin took several breaths, perhaps just seeing if he still could. "I don't know how it happened. The water got deeper and deeper, and I just . . . walked under it. It didn't hurt. I kind of went to sleep, although I was still aware of things. It was strange. Confusing; everything was spread out and muddled, as though I was seeing and hearing everything at once. I even felt you pulling at me, but I didn't want to go bad enough to help."

Fear tightened Alex's throat; for just a short time Justin had *been* Wildwood. "I wouldn't go walking out there again, if I were you."

"Hey, tell me about it. But at least I got this," Justin said, pulling something out from beneath his T-shirt.

The crystal. Alex took it from him, gently wiping mud from its smooth sides. It glimmered back at him, singing its song of pain into the back of his mind.

"A good job," he said. "A very good job. Now let's collect Francine and see if we can locate Kelli."

"What're we going to do with the lieutenant? Even if we could think of a way to convince him to leave, there's no way he could drive in this fog."

Alex hauled the young man to his feet and steadied him until he regained his balance. "I'll think of something."

"Famous last words," Elizabeth said.

Lydia held the candle in front of her eyes, watching the flame leap and dance, then tilted it so that the melted wax ran out onto the floor beside the mattress.

"Please," the girl said. "Don't hurt me. I'm going to have a baby—"

"I'm not going to hurt you." Lydia pressed the base of the candle into the swiftly hardening puddle of wax.

From the look in the girl's brown eyes, she didn't believe it. She wanted to, but couldn't. Lydia smiled. Lighting another candle, she placed it about a foot beside the other, completing a circle around the mattress. The girl . . . what was her name? Oh, yes, Kelli . . . shifted to watch her. Her eyes reflected the flames, and the knowledge that the completed circle meant that something was about to happen.

Oh, yes.

"Are you afraid, Kelli?"

"Why are you doing this to me?" Fear made her voice rise unnaturally high.

"It's got nothing to do with you," Lydia said. "You just happened to be in the wrong place at the wrong time. And to have gotten pregnant by the wrong man."

"What do you mean?"

"My name is Lydia Danilov."

Kelli gasped. "But I thought you were dead!"

"I am." The room seemed to darken and press closer. "But I want to live again. A new life, Kelli."

"You're . . . going to take my body."

Lydia laughed. The sound bounced around the room, tasting more of malice than humor. "Not yours."

Horror widened the girl's eyes as she realized the implications. "No! I'll . . . abort you."

"You won't remember a thing about tonight. You'll be a good little mother, and you'll take good care of your little girl."

The girl began twisting her bound wrists. Savagely, determinedly. Blood dotted the cord and dripped on the mattress. Lydia watched for a while, then leaned over and caught a crimson drop.

"It won't do any good," she said, raising her finger to her mouth. The blood tasted sweet and metallic; the essence of life, her salvation.

"Let me go," Kelli panted. "Let . . . me . . . go!"

Lydia stepped back to admire her handiwork. Not bad. Of course, the dingy mattress made a poor altar, the abandoned warehouse an even poorer sanctuary, but it would do.

"Time to go to sleep now," she said. Grasping the ghost crystal, she sent the girl into unconsciousness.

Almost ready. She retrieved the crossbow she'd obtained this morning, rolling it over and over in her hands. The collector had been very proud of it; he'd died before giving it up. She shivered, remembering how the bolts had driven into the target with solid, meaty thunks. Imagining how it would be like to hear one slam into Alex's chest . . . She'd replaced the metal bolts with wooden ones, of course.

She stepped into the circle of candles and set the crossbow on the floor at her feet. Gripping the crystal, she tapped the black well of its power. *Now.* She called to the small, fragile consciousness that lay deep in Kelli's belly. Touched it. It fled from her, darting this way and that, crying out in fear and pain. She chased it down, dug invisible, powerful claws into it. With surprising strength, it wrenched free.

She needed more power. Recklessly, she tore strength straight from the stone's dark heart. Sullen light pulsed in it, forming an apex within the circle of candle flames. Her mind seemed to split, giving her a view both of the outer world and the inner. She watched the flesh shrink from her hands and arms, the skin shrivel, the bones knot and bend as she tapped the full stretch of her power. And she saw her quarry, a tiny, bright spark, fleeing ahead of her like a frightened rabbit.

I'm the wolf at the door, little one. And I'm going to eat you.

A dank wind sprang to life. It plucked at Lydia's hair, then went skittering around the room. Pieces of paper whirled into the air, and glass crashed as the wind upset the table at the far end of the room. The candles guttered. Sweat broke out on her upper lip as she strove to hold them. After a moment the flames steadied.

The darkness pressed close against the edges of light. Eager. Hungry. Half-seen shapes prowled the blackness, a flash of claws here, the red glow of an eye there. Fear nibbled at her mind; she'd gone mostly on instinct here, augmenting it with memories of Suldris's ceremonies and what little knowledge she'd learned along the way. For the first time she realized what she'd called into being here, and the price of failure.

"I won't fail," she said.

Closing her eyes, she reached for the child again.

Cloaked in revenant power, Alex stood in the doorway and watched Rhudwyn and Francine Dey. They sat facing each other, but their closed faces and crossed arms showed that their conversation hadn't been exactly amicable. The room reeked of emotion—the detective's frustration, the psychic's fear. They mixed and soured.

"You better take it easy on that," Rhudwyn said, pointing to the glass in the woman's hand. "That's your third in fifteen minutes. You're going to be flat on your back if you don't slow down."

She smiled, then raised the glass and took a long drink. Defiantly. Rhudwyn stared at her for a moment, then raked his hand through his hair and looked away.

"Where'd they go?" he muttered.

Francine swirled her drink—sloppily, so that some sloshed out onto her hand. "Probably to hell."

"What's your problem tonight?"

"Maybe it's the full moon." Her voice had begun to slur. "Nope, that's werewolves. What is it vampires do?"

"Shit," Rhudwyn growled. Leaning his head against the back of his seat, he closed his eyes.

Perfect, Alex thought. He eased into the detective's mind. Gently, with a light touch that would neither alert the man nor leave obvious traces, he slowed the brain's activity. Rhudwyn slipped painlessly over the edge into sleep.

Alex dropped the illusion that had hidden him. Francine's glass fell amid a spray of bourbon and ice cubes. She made no attempt to pick it up, merely stared at him as though death himself had come to claim her. He raised his finger to his lips, cautioning silence, then beckoned her.

She groped blindly for a moment, then braced her hands on the arms of the chair and pushed herself upright. The smell of bourbon rolled through the room. Alex stood, arm outstretched, until she reached him.

He ushered her into the hallway, closing the door softly behind him. "If you hadn't clouded your mind with bourbon," he said, "you wouldn't have been so surprised."

"If you'd stayed away another half hour, I wouldn't have had to feel anything at all."

"I expected more of you."

"So did I." She took a deep breath, let it out with a harsh sound. "What'd you do to the lieutenant?"

"Ah, merely suggested he take a nap."

"Can you do that anytime you want to?"

"Usually."

"Why didn't you do something to me?" she asked. "You know, to make me forget you existed."

He felt her shudder as he put his hand on her shoulder and turned her toward the back of the house. "That goes deeper than merely causing a snooze, and leaves a great deal of damage behind. Your gift is too precious to be lost—or dulled with liquor. Besides, I need you."

"Where are we going?" she asked, her voice unnaturally high.

Fear: his Blood-Hunger recognized it, beat in time to the hammering of her heart. "Outside, to the garden. The others are waiting for us."

The fog swirled close, grasping them the moment they stepped out of the house. It was eerie, like stepping off the edge of the world.

"Justin?" Alex called.

"Here."

The young man stepped out of the whiteness, followed a moment later by Elizabeth. Justin looked darkly human;

Liz, with her sun-colored eyes and pale, pale skin, like an angel come to earth.

Fallen angel.

She made his soul ache with need, with guilt, and with the knowledge that something beautiful and fragile had been shattered beyond repair. Once, he could have cherished her; now he could only hope to teach her to survive long enough to love him again.

And she held the big crystal in her cupped hands. It sang its song of pain into the shrouded night.

"Oh, God," Francine moaned.

"Whew." Justin waved at the bourbon-scented air. "She's loaded."

"Not enough," she retorted.

Alex didn't need sight to find the gazebo; he'd walked this way—either with his feet or his mind—every day for two hundred years. The building appeared ahead of them, seeming to hang like lace upon the fog. Francine was leaning on him heavily now, and he lifted her into his arms to get her up the stairs.

"Hold out your hands, Francine," he said, settling her in one of the chairs.

She put them behind her back. "I'd rather not."

"Lydia wants my kid's soul," Justin hissed, thrusting his face close to hers. *"Hold out your hands."*

The psychic looked deeply into his eyes. For a moment the alcohol haze vanished, leaving the sharp-edged, intelligent woman she'd been such a short time ago.

How great a difference a day makes, Alex thought. Twenty-four hours. And a taste of hell.

Squeezing her eyes shut, she slowly extended her hands. Tears leaked out from beneath her eyelids as Elizabeth dropped the big crystal into her palms.

Alex felt it happen to her, felt the swift spiral into the faceted, fractured depths. The crystal was no longer clear. Mist permeated it, Wildwood's essence caught in the very substance of the stone itself. Dread spiked his mind; Wildwood was the wild card, that which could not be understood or defeated. He didn't like its presence here.

I thought you couldn't do this yourself.

Francine's thought singed through his mind, caustic and hopeful at the same time.

Sorry, Francine. I've only come riding on your coattails.

I'll get you for this.

As long as you find Kelli first.

With a mental flounce, she left him behind. He tried to follow, but couldn't; his powers were revenant only. So he waited in the pain-haunted corridors of the crystal's empty heart, ready to pull her out if she got into trouble. Hoping, rather, to be able to pull her out.

Suddenly she came howling back, her fear and horror shrieking like a siren along the broken-rainbow corridors. Alex spun helplessly in the black wash of terror, then was left behind as she fled into herself and slammed all the doors and windows closed.

He opened his eyes. "Francine."

She remained unreadable. The tears fell freely from her closed eyes. They splashed down on the crystal and ran unheeded down its sides. Frustration burned in his chest, igniting his anger; there was so much at stake here, things that, if lost, could never be retrieved again.

"Francine!" he snapped. "What was it? What did you see?"

She shook her head. Her Adam's apple went up and down convulsively as she struggled to swallow. He grasped her by the arms, no longer gentle, and lifted her from the chair.

"Tell me!"

"Alex." Elizabeth put her hand on his shoulder. "You're frightening her. Let me talk to her."

With a sigh of frustration, he lowered the woman onto the chair. Then he spun away, seeking balance for his careening emotions.

Elizabeth knelt in front of the psychic, taking the woman's trembling hands in hers. "Take a deep breath, Francine. Yes, that's right. Now another. Calm yourself. You're safe now. No one can get to you, no one can hurt you."

Francine opened her eyes. Her pupils were enormous, endless black pools ringed with jade. Tears spiked her lashes all around. Loathing twisted her face, pulled the corners of her mouth upward in a snarl. "You *liar*! I feel it now. No one can stop it, not you, not him, not anybody! I'll never be able to forget it, never stop the pain."

Surprise plain on her face, Elizabeth stood up and backed away. "I—"

"The darkness, the tearing . . ." Francine's whisper seemed to cut the air between them, the agony stark and powerful. "It's calling out to me, begging. . . . I can't do it. I can't stand the pain, don't have the strength. . . ." Francine slid out of the chair onto her knees and pressed her face to the wood floor. "Oh, God! Somebody help me. Somebody help *her*!"

Realization sank red-hot pincers in Alex's mind.

It was happening, and it was happening *now*.

24

"Francine," Alex said.

She pressed her face harder against the floor.

"Francine," he repeated.

"No," she sobbed. "No more. I can't stand any more."

The violence left him. Bending, he lifted the psychic to her feet. She sagged between his hands, eyes closed, mind closed.

"I'm sorry," he said. "I had to make you do it."

He pulled her into his arms, folding her in the circle of his revenant power. Her terror beat at him like a trapped bird. He bore it, pulled it away from her and into himself, where it became lost in the darkness of a thousand years of fear.

"Come back. For the child's sake," he said. "For the sake of its immortal soul."

"What the hell do you know about souls?" she asked.

"Enough to fight for this one."

She opened her eyes, stared unblinking into his. He felt her reach deep. Searching. And finding a core of strength within her. Enough, perhaps, to see her through.

"What do you want from me?" she whispered.

"There's no time for us to get to Savannah by conventional means. But the crystal can be a doorway—to one who can touch it properly."

"I'm no crystal gazer. My talents lie elsewhere."

"Yes," he agreed. "But you seem to be able to sense death's touch, which is why you help out in homicides. And why it hurts you so much. At the other end of this"—he touched the stone, felt its wail in the flesh of his fingertips—"is death in the guise of Lydia Danilov. It doesn't want you or Justin or Liz, or even me. It wants the soul of a child, the one truly pure thing in this damned, fouled-up world."

She took a deep breath. Then she pushed away from him and gained her own feet. A little unsteadily, but she made it. Justin retrieved the crystal from the floor and held it out to her.

"I'm completely sober, you know." Her smile twisted. "That was a hell of a way to lose a nice, roaring high."

"Come *on*," Justin hissed.

Francine took the crystal from him. It looked like a chunk of captured mist, only its hardness setting it apart from the fog around them. "What do I do?"

"Reach for what frightens you the most," Alex said. "Touch it, embrace it, hold it close. It will pull you through. And I'll bring the others after you."

He could feel her fear. Reaching out, he took her hand in his. Her skin was cold, her grip firm. Then her eyes unfocused, and he knew she'd gone into the crystal.

The fog thickened, pressing close, running warm, damp tendrils along his skin. It felt like a caress, smelled like terror. The crystal began to pulse with light, and mist-shrouded broken rainbows darted along its smooth sides. The flesh of Francine's hands turned translucent, showing the solid lines of the bones beneath. Her eyes drifted closed. The glow spread, creeping up her arms to her shoulders, to her face.

"Justin, Elizabeth, come to me," Alex said.

Liz grasped his free hand; Justin grasped hers, completing the link. Power hummed along Alex's nerves. The fog nearest Francine began to rotate. It grew thicker and more substantial, fraught with a dark, rushing wind that plucked at their hair and clothes, passed chill fingers across their skin.

"I'd be scared to my soul if I had one," Elizabeth said.

Francine cried out. Alex did, too, as the wind snatched him up and sucked him toward the spot where the fog was thickest. He plunged into pain. Rainbow shards whirled around him, through him; the voice of the crystal, wailing as it reached out for its lost, dark heart.

He shifted his grip to the psychic's wrist. Liz clung to his left hand, her free arm circling Justin's waist. Suddenly, astonishingly, Alex sensed a third human presence. One that shouldn't have been there: Rhudwyn. Untethered, the detective began to flounder.

"Martin! Grab Justin's hand!" Alex shouted.

The wind tore the words from his mouth, ran tittering off with them. But Justin heard. He lunged at the other man, catching him by the collar and hauling him in.

"What the hell is going on?" Rhudwyn screamed.

Alex ignored him; there was no time for explanations, only survival. He and Liz were the only ones with the strength to hold the group together. If the revenants faltered for even a moment, they'd all be lost.

The wind beat at them, spun them like dry leaves as it tried to tear them apart. Crystal song surrounded them, sank pain into their flesh, their minds, their souls. Francine arched in Alex's arms, her eyes wild.

"I can't . . . hold it anymore," she shrieked.

He pulled her close. "You can. You have to."

"I can't! It hurts too much." Her chest fluttered with panting breaths. "She's too strong."

Suddenly Elizabeth reached around Alex and slapped

the psychic across the face. Shockingly. A measure of sanity came into Francine's eyes.

"You can do it," Liz said. "We're almost there; feel her black heart!"

It was true; Alex could feel the malice all around them, almost hear Lydia's sweet, vicious laugh upon the wind. Francine nodded. She lifted her chin, her green eyes looking like backlit glass as she fell toward the wind's source. Like rags on a kite's tail, the rest of them went with her.

The fog shattered. Alex lost his hold on Elizabeth as he rolled onto a hard wooden floor with enough force to rattle his teeth. Francine landed on top of him, driving the breath from his lungs.

"Liz!" he gasped, sucking for air. "Justin! Martin!"

"They're not here." The psychic clutched his shirtfront. "Alex, I'm scared."

He disengaged her hands and stood up. They'd been dumped into a big, musty-smelling room that seemed overfull of shadows. Evil filled the place, suffocating and rank, creeping into the nose and laying the taint of corruption on the skin. Candles burned in a circle around a mattress, and upon the mattress . . .

"Kelli," he said.

But he didn't move toward her, for something shared that circle of light with Kelli, something that had once been Lydia Danilov. The hair was the same; lovely, shining tresses as bright as flame. But the face beneath it had fallen in on itself, wrinkles layered upon wrinkles, wattles of spotted flesh hanging from its pointed jaw, spreading patches of rot oozing in from the scalp. She raised her hand, and he saw the pale flash of bone where her fingers should have been.

"Hello, Alex."

The voice was the same; low, beautiful, mocking. His Blood-Hunger responded even through his horror.

"It's been a long time, lover," she said.

"Oh, God," Francine moaned, grabbing at Alex's shirt again. "What is that?"

He shook her off, less gently this time. "What have you done, Lydia?"

"Your friends didn't make it," she said. "And that old woman isn't going to help you."

"Then I'll deal with you alone."

"Better get started, then." She grasped the dark stone she wore, and for a moment a small tornado whirled through the room. It sucked the candle flames into oblivion. Then it disappeared, and the room's dimness became mere shadows again.

But the evil remained; it centered on Lydia. *Was* her.

"Let the girl go," he said.

"Fuck you."

"If there's anything human left in you—"

So swiftly that he had no time to react, she knelt, jerked a crossbow up from the floor, and loosed a bolt straight toward his chest.

"No!" Francine shrieked.

He spun, as though pulled by her voice. Instead of hitting his heart, the bolt lanced into his shoulder, breaking his collarbone and bringing blood spurting out. Agony shot through him, the burn of something more than mere pain. Ash. It was ash.

"Ahhhhh!" he cried, ripping the bolt out. He went down on one knee, gasping.

Lydia sprang at him, her mouth avid for the blood flowing down his chest. She snapped at him like a rabid animal as he held her away. With a galvanic effort, he surged to his feet. Lydia still clung to him, ravening, her mad gaze focused on his wound.

"Get . . . off!" He flung her away with all his strength.

She landed hard. But she managed to retrieve the crossbow as she skidded past it, then leapt to her feet. Skin and flesh had been lost to that slide across the wooden floor. She ignored it, the zombie's unconcern for self.

"How do you like the crossbow?" she asked, laying another bolt in place. "I took it from a collector. He was a real connoisseur of medieval weapons, that guy. Really knew his stuff. This one's sixteenth century. I wanted you to feel right at home."

Alex pressed his hand to his wound. Blood still flowed freely; his swift revenant healing had been inhibited by the sacred wood. Jagged patches swam across his vision. Pain ran in red waves from his shoulder and down his arm as he pushed Francine away from him.

"Stay away," he gasped.

"But you're hurt—"

"Move!"

Something in his tone must have convinced her; she stepped away, pressing her back against the wall. He took a deep breath, then another, trying to bring the pain to a manageable level.

"I don't want to kill you," Lydia said as she cranked. "At least not as much as I want something else. You know what that is."

He knew. He'd always known. Poor Lydia, always reaching for what couldn't be had.

"You want to remain like this forever?" he asked.

"Of course not. I know how to heal myself. I'll be Lydia again. And I'll be Lydia forever, and I'll be happy."

He shook his head, denying not her abilities, but the premise. "There is no happiness in immortality," he said. "It's a curse."

"So's this." She finished cranking. "You know what I want. And I want it from *you*."

He inclined his head, understanding the distinction. "I know what you want. But no."

"You're too late to help the kid, you know. I've already sent her to wherever good little unborn souls go."

A moment ago he wouldn't have been able to move. But the creamy satisfaction in Lydia's eyes brought his outrage surging high, and he took a step forward. She snapped the crossbow up, centering the quarrel on his chest.

"I wouldn't," she said.

He took another step. The struts of the crossbow quivered as she put tension on them. Alex watched her hands, trying to judge his own ability to dodge if she let fly. The prospects weren't good; he couldn't move his left arm at all, and pain sapped his strength and reflexes. If he ended here, the child was lost for certain.

"We'll bargain, then," he said.

"You're not in a position to make demands."

Alex stared at the crossbow bolt, at the pale, deadly wood aimed at his heart. And he smiled. "But I am," he said.

"I'll kill you."

"So?"

"You're not fooling me," she said, low and deadly. "You don't want to die any more than I do."

"The biggest mistake you can make, Lydia, is to judge an enemy by your own standards."

The corners of her lips lifted, a travesty of a smile. "I can drink your blood after you're dead."

"I'll be ash before you take three steps."

"I don't believe you."

He held his good arm out. "Then do it."

The pale wood of the bolt glimmered at him as though hungry for his flesh. His vision narrowed to that single, sharp point; he could see the whorls of graining, the hatch marks of the knife Lydia had used to sharpen it. For a moment it held steady, and he waited for it to come for him. Then it wavered. A fraction of an inch only, but a great telling of Lydia's indecision.

"I'll give you what you want," he said, "but only if you release the child's soul first."

"Make me immortal, and *then* you can have the kid."

"Don't!" Justin's voice rang from the doorway.

Lydia spun, releasing the bolt at Justin in the same movement. Alex leapt for the young man, knowing he'd be too late. He cried out against the loss.

Elizabeth appeared in the doorway behind Justin. She slung him aside. Her arm blurred as she knocked the bolt up and away, letting it clatter harmlessly to the floor behind her. Lydia slapped another bolt into place and cranked swiftly. The sound seemed to echo around the room.

"You're too late," she said. "You're all too late."

Justin struggled to a sitting position. "She already did it, didn't she?" His voice sounded raw, desperate.

"Yes," Alex said.

"You bitch!" Justin screamed, springing to his feet. "I'm going to—"

Lydia snarled. Power exploded out from the ghost crystal, a pile-driver blow that smashed him backward against the wall. He slid to the floor. Alex started toward the young man, heedless of the crossbow, but was flung away by another blast of power. He slid along the floor helplessly as blood spurted from his reopened wound.

"Alex!" Liz cried.

Lydia swung the crossbow around, training it again on Alex's heart. "Move, and I'll send this into his heart."

Alex probed Justin, found his life beating steady and slow. His breath went out in a gasp of relief. Turning, he looked into Liz's eyes. "Take her," he said.

She met his gaze levelly. He gave her everything he had, everything he was. A thousand years of civilization dropped away, leaving the pure, cold ferocity of the man who had pledged his sword—and life—to God, and had walked onto the battlefield careless of anything but taking as many enemy as possible with him when he died.

And he was willing to die now, as long as Lydia went to hell with him.

Liz nodded, her amber eyes warming to gold. Then she smiled, as reckless as he. It was worth it, that one glorious moment, worth everything.

She turned back to Lydia. "You made me kill," she said.

"It's your nature to kill," Lydia replied, keeping the bolt aimed at Alex. With her free hand, she reached up to clasp the crystal. It throbbed with dark power, cast sullen light through her fingers to throw grotesque shadows on her ruined face. "Come get me, if you can."

Liz stalked forward with deadly grace. "You won't have time to reload, you know. Either Alex will get you, or I will."

Lydia smiled, a grimace from hell itself. "I don't need a crossbow to stop you, my sister."

"I am not your sister!"

"But you are," Lydia said. "Suldris was our father. Don't you remember, Liz? Don't you feel him?"

"No! I . . ." Elizabeth's smooth movements slowed, became jerky, as though the spring in a windup doll had lost its tension. She stuttered to a halt. Alex saw that she was fighting it; her hands were clenched into fists, and outrage flared in her eyes.

"You see?" Lydia taunted. "We're the same. *He* made us the same. Feel the darkness deep inside. Look in it. You'll see his face, and you'll see mine."

Slowly, with an effort that was painful to see, Liz shook her head.

"Oh, yes." Lydia's smile had turned to a rictus of hate, and her breathing rasped through the room. "You can never get away, no matter how fast you run or how far you go. He'll always be there waiting."

The silent battle continued. Alex struggled against his

own weakness, pushing himself to a sitting position, to his knees. If he could just reach Liz, touch her, he could pull her out of the darkness. His breath rasped with effort. He managed to get one foot under him.

Lydia slashed at him again with the crystal's power, knocking him backward with tremendous force. Red agony bloomed in his body, his mind. Unconsciousness hovered close, a vast black hand waiting to take him. He fought it savagely. Managed, through revenant strength or pure, human stubbornness, to push it away. He tried to rise, but his body refused his commands. Helpless, he could only watch as the light died in Elizabeth's eyes.

"Now, where were we?" Lydia asked. "Oh, yes."

Her hand tightened on the crystal. Elizabeth's head turned, an alien, inhuman movement. Her gaze went to Justin's motionless form.

Alex felt her Blood-Hunger rise, and his with it. A human life; his mind filled with the beat of Justin's heart, the warm rush of blood in his veins. The need pressed him down, roared through his body in a red scar of heat.

"No, Liz," he panted.

She didn't look at him. The candlelight cast trails of gold in her hair as she turned toward Justin. With terrible grace, she began to move.

Lydia's sweet, malevolent laugh seemed to bounce around the room. "That's right, sister mine. Time for dinner."

25

"Everybody freeze!"

Rhudwyn's shout crashed through the suffocating tension. He edged through the doorway, both arms braced in front of him to support his gun. Candlelight whorled blue-steel glints along the barrel. His gaze made knife-edged shifts from Lydia to Elizabeth and back again, but the gun didn't waver.

"Put that crossbow down, lady," he barked.

Lydia laughed. "Is this your cavalry, Alex?"

"Martin, get out of here!" Alex drove the words at him, trying to communicate his urgency, and the danger. But he knew Rhudwyn didn't realize he'd entered a different world here, one where guns and badges had no meaning.

"The bow!" the lieutenant shouted. "Drop it!"

Lydia moved forward into the light. Rhudwyn's face paled, and his knuckles whitened as his grip on the gun tightened.

"Goddamn," he whispered. "Goddamn."

"Very," she said. With a contemptuous curl of lip, she pointed at him. The gun glowed a sudden cherry red, and Rhudwyn dropped it with a yelp. Alex's nostrils flared

at the reek of scorched skin. Then he saw Lydia pull her
arm back again.

"Martin, *move!*" he shouted.

The detective dove to one side. A blast of power hit the
floor where he'd stood, making the wood buck and groan.
Rhudwyn kept moving, scooping up the still-hot gun as
he went past. The smell of singed skin grew stronger.
He came up hard against the wall near Justin, raised the
weapon in both hands.

Two quick shots exploded in the room, and two neat,
round holes appeared in the left center of Lydia's chest.
She half turned, spun by the bullets' velocity, and Alex
saw that the exit holes weren't nearly as neat and round
as the others. Her back had become a mass of chopped
flesh and pale bits of bone. Black blood welled out,
dripped in thick licorice driblets down her body. Then
she straightened and turned, bringing the business end
of the crossbow back to bear on Alex.

"What the . . ." White showed all around Rhudwyn's
yellow-brown irises. He shook his head like a punch-
drunk fighter, then leveled the gun and popped off two
more shots. Both hit Lydia in the chest again, and both
did nothing more than send her staggering back a step.

"Run, you fool!" Alex shouted, struggling to rise. He
made it to his knees, knowing it was too little, too late.
"Get out of here!"

Rhudwyn started to move, instinct apparently overriding his shock. Lydia struck at him, her face twisted with
hate and dark power. Connected. Even at this distance,
Alex felt the terrible impact. Martin's body spasmed. The
gun clattered to the floor at his feet as he continued to
jerk uncontrollably. He screamed once, sharply, and the
echoes of it seemed to hang in the charged air.

"Ah, Martin," Alex muttered.

Lydia dropped her arm to her side. Released, Rhudwyn
fell, arms and legs flopping uselessly. Lifelessly. Outrage

washed through Alex, bringing with it a black surge of ferocity. It pulled him to his feet, staggering, weak, but upright.

"How many people have to die to give you your damned immortality?" he shouted.

"As many as necessary." Lydia bared her teeth, an animal's grimace. "If you hadn't been so damned stiff-necked, none of this would have happened. I went to Suldris because you wouldn't help me. Because you wouldn't help me, I became *this*."

"You weren't satisfied with wealth and beauty," he said, "and you wouldn't have been satisfied with immortality. That's not your nature."

Out of the corner of his eye, he saw Francine edge along the wall toward Rhudwyn. Lydia's gaze flickered toward the psychic, and he rushed to distract her.

"Give me back the child's soul," he said.

"Give me immortality."

Alex knew she'd drain him the way she'd drained Roger Essler; youth and beauty and eternal life in one moment. He'd allow it—if he could take her with him. "And what would you do with immortality, Lydia? Continue to kill?"

"Isn't that what vampires do?"

"Some."

She studied him from beneath her lashes, a coquettish look that was horrible in her ruined face. "It's not the same without the killing. You know that."

"There's more to be considered than merely pleasure."

"Ah, morality again. What has it gained you, Alex? Did it buy you happiness? Did it buy you love?" She pointed a crooked finger at Elizabeth, who stood like a beautiful robot waiting for the next command. "Look at her. She didn't help you. Right now, she doesn't even know you exist. Feel her, Alex. There's nothing inside her but Blood-Hunger. Just like yours."

Just like his. True. But Lydia was too impulsive, always had been; she never quite saw the whole picture. She might hold Elizabeth's body, but he knew the woman behind the revenant mask. And that woman would never give up, never willingly let herself become Lydia's creature.

"Fight her, Liz," he said. "Remember what she did to you."

Lydia's lip lifted in a sneer. "Do you see those three over there, Elizabeth? Those are yours."

"No!" Alex shouted.

Light bloomed in the ghost crystal, as dark and malevolent as Lydia's heart. She hurled power at him again. He groaned in pain as he smashed into the wall with brutal force.

When his vision cleared, he saw that Elizabeth had reached Francine. Bending, she lifted the psychic to her feet. And up, onto her tiptoes and higher still.

Francine's face had gone chalk white with terror. She braced her hands against the vampire's chest, holding herself away. But her arms began to quiver from the pressure, and Alex knew it was only a matter of moments.

He staggered forward. Lydia hit him again, smashing him back to the wall. He shouted out at the impact, but in defiance rather than pain. Agony came, of course, but he welcomed it, absorbed it into the red tide of battle rage that spun through his brain. He'd seen berserkers fight mortally wounded, stepping on their own entrails as they continued to bring enemy after enemy down. Death caught them on their feet, swords flashing as they roared defiance. He'd been awed but, until now, hadn't understood.

"Elizabeth!" he gasped, even as Lydia hit him again, hurling him back against the wall with enough force to break boards. "By my ancestors, this will not be!"

Liz jerked. Her hands opened, and Francine dropped to the floor. Something flickered in the revenant's eyes, something that might be memory.

Alex grasped at it. "Look at me," he said.

"No!" Lydia cried. She pointed at Liz as the crystal beat pulses of light against her chest. Then she closed her hand into a fist, a gesture of possession and domination. "Do what you're told, Elizabeth."

Liz took a halting step forward, bent toward the woman who lay stunned on the floor before her. Confusion, fear, dark Hunger chased one another across her face. But Blood-Hunger dominated those dark amber eyes, a need that drove sharp spikes of agony into the mind, raked jagged claws along the spirit. Alex felt it, for it was his. His creation, his curse.

"Look at me," he said.

With a howl that had nothing human in it, Lydia slashed power at him. But he'd passed beyond pain; he let it roll over him, through him, made it his own.

"Elizabeth," he said.

Slowly she turned. Alex opened himself to the raging storm of revenant need, riding it into her mind, her heart. He touched something dark and powerful, something that called to him beyond the boundaries of Blood-Hunger. Woman/revenant, revenant/woman. Both courageous, both fiercely independent. Both frightened of being lost forever in the abyss of Lydia's power.

Lydia pointed at Francine. "Do it," she commanded. "You want to."

Liz did want to; Alex could feel her need in the depths of his being. But the beginnings of awareness had bloomed in her eyes, and strain as she searched for the strength to deny her Blood-Hunger.

The ghost crystal beat like a heart on Lydia's chest, demanding obedience. "Do what *I say*." Her voice broke on a note that almost sounded like a sob. "Damn you, I *own* you!"

Alex laughed, a savage, mocking laugh that echoed in the far reaches of the room. She swung around to glare at him. Her eyes had become black pits of hate, and spittle ran down her chin and dripped upon the floor.

"Don't laugh at me!" she shrieked.

Darkness swam in her eyes, and all the shadows in the room seemed to contract as she pulled still more power from the crystal. A great hunk of hair fell from the right side of her head, lay like a pool of flame upon the floor. Then she turned, and Alex realized in disgust that she'd lost more than hair; a handbreadth of bare skull gleamed in the dim light.

"Do what I say, Elizabeth. Suldris made you, made me. He's our master. If you reach inside, you can feel him."

"Ah, Lydia," Alex said. "Liz is revenant. She belongs to herself, answers to no master like a cringing dog."

Lydia's mouth twisted. "Are you calling me a dog? A bitch, perhaps?"

"Not at all. A dog, at least, knows how to love."

She came up on her toes, and he braced himself for the blow that was sure to come. Then she shook her head. "Oh, no, you're not going to distract me. And don't give me any of that revenant bullshit, either. I made her, and she's going to do what I tell her."

He smiled. "Will she?"

"Yes!" Her face twisted with terrible rage, she stabbed her forefinger at Liz. "Do it! Kill them! Kill them all!"

Liz bent, reached again for Francine.

"Elizabeth," Alex said, "remember who you are."

She stopped, straightened. The candle flared brighter, bringing more light into her eyes. Slowly, haltingly, she reached up to clasp the griffin medallion. Bloodred fire glimmered in the stone, shone through her hand as she clasped it. Alex watched the glow spread up her arms and over her body. Her hair whipped around her as though raked by a sudden wind, casting ruby sparks into the air.

"By my ancestors," he whispered for the second time, understanding, "come to me!"

The sparks swirled toward him. He closed his eyes and breathed them in. Power hummed along his nerves, coiled most strongly in his wounded shoulder. The ash burn faded. Torn flesh and skin healed. Danilov strength, Danilov power, forged in fire and violence more than a thousand years ago.

He was whole again.

Warrior's instinct brought him spinning around to knock the quarrel aside with his forearm. Liz had already begun moving; with a cry that echoed the clear, high call of the hunting falcon, she sprang at Lydia.

And was blasted aside. She rose to her hands and knees, shaking her head groggily. Seeing Lydia ready herself for another blow, Alex tensed to leap.

"Alex, wait!" Francine shouted.

He glanced at her, saw her draw back her arm and hurl something at Lydia. It spun end over end through the air, its speed increasing far beyond the impetus it had first been given. The candlelight caught in its smooth-faceted sides and was cast back in whorls of rainbow color.

"The crystal," he whispered.

Time seemed to stutter and slow. He watched terror bloom in Lydia's face, watched her arm come up as though to ward off a blow. The crystal wailed, the cry going up and up the scale until it passed from human hearing into a teeth-clenching vibration. And then it struck—a direct hit on the dark ghost crystal. Light exploded outward. Something black and howling came into being in the center of the incandescence.

"No!" Lydia shrieked. "Nooooo!"

The Abyss. The realization settled in Alex's mind, as inevitable as death.

The blackness grew and spread, becoming a great, yawning mouth that gobbled hungrily at the fabric of this world. A sound came from that dark, endless pit, a sound that raked the nerves and tore at the spirit: a child crying. A tiny soul, spinning helplessly in the blackness of the Abyss.

"Do you hear it?" Francine cried. "Oh, God, can you hear it?"

Alex took a deep breath. This was his destiny, the price exacted for a thousand years of existence. A small price to pay for what might be gained.

"Yes," he said. "I hear it."

With a roar of defiance, he leapt straight into that dark maw.

26

The Abyss closed around Alex. He spun in blackness, robbed of light and the world of man. The wail of a lost child echoed in his ears. As he extended his senses, he caught a trace of something long lost and very welcome. Lavender. He took a deep breath, trying to pinpoint the source.

"Catherine?" he called.

The child's voice stopped. Silence closed in, as thick as velvet.

Something hit his back with stunning force, hit and clung and chopped at him. The stench of rot filled his nose. He reached back, grasping his attacker. His hand closed on hair, came away with a fistful of shining red tresses and parchment skin.

"Lydia!" he rasped.

With a convulsive effort, he managed to haul her over his shoulder. He would have thrown her from him, but she grabbed his arms and hung on with zombie strength. Her once lovely face had turned into something inhuman and horrible. Rotting flesh and exposed bone, teeth bared between shriveled lips—her greed and perversion entombed in her flesh. The real Lydia.

"I'll have what I want," she hissed.

"Not from me."

"Yes! From you." Terrible certainty steeled her voice, stared out at him from her eyes. "Don't you know? I'm stronger here than you are."

Her grip tightened. He looked into her eyes, smiling, as his bones grated beneath her hands.

"You can become the most beautiful woman in the world, Lydia, but you can't do a thing about that rotten black hole you call a heart. You'll still be a monster. You always were, and you always will be."

He arched beneath the terrible lash of the crystal's power. It sank into his chest, pulling at him, sucking his vitality with avid dark pleasure. He fought it, there in the black nothingness of the Abyss, and clutched desperately at the seeping tide of his essence.

"Yes," Lydia whispered. The image of the woman she'd been flickered over the shattered zombie's face, youth superimposed over corruption. It disappeared, then appeared again, more substantial this time.

She pulled herself closer, her gaze focused unblinkingly on his throat. Desperation stabbed deep in his belly; once she fastened on that spot, she'd drain him of everything he was. Alex jabbed at her, felt flesh slough away beneath his hands. It didn't stop her. Nothing stopped her.

And then the child began crying again, a sweet, pure sound of loss. It touched something in him, something deep and primal and utterly savage. With a snarl to match Lydia's, he clamped his hands on her forearms. A thousand years of Blood-Hunger flared through his body as he wrenched at her arms with all his strength.

Her mouth opened in an O of surprise as her elbows gave way with a sickening crunch of bone. Crippled, she snapped at him with her teeth as she drifted away. A breeze sprang to life somewhere behind her—a doorway had opened, pulling her back toward the world from which she'd come.

"Help me, Alex!" she shrieked, holding the stumps of her arms out to him beseechingly. "I'll die there."

If she'd shown pity to anyone else, he would have pitied her. If she'd shown mercy to others, he would have been merciful. But not now. Not with that child's soul lost in blackness.

"Good-bye, Lydia," he said.

"Damn you!"

"I was damned long before you met me, Lydia. Save me a spot in hell."

Ugly light spewed out of the ghost crystal, her last attempt to escape. But the wind caught it up, tore it asunder, and absorbed it into the spiraling tunnel of force that was pulling her away. Shrieking, she fell into the tunnel. Light blossomed at the far end, silhouetting her swiftly dwindling figure.

She seemed to grow larger suddenly. Alex let his breath out with a hiss, thinking she'd managed to get away somehow. But then light flared between shoulders and arms, legs and torso, and he realized that she'd begun to break up. Drifted apart from herself as the ghost crystal's power drained away.

"Give my regards to Suldris," Alex said.

The scent of lavender swirled around him, stronger this time. Real. Alex turned to find Catherine hovering in nothingness, her hair blending with the endless dark of the Abyss. Her face held the same serenity he remembered from their last encounter, and she carried something small in her arms.

"You look very fierce," she said.

"Evil offends me."

" 'Sufficient unto the day is the evil thereof.' "

He smiled at her. "Today's evil, however, was a bit

more than sufficient. What have you got there, heart of my heart?"

"A young Danilov," she said. "And a very special one."

He looked down at the small being she held in her arms. It wasn't quite human; it still carried too much of the brightness of heaven. "I should have known you'd find a lost child, even in the Abyss."

"It doesn't belong here."

"Neither do you."

She didn't answer, only smiled at him. It was then that he realized the wind had come after him; it sifted over his skin, barely felt, but demanding nonetheless.

"You have to go back," Catherine said.

"Yes. But this time I'm taking you with me." He reached out to grasp her arm.

His hand passed through her.

His throat ached with something that might have been anger, might equally have been tears. She looked so real. He could see the texture of her skin, each curling strand of dark hair, smell her perfume. He wanted to hold her, touch her. How long, he wondered, until the fabric of her soul unraveled completely?

She smiled, an echo of his own sadness. "Would you stay here with me if it were possible?"

He looked deeply into her eyes as he began to drift away from her, those blue, blue eyes that seemed to pull his heart out of his chest. She'd always had that effect on him. Always would. Ah, Lord, he still loved her. But he loved Elizabeth, too, and she had so little to live for. If he stayed here, he'd be condemning her to the dawn. "I—"

"Shhh," she said. Her smile was no longer sad. "I know the answer. Staying here would be death, and life has always beckoned you too strongly."

"Except once."

"Alex, love, I know you better than anyone in the world. And I don't believe—cannot believe—you would have taken your own life, then or ever."

Astonishment spread through him. "What?"

"You ought to believe me," she said. "I've had a great deal of time to think about it."

The wind pulled him backward, plucked imperatively at his clothing, his hair. The distance between them increased. And although he fought to reclaim those lost yards, he might as well have stormed the gates of heaven, asking admittance.

"I haven't given up, Catherine," he shouted. "I'm going to get you out of here!"

"Tend to the things in your world." The blue of her eyes brightened, and the scent of lavender wrapped around him like a benediction. "Leave the impossible to God."

"My word as a Danilov!"

She laughed. "Catch!" she called, tossing the child's soul after him.

He caught it in his hands. It clung to him, a bright spark of innocence in an ocean of darkness. Infinitely precious. Then the wind swept him up, whirled him into the roaring tunnel that had swallowed Lydia a few moments before.

"Her name is Aileen!" Catherine's clear, sweet voice came after him. "Farewell, my love!"

Everything seemed to break up around him, shards of light and dark whirling, colliding, shattering into ever smaller pieces. Alex curled protectively around the fragile soul that rested so trustingly in his arms. The wind tore at him, buffeted him, sent him spinning like a leaf in a hurricane.

Suddenly, without warning, he was spewed out into reality. He landed on the hard wooden floor of the warehouse. With a grunt, he rolled over onto his back.

He felt the child's soul leave him, drawn back to where it belonged. It left echoes of Catherine's laughter in his mind.

"Alex!"

He opened his eyes, saw Elizabeth and Justin standing over him. Justin's face held grim concern; Liz's, nothing at all. Yet Alex sensed powerful emotions churning beneath that expressionless mask, and knew she was holding on to herself as tightly as she could.

With a sigh, he sat up. "How long was I gone?"

"A couple of minutes," Justin said. "Did you . . . find it?"

Alex glanced past him, to the mattress where Kelli lay curled around herself in private misery. Then he smiled. "Her name is Aileen."

"What are you talk—" Suddenly the grimness fell away. "Kel!" he shouted. "Kel!"

Alex watched him pull the girl into his arms, watched the joy dawn on her face. Then she burst into tears, great, racking sobs that sounded like pain and fear and joy all rolled together.

"Ah, youth," he murmured.

"She'll be okay," Liz said. "She's tougher than she looks."

With a groan, Alex climbed to his feet. Every muscle in his body protested the movement. Gently he brushed some stray hairs from her forehead. "Are you all right?"

She pulled away. "Of course."

"Liz—" He broke off, sensing two human presences behind him.

Turning, he saw Francine and Rhudwyn walking toward him. She supported much of Martin's weight, but the detective looked remarkably foul-tempered for a man who'd just beaten death.

"You were dead last time I saw you," Alex said.

"CPR," Martin growled. "I want some explanations."

Alex looked at Francine, saw trust in her eyes. She'd back whatever he said; they all would.

"I'm sorry, Martin, but there are no explanations."

"Yeah? What was that . . . thing I shot at?"

"What thing?"

Rhudwyn pushed away from Francine. He stood, listing a bit to one side, but stood nonetheless. He thrust his burned hands out. "Then where did I get these?"

"Pulling a drunk out of a burning Dumpster, perhaps."

"I wonder if there are any burned drunks in the hospital tonight."

"Let it go, Martin."

"I can't do that."

Alex sighed. "What are you going to tell your captain? That you traveled through a crystal's heart and confronted a monster that struck you with unseen power? Even if the rest of us confirmed that, they'd just call us *all* crazy."

"And what about Liz Garry just appearing out of nowhere a year after she disappeared?"

"Amnesia," Francine said. "She woke up in an Atlanta alley without a clue as to where she's been."

He turned to look at her. "You, too?"

"I have no choice, Martin," she said. "The reality is too incredible. I'm going to go home, keep my mouth shut, and be satisfied that the good guys won. If you're wise, you'll do the same." She slid her hand beneath his elbow. "Now let's get you to a hospital; those burns need attention."

"I'm fine." He flexed his hands, drew breath in a long inhalation of pain. "Then again," he gasped, "maybe you're right."

"Of course I'm right," she said.

Rhudwyn pinned Alex with a challenging, yellow-brown stare. "I'm not finished, Alex. Not by a long shot. I'm going to dig until I get to the truth."

He turned away. Francine hurried after him, slipping her arm around his waist to support him.

Sudden impulse caught Alex, made him call out as the pair reached the doorway. "Hey, Martin!"

Rhudwyn stopped and turned, wariness in his eyes. "Yeah?"

"We left you asleep in the house. What brought you out into the garden at just the time we entered the crystal doorway?"

"Are you kidding? It felt like a bomb went off—" He broke off, clamping his teeth with an audible sound.

"Ah," Alex said. "Intuition?"

With a grunt, Rhudwyn turned back around. Francine shot Alex a glance over her shoulder, laughter sparkling in her eyes.

"He's going to be a problem," Elizabeth said.

"True. But he plays an excellent game of chess."

"Don't underestimate him, Alex."

"I never have," he said. "Where's Lydia?"

Elizabeth took his elbow and turned him. Now he could see the scattered bones that were all that remained of Lydia Danilov. But her legacy lived on in the shattered lives of Kelli's parents, the legion of bodies lying in the morgue, and in the guilt Liz Garry would struggle with for the rest of her life.

He crouched beside the skull. It lay on its side, staring at him with blank, accusing eyeholes. He crouched and picked it up. A dank smell of malice clung to it, and it almost seemed to slither in his hands.

"She came through in pieces," Liz said. Remembered horror darkened her eyes. "Her head screamed for a while."

"A fitting end."

Liz ducked her head, hiding her face from him. "Are you satisfied?"

He exerted pressure. The dome of the skull crumbled inward, collapsing the eye sockets and sending teeth clattering to the floor. Alex stood, letting the shards of bone drop. "Now I am," he said.

"Is that what happens to those who cross Alex Danilov?"

"Being crossed only annoys me. Those who attack my family, however, I will crush. Always."

Her breath hissed as she drew it in. "It's so easy to forget how old you are. Until you say something like that."

"I'm sorry you don't approve."

"I never said I didn't."

She walked away from him, bent to pick something up from the floor. When she came back again, he saw that she was carrying the big quartz crystal.

He held out his hands, and she dropped the stone into them. It had turned clear again. The shadowy, perfect shape of the ghost crystal hovered in its center. Dark heart, he thought, running his fingertips along its smooth sides. The song of pain had stilled.

"Alex."

Something in Liz's voice startled him, and he looked up at her.

"I waited for you," she said. "I sat beside that damned howling skull and waited, not knowing what had happened, how long you'd be gone, or"—her voice faltered just a bit—"if you'd be back at all."

"And how did you feel about that?"

Tears glittered in her lashes. "I don't know."

His throat tightened. Had there been anything to say, he couldn't have spoken. Instead he reached for the medallion, taking its smooth golden weight in his palm. Light sparked briefly in the ruby.

"Do you want it back?" Liz asked.

He shook his head. "Ten years from now or a hundred years from now, I want you to look at that and remember the night I gave it to you."

"A hundred years." Her breath caught on something that might have been a sob. "I'm not sure I can make it past tonight. And the dawn comes every day."

He held his hand out to her. If he could give her nothing else, he could at least give her this. "Then let me make the decision for you—tonight you will live."

"And tomorrow?"

"Tomorrow, we'll make that decision again."

She sighed. "Is that all there is?"

"It's all anyone has, revenant or human. The joy must be found somewhere in the chaos of existence, found and recognized and held precious."

Slowly she reached out. He grasped her hand, accepted her faith.

"Come, Elizabeth. As the cliché goes, we've miles to go before we sleep."

She smiled, and it was like sunlight dawning across a nighttime sea. "And a piper to pay," she countered.

"That, too."

27

Alex stood with Justin at Wildwood's edge, taking turns skipping stones into the dark water.

"Two, three, four," Justin said. "Not bad. Have you noticed there hasn't been any fog since Lydia died?"

"I noticed." Alex paused to watch a pair of white owls skim soundlessly through the trees. "We'll probably never know why."

"It's strange. I ought to be afraid of it, but I'm not. I just wish I could understand what it wanted from me."

"Wildwood is too big to be understood, and too old."

"Yeah." With an expert flip, Justin tossed another stone out across the water. "Five," he said. "Francine's coming."

Astonishment shot through Alex. He'd registered the psychic's remarkable mind the moment she'd stepped out of the house. Justin, however, shouldn't have been able to.

"You ought to see your face," the young man said.

"How long?"

"Have I been able to do that?" Justin shrugged. "Since the night Wildwood swallowed me up."

It troubled Alex. He tossed another stone, but gracelessly, and it fell into the water with a dull plop.

"You don't like it," Justin said.

"I don't like it."

Bending, Justin retrieved another stone. He tossed it up, caught it, tossed it again. The starlight reflected in his dark eyes. A new breed of Danilov, Alex thought. This young man had passed beyond the boundaries of this world, exceeded them, and now straddled both.

A disturbing notion. But then, perhaps this was the only sort of father Aileen could have.

"Are you happy with it?" Alex asked softly.

"I've got Kelli, and I'll have Aileen when she's born. The rest I'll live with."

"Yoo-hoo!" Francine called. "Where are you guys?"

Alex turned. "Here, by the marsh."

The pop of breaking twigs marked her passage. Her footsteps were a bit unsteady, and Alex knew she'd been hitting the bourbon again.

"Need some help?" he asked as she paused at the top of the incline.

"Thanks." She grasped his outstretched hands and came down in a rush. Her purse batted him in the side. "Sorry about that. What have you been doing out here for the past two hours?"

"Skipping stones," Justin said.

"Let me make a suggestion." She opened her purse and took out the big quartz crystal, then handed it to Alex.

He looked down at it. Mist still coiled gently in its depths, half obscuring the dark ghost crystal that was its heart. "Why?" he asked. "It's harmless now."

"Trust me on this." She thrust her thumb at the marsh.

He ran his fingertips over the stone, feeling now, as he had before, that it was too important to be cast away. But Francine had trusted him when it really counted, and he owed her this. With a smooth, powerful overhand swing, he threw it far into the marsh.

For a moment the spiky grass rippled and bent, the blades bowing gracefully against the wind. Then Wildwood settled in on itself, returning once again to its eternal business of life and death and renewal.

"Can you feel it?" Justin asked. "It's over. Finally."

Francine took a deep breath. Awe smoothed her face, made her look almost young again. Then she looked away, toward Justin, and the lines settled in again.

"Justin, I . . ." She thrust her hands into the pockets of her white cotton pants. "Your mother got a call tonight from someone named Philippe. He wants her to meet him in Paris tomorrow."

"I suppose she'll be leaving."

"She's packing now. She asked me to tell you."

He let his breath out with a hiss. "Didn't have the guts to do it herself, huh?"

"She's fragile, Justin," Francine said softly. "She's not like you. That woman needs something to cling to. And I can tell you from experience that this family moves way too fast for clinging."

"I don't blame her for being what she is. I just wanted . . ." He chopped at the air with the edge of his hand. "I'd better go say good-bye."

He swung around and strode toward the house. Alex started to follow, but Francine caught his arm, holding him back.

"Let him go alone," she said. "You can't help him with this."

For a moment he stood stiffly, then acquiesced. "What will he be, Francine? Can you see?"

"There's something very powerful inside him," she said, some of the awe returning to her face. "We can only hope he learns to grow large enough to contain it."

"And if he doesn't?"

"Then it will probably destroy him."

Alex turned back to the marsh. "Not a comforting thought."

"It's not a comforting talent. I should know."

"What are your plans?"

She moved up beside him, planting her feet firmly on the dew-wet grass. "I'm going back to Philadelphia tomorrow. I've been here two weeks, and it's time to go."

"We'd like you to stay."

"No, sir. Pardon me, but I've had my fill of Savannah. And I'm finished with police work, too."

"Going to put yourself out to pasture, hmm?"

"Yup. Give me a recliner and a nice, tall drink, and I'll be all set."

"You'll never do it."

"I'm going to give it a hell of a try." She glanced at him again. "Rhudwyn's nuts about this thing. He's not going to leave you alone."

Alex smiled. "He never has before, why start now?"

"Yeah, well . . . just be careful." She fidgeted for a moment, then asked, "What about you? Any plans?"

"Not really. Kelli's father is supposed to be getting out of the hospital sometime next week, and we've asked him to stay here until he recuperates fully."

"Oh, right. Kelli told me." She glanced at him again. "That girl worships you, Alex. Oh, she *loves* Justin, don't look so alarmed. But you brought Aileen back to her, and she'll never forget it."

"Catherine found the child's soul, not me."

"Catherine . . . Oh. It's just like you to give the credit to a dead woman."

He was surprised into laughter. "I *will* miss you."

"So, what will you do with yourself now?"

He shrugged. "My life will settle into suburban boredom, I expect. With you and Sonya both gone, it'll be a very quiet household."

And with Elizabeth gone. The thought seemed to hang in the air between them, and for a moment it took the shine from the moonlight.

"Have you heard from her?"

He shook his head. "Charles said she hardly leaves the safe room, even at night."

"Why did she leave?"

"She . . . said she needed time away from me, where she could think without our Blood-Hunger getting in the way."

"It's only been five days."

"It seems longer." He turned and offered his arm. "Shall we go in?"

She nodded, tucking her hand into the crook of his arm. He didn't talk as they walked toward the house, and Francine respected his need for silence. The Arbor gleamed in the moonlight, the lit windows golden rectangles of welcome. He paused at the back door, tilting his head back to look up at the hovering live oaks.

"It's just a house," he said. "I wonder, sometimes, why I keep coming back."

"Maybe because you don't have anywhere else to go."

He let his breath out in a harsh sigh. "It can be a very uncomfortable thing to talk to a psychic."

"Why do you think I never married?" she asked. "Open the door, will you? My hair's starting to go limp."

He sensed Elizabeth's presence the moment he walked into the house. His Blood-Hunger leapt, and so did his heart. She'd come back to him. The promise of her filled the house, ran like foxfire through his veins. It tasted like sunlight.

He turned to look at the woman beside him. "You knew."

"I wanted to surprise you," she said.

He started up the stairs. Then he paused, turned, and ran down again. Grasping Francine by the waist, he lifted her up and kissed her on both cheeks. "Thank you."

"Save it," she growled.

"Visit?"

"Only if you promise me no zombies, crystals, or bizarre murders."

He set her gently on her feet. "How about a christening?"

"That I could handle."

"Good-bye, Francine Dey," he said, bowing before her like a courtier. "Fare thee well."

"Good-bye, Alexi Danilovich." She dipped into a surprisingly good curtsy.

He found Liz sitting on the fine old bed in his room, her eyes less shadowed than they'd been when she left. Although he wanted to sweep her into his arms, he forced himself to only take her hands in his.

"So, Liz Garry. Have you decided on me?"

"I'm . . . flawed, Alex. Eighteen lives stain my soul, lives I can never give back. Every night I want to walk out to meet the sun."

"Live for me, if not for yourself."

"One day at a time?"

"The healing creeps up on one," he said. "And sometimes comes when you least expect it."

"Help me see it." Her hands tightened on his. "Hold me, Alex, before I lose myself."

He pulled her up into his arms. She came to him with sweetness, with Blood-Hunger, and with desperation. It wasn't happiness. Not yet.

But for now, it was enough.

Epilogue

"Don't you ever bring light down here?" Elizabeth asked, coming into the underground room.

He looked up from the manuscript he'd been reading. "It never occurred to me."

"I've never gotten out of the habit of flipping the light switch when I enter a room."

"I have no such reflexes, having predated electricity."

Her smile was brief, but precious. He'd learned to treasure them; they'd been rare in the three months since Lydia died. Liz hadn't come to terms yet with the killing she'd done. But she'd managed to find occasional contentment, and he'd been satisfied with that.

"A package came for you today," she said, taking a flat, rectangular box out of her pocket.

"Is it yet another electronic gizmo from Charles?"

"No. It's from France."

He pushed his chair back and got up. Taking the package from her, he turned it over and over in his hands. It had been more than securely wrapped in strapping tape. An aura of age wafted from it, something apart from the scent of mildew and old leather.

He tore it open. Inside, a sheaf of yellowed manuscript and a small, leather-bound book lay in a swaddle of bubble wrap. A note accompanied them. Written in the spidery, unsure hand of the very old, it said, *Monsieur Danilov, these were found in the cellar of the Abbey deGuisinard. Knowing you were searching for such things, I obtained them and sent them along. You will know what they are worth. Your servant, Marie Oudres.*

Ah, Marie always made it seem so easy. For sixty years she'd been a purveyor of things no one else believed in, let alone found.

Reverently, Alex unwrapped the manuscript, titled *Claviculae Salomonis ad Filium Roboam.* "A copy of the Latin manuscript," he murmured. "A treasure, indeed."

The diary, however, was potentially more interesting. It contained the story of a man who claimed to have befriended the Jew Eleazar.

Alex hefted the slim book, weighing its antiquity. "Was Flavius Josephus right, Eleazar? Did you actually possess the Book of Solomon when you performed your tricks for Vespasian?"

"Good God, Alex, what is it?"

"A lever, perhaps, to pry Catherine out of the Abyss."

"Let me help you."

He smiled at her. As a woman, she'd had a generous soul; as a revenant, she'd learned to give even more deeply, even if she wasn't able to see it for herself. "Can you read Latin?"

"Do you think my father would have let me grow to adulthood without it?"

Something bloomed in her dark amber eyes. Interest, perhaps, a sense of purpose, or response to a challenge. Whichever, it looked enough like joy to make his heart pound.

"A quest, then?" he asked.

"You are, after all, a knight," she said, smiling. "And knights are supposed to go on quests."

He turned back to the table. Pouring two glasses of fine claret from the decanter, he handed Liz one and raised the other in a toast. "Onward, then. To wherever it may lead us."

"To wherever."

They clinked glasses. The griffin's ruby eye seemed to twinkle.

A trick of the light, perhaps.

> *I will instruct my sorrows to be proud;*
> *For grief is proud, and makes his owner stoop.*
>
> —**Shakespeare,** *King John*